The Maid's Forbidden Heart

A Clean Regency Romance Novel

Amanda Stones

Copyright © 2025 by Amanda Stones
All Rights Reserved.
This book may not be reproduced or transmitted in any form without the written permission of the publisher. In no way is it legal to reproduce, duplicate, or transmit any part of this document in either electronic means or in printed format. Recording of this publication is strictly prohibited and any storage of this document is not allowed unless with written permission from the publisher.

Peter Brookfield
Penelope Matthews

Table of Contents

Chapter 1 4
Chapter 2 12
Chapter 3 19
Chapter 4 26
Chapter 5 31
Chapter 6 38
Chapter 7 43
Chapter 8 51
Chapter 9 57
Chapter 10 66
Chapter 11 73
Chapter 12 80
Chapter 13 86
Chapter 14 93
Chapter 15 99
Chapter 16 105
Chapter 17 112
Chapter 18 118
Chapter 19 125
Chapter 20 133
Chapter 21 138
Chapter 22 144
Chapter 23 150
Chapter 24 156
Chapter 25 160
Chapter 26 171
Epilogue 178

Extended Epilogue 185

Chapter 1

"I hate storms," Peter muttered where he stood at the window of his study. The thunder rattled the windowpanes loudly, drowning out his words. Without warning, his mind filled with the memories of London on that terrible night.

"My lord?" Mr Preston, Peter's butler, called from the doorway of his London study, his voice raised to carry across the sound of the rain and thunder. The lamplight flickered on the walls as the door opened.

"What is it?" Peter asked, his grey eyes widening to take in the tense, hunched figure of the man who waited outside with Preston.

"I apologise for interrupting you so late, my lord," Preston demurred. "But this man has urgent news. He rode from Holway Manor post-haste."

"Holway Manor?" Peter snapped. That was where his cousin and best friend, Charles, resided; a secluded estate around eight miles from London. "In this storm?" Rain lashed at the windows, and thunder rumbled outside. Peter's heart thudded. He had expected to hear that his cousin had returned from the opera an hour ago. Charles had borrowed the Landau so that he and his wife, Eliza, might attend the theater in comfort. The coach had gone out to fetch them almost two hours previous, and, even with bad conditions on the road to Holway Manor, one would have expected that they would have arrived at home.

"Yes, my lord." Mr Preston was fidgeting with his shirt-cuff, a habit when he was tense. Peter swallowed. Clearly, the butler had some knowledge of the matter at hand, and his unease was far from reassuring.

"Send him in," Peter tried to say, but his voice came out almost as a whisper, tension tightening his throat too much for speech.

The butler nodded to the man and withdrew.

"Shut the door," Peter commanded. His heart was thudding. Somehow, he knew without being told that something terrible had happened.

The man stood with his cap in his hands, clearly deeply distressed. Peter nodded to him.

"State your message," he said as gently as he could. The man began speaking.

"My lord. I am sorry. So very sorry," he began. His voice wavered, and he seemed on the verge of tears. A servant from Charles' household, Peter surmised. His heart froze. He already knew before the man told him. "My lord, I am so sorry to have to tell you. Your cousin, Viscount Holway, was shot in a highway robbery. Her ladyship too."

Peter gripped the desk. Unreality surged in. He could not believe it. The man was talking, and he was trying to listen, but he could not think. His mind was entirely blank. The words made no sense. Charles was his dearest friend, like a brother to him. A light in the darkness that had followed the death of his own parents. He could not be dead too. He could not.

"...and you will have charge of their son. Thomas." The man concluded, voice shaking.

Peter stared at him. Without consciously trying, words poured out of him—commands and instructions were at his lips, delivering orders and organising meetings and coaches and all manner of necessities. He was barely present, diving into the world of bureaucracy and duty because it was something he understood, somewhere safe.

A crash from the hallway brought him sharply back to the moment. He blinked. His mind was still usually locked, after six months, in the world of bureaucracy and duty, his heart still achingly empty of any feelings at all. This was the first time in a long while that he had recalled that night.

"My lord?"

Peter turned to the door. His butler—not Preston, because Preston staffed the London house, where Peter had not returned since the accident—was there.

"Yes? What is it?" Peter asked a little sharply.

"My lord? The new maidservant has requested that a room in the east wing be prepared for young Master Thomas." Mr Harris answered tensely.

"What?" Peter asked harshly. The new maidservant had arrived two days ago. Was she already causing trouble? He tensed. "To what purpose has she requested such an odd thing?" He ran a hand through his thick, dark hair, feeling tense and weary.

"The roof in the nursery leaks, my lord. She fears it may be unwholesome for Master Thomas." The butler sounded apologetic.

"Oh." Peter bit his lip. The west side of the house was drafty. He could not argue with the young woman's estimate—it probably was unhealthy. "Well? See that it is done." He lifted his shoulder.

The butler, Mr Harris, bowed. "Yes, my lord."

When the butler had departed, Peter ran a hand wearily down his face, allowing his rigid posture to slump. He was exhausted. His ten-day journey from London to his country home, his sister's arrival at the family estate, and the need to find a replacement for Mrs Milnerton, who had cared for Thomas, had thrown him badly. He looked up, seeing his face reflected in the window pane against the dark sky outside.

He looked thinner than he recalled, his cheeks hollow, his eyes ringed with dark bags. His thick, dark brown hair was tousled from lack of sleep, and his skin seemed even paler in contrast to its darkness. His grey eyes stared back at him, blank and weary. His tall height was masked by his weary, stooping posture. He looked much older than his seven-and-twenty years.

"I need to go to bed," he told himself firmly, stifling a yawn. It was only seven o'clock in the evening, and he had not yet eaten dinner, but already the need to sleep dragged at him. He had not yet recovered from the journey, though he had been at Brentdale Manor, his home and the country seat of the Earls of Brentdale, for three days. There had simply been too much to organize in that time.

He walked to the study door and paused there. There was noise in the hallway—the sound of servants moving something heavy. He wandered towards the sound.

"And pull! Oh! My lord!" Mr Samuel, the footman, tensed, shooting Peter a worried glance. "Men, that'll do," he added to the team of three men who were pushing a vast dresser, the legs wrapped in cloth, across the hallway.

"What is the meaning of this?" Peter demanded. His voice was cold. The sound brought instant silence to the hallway as four pairs of eyes gazed at him with fear.

Mr Samuel looked down uncomfortably. "My lord, we are moving the furniture. Miss Matthews requested that we move it all from the nursery into the Green Room. So, we moved it." He stepped in place, seeming awkward.

Peter blinked mildly. "If it is needed, then, pray, continue," he said lightly. Mr Samuel nodded formally.

"Yes, my lord. Men! Keep moving," he added, addressing the three men, who grunted with effort as they pushed the dresser across the floor.

The former nursery was in the west wing, the corridor that led to it opening off just after the drawing room. Peter walked in that direction. His ancestors had been adding to Brentdale since its original building two hundred years before, and the place was a warren of hallways. He could have found his way in the house blind, so it was easy enough even in the stormy darkness of the hallway where the butler had not yet lit the lamps.

"Hush. Hush, now," a woman's voice was saying as Peter approached the open door. A candle was flickering, casting shadows through the door and onto the hallway floor. He tensed, hearing the woman's soft voice and the sound of fretful crying. He did not want to intrude. He stopped in the hallway, the need to remain out of the way warring with curiosity.

As he stood there, the shadow moved, and a woman stepped into view. Her long chocolate-brown hair was coming loose from its thick bun; some thick, wavy locks framing her pale face. She was slim and quite tall, her arms wrapped protectively around the bundled form of an infant in her arms. She wore a neat white uniform. Her thin face looked oddly calm, despite the fretting baby in her arms. He could see high cheekbones and a determined chin below a soft, generous mouth. Her nose was slender and well-formed, her face a longish oval shape. She was pretty. The thought filled him with surprise. It was the first time he had thought anything like that since the night his cousin was killed.

She looked up. Her eyes locked with his. They were green, a rich, dark green like emeralds. He froze in place, startled as much by the shock in her own gaze as by its riveting effect.

"My lord!" she gasped. "I apologise. I did not see you there."

The baby in her arms wailed, seeming to sense her distress.

Peter tensed awkwardly. He avoided visiting the nursery, preferring to allow others—more capable than himself—to tend to the small child. Seeing that innocent, childish face with its hazel eyes and mop of honey-coloured hair was like being stabbed in the heart. He could see Charles in the baby's squarish countenance and friendly smile and Charles' wife, Eliza, in those hazel eyes. He could not bear the reminder.

"He's fretting. It is because of the storm."

Peter blinked. The young woman was talking to him again, and this time he listened more carefully and noticed something. Her speech was oddly unaccented, like his own. She had a cultured voice, neither low nor high-pitched. Somehow, it was not the voice he had expected, and he tensed, listening.

"Yes?" he asked after a moment when she looked up at him expectantly. Her green eyes were mesmerising, not just because of the colour but because of the strange calm in their depths. Even when he had startled her, that calm had shifted only for a moment, returning instantly.

"I just meant to say that when the storm settles, he will settle too."

Her voice was calming, and he noticed again that peculiar lack of an accent. Everyone on their staff had a regional Devon accent, as far as he was aware. She had none.

"I suppose that you are correct," he managed to say after tearing his focus from her eyes and the unusual quality of her voice. "I must confess that I do not know much of infants." His lip lifted at the corner in an ironic smile. Her eyes brightened and, blushing, he schooled his face to neutrality.

"Infants are like weather-vanes, my grandmother used to say," the young woman replied, her green eyes holding his. "And sometimes, the stormy weather that they respond to is in our own souls."

The words intrigued him. The thought of stormy weather in his soul disturbed him. In some way, it was as though a terrible storm had been raging inside him since the time of his cousin's death. His helplessness and fear, shock and pain, were like the raging thunder and rain of a wild summer downpour. He pushed the thought away. It was a silly notion.

"Perhaps that is so," he managed stiffly.

The young maidservant said nothing. Her gaze held his. His heart thudded loudly in his chest, the noise filling his ears. Her eyes were so mesmerising, and their expression called to him, making him want to confess more. He looked away, his cheeks flushing awkwardly.

"You did a good job in moving the nursery," he said, coughing to clear his throat and return to his formal tone. "I trust you will continue in the same diligent manner."

"Thank you, my lord," she replied.

Peter turned away and walked out into the hallway, his eyes focused on the wall outside. He drifted past where the men had been pushing the dresser. There was noise from the Green Room, where they were clearly still working. He did not stop to look in. He walked down the cold hallway to the drawing room.

When he got there, he sighed in relief. A fire was burning in the grate, and someone—Mr Harris, he presumed—had drawn the velvet curtains over the windows. It was warm and comforting, and he breathed out. He felt in need of refuge.

The new maidservant had discomforted him. He could not get those green eyes out of his thoughts. Her slender form, her long, oval face, and her thick, glossy hair played through his mind. Altogether, in combination with that strange, neutral voice, she captivated him in ways that nobody else had for a long time. Even before his cousin's death, he had found high society repellant—overly formal, restrictive and uninteresting—and had socialised with few others outside his immediate family.

He walked across the room to the fireplace, staring into the flames. He had been only briefly into the nursery where Thomas was accommodated in the Devon house—this was the first time he had really looked at him since their arrival. It always unsettled him.

It is just that, he told himself firmly. *Just seeing the baby again.* It couldn't have been the maidservant and her enchanting green eyes. He could not be so interested in someone on his own staff.

A voice, middle-pitched and authoritative, echoed in the hallway. Peter tensed.

"... Anna? Bring my things to the drawing room, please. I will sew here."

He recognised the voice at once. His elder sister, Millicent, had arrived at the manor a day after he had, along with her husband Edmund. He had not seen Millicent in several years—outside brief exchanges in London—and it felt strange to be sharing a house with her. She was five years his senior, and she seemed to assume instant control wherever she went, including at the family's ancestral home, which felt wrong because he was the earl.

"Yes, my lady," a woman's voice replied to Millicent's request.

"And if you could...Oh! Peter!" Millicent had stepped through the door, and her hazel-eyed gaze fixed on him. "I thought you were occupied in your study."

"My business is concluded for the day," Peter said a trifle formally. He did not feel comfortable with his sister dictating anything about him, including where she did and did not expect him to be.

"Ah! Well! How grand! Then I can discuss matters about the house-party with you. I am so glad you have time."

"Millicent..." Peter began a little desperately. He did not want to think about the house-party. It was Millicent's terrible idea. Designed to bring him out of himself—her words—and keep him aware of what was happening in society, Millicent's house-party consisted of more than twenty guests and was planned to take place over three weeks. He did not like the idea of twenty strangers lodged at the Brentdale estate. He did not like the idea of a three-week house-party. And he especially did not like the fact that his sister was planning all of it without consulting him.

Though I expect that is all my own fault, he thought with some irony. He was the one who evaded discussing it whenever he could.

"You have time now. You just said so," Millicent said insistently. Her hazel eyes narrowed just a little. She had a squarish face, like his own, with the same high cheekbones and chiseled nose and with their father's dark brown hair. Her mouth was a little fuller than his own, and her eyes were entirely their father's. She had a firm chin and somehow altogether more intensity about her. She was also quite short, whereas he was tall. She drew herself up to her full height, which was not particularly imposing but nevertheless had the desired effect.

"What is it, Millicent?" he asked wearily. He gestured her to a chair, and she sat down. He took a seat opposite her.

"We will be housing the guests in the west wing," Millicent said instantly. "I believe there are enough rooms between the west wing and the three in the east quarters."

"Millicent..." Peter began. Until recently, Thomas had been housed in the west wing, and he did not like the thought of the poor baby being disturbed at night when the guests returned late from balls and parties. But, with the baby safely moved, he realised slowly, there was nothing to stop her.

"What, brother?" Millicent asked firmly. "If you have an objection, inform me."

Peter sighed. "The roof leaks, Millicent," he said, feeling exhausted. "In at least two of the rooms."

"What? Well, then! We shall have it fixed. How long have you let this place fall into neglect, Peter?" She chided.

Peter made a face. "I have been in London for a year, sister," he said slowly. "The house has not fallen into neglect. Two rooms have slightly leaky roofs. Given the fact that they face the side where the storms come from, that is unsurprising. They were built two hundred years ago," he added, feeling the need to support his argument. Only his sister could make him feel so defenseless.

Millicent shrugged. "We have the means to hire the best craftsmen. They will be hired, and by the time the guests arrive the day after tomorrow, the house will be fit for them. *All* the rooms," she added, one brow raised.

"The day after... sister!" Peter gaped at her. She had not once hinted that the party would commence so soon. "Is it truly supposed to be then?"

Millicent looked surprised. "The day after tomorrow is Friday," she reminded him, as though that made it all make sense. "I thought that it would be pleasant to have the ball on Friday, so that the guests have two days to recover and spend on lighter entertainments before our next event."

"Which is what?" Peter asked a little nervously.

"A garden party, of course. It's summer. Do try to enjoy it?" Millicent asked, her eyes wide.

Peter sighed. "I commend your effort," he added, not sure what else to say. There was somewhere within him a box of pleasantries that seemed to open whenever there was nothing left to say. When he reached the point where he was talking with meaningless polite phrases, he knew that he was too tired to express anything else.

"Thank you!" Millicent smiled, as though the words were genuinely pleasing. "I am so glad to hear it."

Peter sighed again. "I think I will retire to bed, sister," he said after a moment. "I feel unwell. The storm," he added, waving a vague hand at the window as if the state of the weather explained his sudden sickness.

"Oh! Of course, Peter. Of course, we will miss your presence in the dining room," she added politely.

"Thank you, sister," he managed to say. He stood and went to the door.

In his chamber, he sat down heavily on the bed. He truly was exhausted, and, though he had made up the sickness as an excuse, he really did feel unwell. He shut his eyes, relaxing for the first time all day.

As he lay there, an image of the maidservant in the nursery drifted into his thoughts. Her green eyes watched him thoughtfully, that strange calm anchoring him despite all the uncertainty and upheaval around him. He pushed the thought away, his mind drifting. As he fell into an exhausted sleep, the tempests within his soul merged with the rhythm of the falling rain and that watchful green gaze. His last thought before dreams claimed him was that he had not seen someone so unusual, so intriguing, in a long time.

Chapter 2

"Shh, little one. Rest, now," Penelope murmured softly. She felt abandoned and afraid herself—unsure of what she was doing and very alone. It did no good to let fear take hold, knowing it would only seep into her manner and unsettle the little child.

She rocked the little baby in her arms, trying to still his wails. He was eleven months old—quite able to sit up, crawl about and play with the few playthings she had found in the nursery. He babbled freely—when he was not wailing in distress—and said a few words, and she knew that he could understand a great deal more of what she said, even if he could not respond verbally to everything. She had also noticed that he was uncomfortable, frightened and uneasy far more than he was calm. She stroked his soft, downy blond hair.

"I wish I knew more about you, little one," she said gently.

Something had upset the child a great deal—that was plain from the moment that Penelope had arrived, just two days before. After receiving a letter inviting her to the manor, she had spoken to Mrs Harwell, the housekeeper, and had been advised to move in the very next day. She had done so. After the terrible lies that her former employer had spread about her; she had been amazed to be offered a position. She had not asked any questions, and nobody, in all that time, had told her anything about the child, other than his name and age. His origins were a mystery. Was he the earl's son? If he was, she had no idea of his story.

"He's a strange fellow, the earl. Isn't he, little baby?" she murmured, tucking a strand of her dark brown hair behind her ear. The baby gazed up at her, momentarily distracted from his distraught yells by some tone that he heard in her voice. She smiled.

Thomas gazed up at her, seeming to notice her for the first time. She grinned wider, and he gazed back, his eyes lighting with interest for the first time rather than with fear. She could not hide her genuine relief and delight. He chuckled.

"There now, little fellow," she cooed. "Now you feel better. Isn't that grand?"

He giggled again, and she beamed at him, then went to sit down in the upholstered chair by the fire. He was much calmer, and she reached for the glass nursing bottle that she had prepared for him. She had placed it in a bowl of warm water, hoping that the milk would be helped to stay warm, and her heart lifted to see that it was, indeed, still able to be used. She placed the glass spout of the blown-glass object into his mouth and tipped it gently, allowing a slow trickle to enter his mouth. She had already learned to do it slowly and carefully, so as not to provoke a fit of coughing from the poor baby as the milk flowed too quickly down his throat. The nursing bottle was a strange invention, Penelope mused—far from ideal—though Thomas ate porridge and other mashed foods as well, he still needed to nurse and she was grateful for the contraption's presence in the house.

"You poor little fellow," she murmured, stroking his silky hair again. Her mind wandered to thoughts of where he might have come from. Having seen the earl for the first time, she could not help but think that he could not be Thomas's father. The little baby looked nothing like the earl. The earl's hair was very dark brown. Thomas was blond and had hazel eyes, and the earl's eyes were grey. She blushed as she recalled how he had stared at her with that clear-eyed grey stare. She had stared back, her heart thudding in her chest. Her cheeks warmed further as she recalled his face. He was rather handsome with those high cheekbones and that firm chin.

She blushed, chiding herself inwardly, amused by her own inappropriate thoughts. He was her employer, and he seemed a grumpy, distant sort of man. There was certainly nothing appealing about his personality.

All the same, he was handsome, she thought with a smile. *Emily would laugh at me if she knew what I was thinking.*

Her heart ached at the thought. Her younger sister, Emily, just eighteen years old, was employed at Sterling House as a lady's maid. Sterling House was twenty miles away, and Penelope's brow furrowed. She doubted that she would be able to see Emily very often—maybe on important feast days, like Christmas and Easter, they would be given a day off, or at least a few hours, so that they might visit one another.

"Shh. Hush, now," she murmured, looking down at Thomas. Her thoughts of the earl had been replaced by worried ones, and Thomas clearly perceived her distress. He shifted in her arms, turning his head away from the bottle, and his little face crinkled in discomfort.

"Hush, now, little fellow."

He thrashed and turned his head, and Penelope drew a breath, trying to compose herself. She pushed away her thoughts of home, her distress at not seeing Emily, and her worry for her father and for her own future. It was upsetting Thomas. She focused on the sounds around her—the crackle of the fire, the patter of the rain. The storm was less severe than it had been, the thunder rumbling occasionally from far away. As she focused on the room and the present moment, Thomas seemed to relax a little, ceasing to turn or wriggle in her arms.

"Sleep, little baby," she began, singing a song that she recalled her own grandmother singing when Emily was a baby. Emily was born when Penelope was already five years old. It seemed strange to think, sometimes, that Emily was eighteen and she herself three-and-twenty. She pushed the thoughts away again, not wanting to unsettle Thomas.

She sang, rocking back and forth with Thomas clutched in her arms. He began to quieten, his belly full of warm milk and her heartbeat under his ear.

"Sleep, little baby..."

She did not know how long she sat and rocked him, but she noticed, as she stood and tiptoed across the room to settle him in his cradle, that the storm was silent. Not so much as a drop of rain pattered down. She walked to the window and drew back the curtains, staring out.

The night sky was pitch black. It was impossible, through the thick panes, to discern if there were any stars visible, or if it was still overcast. There was a tree close to the window, the boughs glistening in the candlelight that shone through the panes. It was impossible to see anything on the ground below, just absolute blackness.

It was a strange sensation, staring out into the dark—as if she was the only person in the world, or as if she and Thomas were afloat on a vast, black ocean cut off from the mainland.

I feel a bit like that, she thought, leaning on the windowsill. She felt isolated, living in the manor, surrounded by strange, silent servants and the stranger, more silent earl. Nobody seemed to speak, as if the earl's own solemn reserve had cast a hush over them all.

She gazed out. On the road, a light flickered. A coach, she guessed, the lanterns lighting the way to some distant manor or village. Perhaps it was the mail coach, heading to the place where it would stop for the night.

"Miss Matthews?"

Penelope tensed, turning and gesturing sharply to the sleeping baby. The young woman in the door made an apologetic face, hazel eyes squeezing shut for a moment.

"Sorry," she whispered in a loud whisper that would have graced a stage. "I came to see how you fared. You did not dine downstairs with us."

"Thomas was fretting," Penelope explained, smiling at the young woman, who she guessed must be around her own age, perhaps a few years her senior. "Thank you for coming to ask after me," she added warmly. Nobody on the staff had paid her any particular heed since her arrival, though nobody had been unkind, either. It was a relief to talk to someone who seemed friendly and open.

"It was no trouble," the young woman replied, her slim face lit with a sudden, bright grin that transformed her long, angular countenance into something of real beauty. Her hair glowed with coppery highlights in the candlelight. Penelope recalled seeing her in the kitchen for the first time the previous day, at luncheon. Penelope had liked the look of her instantly, but she had hurried through her meal and departed so fast that Penelope had not had a moment to talk to her.

"Thank you," Penelope repeated with genuine appreciation. "He is sleeping soundly now," she added, glancing over at the cot where Thomas slept peacefully for the first time in several hours.

"Good. You did well. Funny little fellow," the young woman replied. She gazed at the cot with real warmth in her hazel eyes.

"He is a funny fellow." Penelope paused. Perhaps the young woman knew something about the boy. "Is he the son of the earl?"

"No. No, I do not think so," her visitor answered, brow lining with a brief frown. "Though, I must admit, I would not know. I only arrived at Brentdale recently myself. I am with Lady Penrith's household."

"Oh?" Penelope smiled, feeling intrigued. "Well, then, we have both been at Brentdale only a short while." That was very comforting, though her heart sank. Perhaps Lady Penrith would stay only for a week.

"That is the case," the young woman replied. "I am afraid I did not introduce myself. I am Anna Peterham. I am pleased to meet you."

"I am pleased to meet you too," Penelope replied, inclining her head politely. "I am Penelope Matthews. Please call me Penelope," she added, recalling that Anna had called her Miss Matthews earlier.

"Thank you, Penelope. And, of course, you may call me Anna."

Penelope smiled warmly at her. The manor did not seem so lonely anymore. She had found someone who could be a friend.

"Thank you, Anna. I hope you will be visiting at Brentdale for many weeks?" she inquired, heart lifting. Having a companion would make it much easier to forget her worries.

"I believe so," Anna said with a dazzling grin. "Lady Penrith will stay for the length of the house-party, which is three weeks long. And I expect that she will remain for at least a week afterwards too, meaning we will remain almost five weeks here. Almost," she added with a small frown.

"House party?" Penelope inquired.

"Yes. Twenty or so guests and three weeks filled with balls, parties and soirees. Lucky things," Anna added, smiling brightly again.

Penelope chuckled. "You would truly enjoy such a thing?" she asked in real surprise. She had never attended a ball—the village where she had grown up held an annual dance, and she and Emily had attended that several times, but she had not particularly enjoyed it. The crowded space, the loud music and the men asking her and Emily to dance had all felt terribly uncomfortable. Her home had been quiet and remote—set outside the village by a hundred yards or so, they hardly ever had visitors at the cottage, except people from the village seeking to talk to her father, who was the local vicar. Being in an enclosed space with many people felt frightening, since she was so unused to it.

Anna nodded. "Oh, most certainly! Who would not love such a thing? Fine music, fine food and the chance to wear a fine dress! Bliss!" She whirled round, letting her skirt billow as she turned. Penelope smiled.

"When you say that, I begin to find it almost appealing," she replied.

Anna giggled. "There! We shall have to attend a ball. Even if we go in disguise. It would not be too difficult," she added with a grin. "You also don't have an accent."

Penelope blushed. She had wondered if anyone in the household had noticed that. Some people had looked at her almost resentfully, and she understood why. Only the gentry and nobility spoke like she did. It was not her fault. Her father, while being the village vicar, was also the Honourable Mr Matthews, the younger son of Baron Alforth. Since he was the younger son, he had not inherited anything at all, and his passion had always been the church, so he had never complained. But, then, father always accepted whatever state he was in with equanimity and grace; his faith too strong to allow him to doubt that all was as it was supposed to be.

"I do not have an accent, no," Penelope admitted, her eyes on the floor. She thought Anna might laugh or make a snide comment, but instead, when she looked up, she found Anna beaming at her.

"Nor do I," Anna replied. "Will you laugh if I tell you a secret?" Her expression was serious again.

"No. Of course not," Penelope replied instantly. The thought of laughing at anything told to her in trust was appalling.

"Mayhap you won't believe me. Not many do," Anna replied quickly. "But my father was the grandson of a viscount. A real viscount! A very poor and obscure one, of course. And Father was the son of the fourth son, so he got not so much as a piece of wood from the floorboards." She smiled. "But, of course, you don't have to believe me." Her hazel gaze was almost challenging.

Penelope gaped. It barely seemed possible. "Your father was the grandson of a viscount?" she asked.

"See? I told you that you would not believe it," Anna said, sounding a little defensive.

"I do. I do," Penelope replied at once. "But may I tell you a secret too?" she asked swiftly. Her heart pounded. Here was someone who might truly understand her.

"Of course. Anything," Anna said at once. "Only not, perhaps, where the buried treasure is. I might go and look." She grinned.

Penelope laughed. "If I had treasure, I would share it with you," she said instantly, knowing it was true. "The secret is that my father is the son of a baron. The second son, like your father was the son of the fourth son. My father also inherited nothing at all. He works as the vicar in the village where I grew up," she added quickly. She glanced at Anna, who beamed.

"I knew straight away that we would be friends," she replied warmly.

Penelope chuckled. "I am so glad," she said at once. Anna held her gaze steadily, and she looked back, her heart lifting. In a house of coldness and isolation, she had found real warmth.

"As am I. You have no idea how much," Anna said at once, grinning her big, warm smile. "Apart from Mrs Harwell, everybody is so serious." She made a disapproving face. Penelope laughed.

"I am glad I met you," she said at once.

"As am I," Anna replied. "Now, if Master Thomas is sleeping, perhaps you can take a moment to enjoy some dinner?"

Penelope glanced at the baby. "I cannot leave him in here by himself," she said swiftly. He was sleeping, but anything might wake him, and she would feel guilty if he awoke to find nobody beside him. "It would be cruel to him if he awoke unattended."

"Nobody said that someone cannot fetch you some cold food," Anna replied firmly. "The kitchen is just down there," she added, gesturing at the door in the wall that led to the servants' corridor. "And I would not mind having a second supper with a friend up here."

Penelope beamed. "That is so kind of you!" she exclaimed, delighted. Her stomach grumbled at the thought of food. It was long past when she would usually have dined.

"I shall not be a moment," Anna replied, going to the door.

"Thank you," Penelope called back, heart lifting.

Anna smiled and disappeared through the door, shutting it behind her. Penelope went to the upholstered chair and sank into it, letting out a slow breath as she closed her eyes. A quiet sense of relief settled over her.

She leaned back, her heart full of appreciation and warmth. As she looked around, her gaze paused on little Thomas, his angelic face aglow in the firelight. She loved the child already. *And even the earl was not terrible,* she recalled. She blushed again, her heart lifting at the thought of him. Life at Brentdale might not be so bad, after all.

Chapter 3

Peter gazed out of the window of the breakfast room. The sky was a clear-washed blue after the storm, brief puffs of cloud dusting the horizon. It was a beautiful summer's day. He drew in a long, slow breath, feeling relieved. He had lain awake until the storm had settled, and then fallen into a surprisingly deep, restorative sleep. He felt energised for the first time since arriving at the manor.

He folded the newspaper, setting it aside. He read it because he ought to, not because the doleful news that it always seemed to carry actually interested him. His gaze fell on an article about an outbreak of cholera in London, mentioning several infant deaths.

"Poor things," he murmured under his breath. His thoughts wandered to Master Thomas in the nursery. He frowned as, along with the little baby's face, the face of the new maid—with those striking green eyes—drifted into his imagination. He pushed the memory away, annoyed with himself. She was a member of his staff. He should not be thinking about her with any sort of interest. And yet, that green-eyed gaze refused to budge from his thoughts.

"My lord?"

Peter looked up, frowning. The butler was in the doorway. Peter did not like to be disturbed at breakfast; a fact everyone on his staff knew. Mr Harris looked up, his long, dignified face a grimace of discomfort.

"Yes?" Peter demanded briskly.

"Beg your pardon for the disturbance, my lord," Mr Harris said awkwardly. "But Lord Chelmsford is here. He requested to be shown to the billiards room."

"George!" Peter exclaimed happily. He smiled. George—or more formally known as Lord Chelmsford—was his cousin on his mother's side and a dear friend as well. He was not like Charles, who had been more of an elder brother to Peter than anything else; but he was a welcome, cheerful presence who had kept Peter sane during the months following the death of his cousin.

"Please show him upstairs, Mr Harris. I will join him directly," Peter replied.

"Very good, my lord," the butler murmured and withdrew.

Peter gulped his tea, dabbing at his lips with the linen napkin by his plate. He had expected George to arrive at some time during the day, but it was a pleasure to have the opportunity to talk to him.

He stood up and strolled down to the billiards room.

George was just preparing his cue when Peter walked in. He turned and grinned.

"Peter! Good morning, old fellow! Delighted to see you." He held out his big, squarish hand for Peter to shake.

"George! Grand to see you." Peter shook his hand, smiling into his cousin's dark brown eyes with real warmth. "How do you fare? I trust the journey was pleasant?" he asked, his gaze scanning George's gentle face. His cousin was tall—the same height as himself—with thick chestnut-coloured hair and dark brown eyes. He had a square face, slightly softened, and his eyes were merry and gentle. One could see straight away that he was kind and friendly. He also looked a little weary; dark rings around his eyes.

"It was good enough. I slept badly last night. I think the weather here was as bad as fifty miles away?" he raised a brow.

Peter nodded, smiling. "I trust it was every bit as bad," he agreed. "We had quite a storm last night."

"Difficult to find rest during a storm," George commented lightly. His gaze scanned Peter's face, as if asking a question.

Peter nodded, keeping his expression neutral. "Quite so," he agreed. He did not wish to worry his cousin, who knew that Peter hated storms, and why. Millicent was concerned enough about his welfare—she said that often as her reason for organising a house-party. He did not want to worry George, whose gentle nature meant that he would take it to heart.

"How fares your sister?" George asked, putting his cue back in its place on the wall.

"Well, I believe," Peter commented, wandering with George towards the door. "I have barely seen her since her arrival—she seems always to be busy somewhere in the house, organising the house-party." He made a wry face. George was included on the guest-list, which was why he was at Brentdale Manor rather than at his own estate fifty miles away.

"It is planned to be quite the event, I think," George replied lightly.

Peter inclined his head. "I believe so. I fully expect half the ton to descend on Brentdale Manor on the morrow." He made a disapproving moue.

George chuckled. "Only half? Would that not be remiss?" he asked playfully.

"Believe me, it probably would," Peter answered. "Which is why I intend to say nothing about it."

George laughed. They reached the drawing room and sat down. A fire burned low in the grate—not for warmth, but to keep the room dry and fresh. Sunlight streamed through the tall south- and east-facing windows, quickly warming the space.

The upholstered chair by the hearth was inviting, and Peter sank into it, only to rise reluctantly a moment later to ring the bell for tea.

"And yourself?" George asked as Peter sank back into the comfortable chair.

"Me?" Peter blinked, confused.

"How do you fare?" George asked gently.

Peter lifted a shoulder, feeling a little uncomfortable. "Well," he said awkwardly. "I suppose," he added.

George smiled. "I do not believe there is a right or wrong answer to that question," he said lightly. "I am glad to hear you fare well."

Peter looked down, reaching for the newspaper. He always felt uneasy when people pried into his business, no matter how pleasant and good-natured the inquiry was.

"My lord?" Mr Harris was in the doorway. Peter looked up, relieved.

"Please bring tea for my guest, Mr Harris. And something light to eat," he added, glancing at George's pale, tired appearance. He suspected that his friend had set out early from whichever inn had housed him the night before. He would have had to in order to arrive at Brentdale by nine o'clock in the morning. And that meant he had likely gone without breakfast.

"At once, my lord," the butler replied and withdrew.

"I believe that Thomas is settling in?" George asked as they waited for the tea.

Peter tensed. He did not like it when people raised the topic of Thomas. Any discussion about the boy was always, in his mind, tinged with a shadow of his terrible guilt. He did not understand it himself, but he felt responsible for the death of the child's parents. Talking about him always darkened his mood. This time, however, it brought with it a picture of the new maid, standing with Thomas tight in her arms. That made it easier to bear. He shrugged.

"He seems well enough," he said lightly. "He has settled in to the Green Room, I believe. Or at least, I have not heard anything to the contrary."

"The Green Room?" George asked, sounding surprised.

"Yes. The new maid suggested that the west wing was too drafty and damp for a baby." Peter kept his voice level. He could not help recalling that wide, green gaze as he thought of the new maid, and imagining her giving orders to the rest of the staff to move the dresser and other things. He wanted to chuckle. She was certainly different.

"Oh?" George blinked. "Well, she is likely not wrong. The bad weather usually comes from there." He shrugged.

"Just so," Peter agreed lightly. He looked up as Mr Harris wheeled the tea-trolley into the room, distracting himself from the uncomfortable conversation.

"She must be quite competent, then," George said as Mr Harris put the teapot on the table. "The new maid, I mean. That shows dedication, moving the baby from unfavourable conditions into better ones. To say nothing of taking some courage on her part," he added, nodding in thanks to the butler as he placed a porcelain teacup on the table.

"I suppose," Peter said awkwardly. He did not want to think about, or discuss, the new maid. His reaction had been confusing, and he did not want to think about it too much.

The butler gave Peter a teacup and saucer as well, then placed a porcelain plate containing slices of raisin loaf, pound cake and little sandwiches with the crusts cut off on the table. He straightened up and wheeled the trolley out.

"It's fine weather, eh?" George asked, reaching for a small sandwich. He bit into it contentedly, shutting his eyes for a moment. Peter smiled to himself. One thing that had remained true of George since their Cambridge days was that he had an admirable appetite. He must have been suffering terribly without his breakfast.

"It is very fine weather," Peter replied, selecting a slice of pound cake. He was not particularly hungry, but it seemed rude to let his guest eat in isolation. Not that George would have minded, he thought wryly. His friend was clearly hungry enough to set etiquette aside for the moment.

"Fine sunshine. Not a cloud up there, eh?" George commented, helping himself to another sandwich. Peter bit back a smile. His sister would probably have been scandalised by George's unashamed appetite. Peter himself merely enjoyed being able to provide his friend with some much-needed victuals.

"Indeed," Peter agreed. "Perhaps going for a ride later would be acceptable?" he asked, pouring himself a cup of tea.

"Most acceptable, old fellow. Most acceptable," George agreed, taking a slice of pound cake.

Peter smiled and looked out of the window. A ride in the afternoon would be very pleasant. It would help to clear his mind. It would also get him out of the house, which was becoming increasingly oppressive as the preparations for the house-party accelerated.

"Brother? Oh! George! What a surprise," Millicent said from the doorway. "You arrived very early." She smiled at George with real warmth in her hazel eyes, inclining her head in greeting as both George and Peter stood up.

"Millicent. Grand to see you," George replied. He inclined his head, a brief bow.

"I am so glad to find you here," Millicent added, turning to Peter. "I was busy overseeing the preparations for the ball tomorrow evening. We will need seating set out for the musicians. I have requested a quintet."

"So many?" Peter asked. Usually, three or four men with stringed instruments were enough to provide the music for a ball.

"I intend this ball to be talked of in London," Millicent said lightly. "Our family has become decidedly provincial in the last years, and we have a need to regain our standing."

"Millicent..." Peter began warningly. He tried to indicate George's presence. He did not want to argue in front of their cousin. He had only just arrived.

"It is no less than the truth. I want to place us right at the top of society. Where we belong. And I also want you to enjoy yourself and become cheerful again." She gave him a firm glance. "So, we need to have a grand ball."

"Millicent," Peter began. How little did she know her own younger brother, if she thought a ball would lift his spirits? He hated balls.

"I will request that Mr Harris help me. He ought to have the capacity to find some seats and oversee the staff to move them," she said swiftly.

"Of course," Peter replied. "Will you not join us for tea?" he added, feeling a little uncomfortable. He should have suggested that earlier.

"Yes. That is very kind of you, Peter."

Peter rang the bell, summoning Mr Harris to bring an extra cup and saucer for Millicent. He arrived almost at once, and Peter instructed him, relieved to have something else to do besides arguing with his sister. Millicent took a seat at the table.

"This is pleasant," she sighed, leaning back. "I have barely sat down all week."

"You are working too hard," Peter told her firmly. "You can trust the household to oversee things."

"This household?" Millicent raised a brow. "They have not been supervised by a countess for a long time. They have become positively lazy. I do not know when Harwell last saw that the silverware got a good polishing." She made a disapproving face.

"The silverware..." Peter began. He could barely believe it. Had his sister truly noticed such a thing? She had barely been there for four days yet! He was perfectly happy with the staff—simply glad to be away from London.

"It's a disgrace! You need to find a countess, Peter. This place will fall apart if you do not do so soon."

"Sister..." Peter said angrily. That was a step too far. He was the earl. She might be his elder sister, but she was not his father. What he chose to do in his personal life was none of her business.

"It is nothing less than the truth, brother," Millicent said firmly. The butler arrived and placed a cup before her. She did not even look up to acknowledge him, but poured her tea and continued talking as though nobody was there. "This estate is going to rack and ruin. Leaks in the roof. Spots on the cutlery. What next?"

Peter said nothing. George was sitting quite still, not speaking. He seemed to be trying to act as though he was not there.

"The estate has been maintained without anybody besides the staff being present for the last six months," Peter reminded his sister firmly. "If certain matters have not been maintained, like the cutlery, that is to be expected. Who would have been using it in all that time?" He held her gaze.

"It does not matter," his sister said airily. "Such things should be maintained. Now, I have invited Lord and Lady Winthrop to the ball. Their daughter Adeline is going to be there as well, of course. I want you to pay special attention to her. She was a shining diamond at the balls of London this year." She held his stare.

"Lady Adeline has just debuted," he reminded his sister, his voice almost a growl. "I would not like to impose on such a young lady." There was not such a great disparity between their ages, just eight years, but that might be the only objection Millicent would be willing to hear.

"Oh, Peter! It's hardly as though you are an old man," Millicent said scornfully. "She is barely younger than you. And she is quite absolutely a paragon."

Peter did not say anything. He had met Lady Adeline, since Lord and Lady Winthrop had been friends of the family while Papa still lived. In his opinion, she was shallow and uninteresting, but he had to admit that he had not seen her in many years. Perhaps he was being unfair.

"I must insist that you dance with her tomorrow at the ball," Millicent continued. "It would be very rude to old friends of the family were you not to," she added, head tilted as though she was chiding a child.

"Millicent..." Peter began. His right hand clenched the arm of the chair, his left hand closing into a fist around the cuff of his jacket. He was fighting his growing rage. She had no right whatsoever to demand anything of him, especially nothing that would, ultimately, affect only himself, such as who became the next countess. "I regret that I have business I must attend to. Pray excuse me," he murmured. He stood up.

"Brother..." Millicent began. Peter walked to the door. He turned, checking to see if George was offended by his abrupt statement. George caught his eye. He looked sad, but not offended.

Peter stalked down the hallway. It felt as though his cheeks were burning, rage flaring up inside him, incandescent and unable to be suppressed. He had to go riding. It was the only thing that he knew of that would calm him.

He hurried around the corner towards his chamber. He had to get out before he lost his temper.

A cry of rage escaped him as he collided, quite forcefully, with someone hurrying the other way. He staggered forwards, just as the person staggered back and fell, hard, onto the hallway floor on their back.

Peter stared in shock. Long brown hair tumbled around the person's face, which was pale and slim. Green eyes, round and frightened, stared up at him from the slender face. It was the new maid.

Chapter 4

Penelope gazed up in horror at the earl, who stood just an inch away from her where she lay on the floor. The bottle that she had been carrying in her hand was smashed on the floor, dropped as she collided with the very firm male body that had hurried around the corner, straight into her.

I'm not even supposed to be here, Penelope thought in terror.

She should have used the servants' corridor. The servants' corridor was dark—a draft had blown out the oil lamps. Not wanting to hurry up darkened stairs carrying the baby's bottle when she could fall, she had chosen to use the manor's main staircase—something that was not really allowed. Her heart raced in shock and fear. Was she going to be thrown out of the house? Using the stairs was a grave enough transgression in most households—but colliding with a nobleman? That was surely far worse.

"I..." she began, struggling to get up. She winced in pain. She had fallen straight over backwards and it was only as she tried to sit that her head started to throb and pound. She had hit it quite badly on the wooden floorboards. Her shock and terror had outweighed the pain, but she blinked, disoriented, unable to see for a moment.

"Miss Matthews. Please, allow me."

Penelope blinked again, trying to clear her vision. The dark grey fog clouding her sight slowly lifted. As it cleared, she found herself staring at an outstretched hand—strong, steady, mere inches from her face.

The earl had bent down beside her.

"My lord! I..." she stammered again, but his hand reached out and, very gently, took hers. She blushed scarlet. His palm was warm, his fingers exceptionally strong. He squeezed his fingers closed and then she was hauled upright as if she was weightless. She blinked, staggering for a moment. He held out his other hand, steadying her by gripping her left arm.

"My lord. I am so sorry..." she murmured, eyes focusing on the toes of her shoes. His feet were an inch away from hers, the dark brown toes of his elegant leather boots just an inch from her white outdoor shoes. Her cheeks were burning. His hand was still firmly closed around her own.

"No need," his voice said, a little rough. "I was as much at fault." His fingers unfurled.

"But, my lord!" She began, about to apologise for using the stairs. He gazed into her eyes. His face was just a few inches away; close enough for her to see his long, dark eyelashes and the very slight wrinkles at the corners of his eyes.

"You were no more at fault than I. Are you harmed?" His voice was serious.

"No," Penelope stammered. She looked down at the mess on the floor. "I will clean..." she tried to say, swallowing hard.

"You are needed in the nursery. I will summon someone to tidy the hallway." His voice was firm.

"Yes, my lord," Penelope managed. Anna was sitting with the baby, lest he woke while Penelope prepared his bottle. She had not meant to be longer than a few minutes. She did need to return. She shut her eyes, her head pounding.

"You are hurt." The earl's voice was firm and insistent. Penelope shook her head.

"I only feel a little unsteady," she murmured. Her own voice sounded as though it was coming from a distance, and her head pounded.

"You need to rest." The earl said firmly. She made herself look up into his gaze. It held hers insistently. His grey eyes were like pools under cloud. Intense and deep.

"Thomas needs me," Penelope said, her voice sounding weary even to her own ears.

"Go and rest," the earl insisted. "I will summon a maid to clean up this mess." He gestured to the broken glass and the wet patch on the floor.

"Thank you," Penelope stammered. She kept her gaze focused on the floor.

"Do not work until your head is clear. Your duties demand your full attentiveness," he added reproachfully.

"Yes, my lord," Penelope replied. Her gaze moved to his. His eyes were not bitter or angry, but held hers gently. She looked away. Her heart was pounding. Her body was suffused with warmth.

The earl turned in the hallway, his back—broad and muscled—turned to her. She hurried away up the hallway towards the new nursery, cheeks burning.

"Anna!" she called as she hurried in. "How does Thomas fare? Is he..."

"Hush, Penelope," Anna replied gently. "He is sleeping. What happened?" She added, frowning.

"I fell," Penelope replied, cheeks flaring again with embarrassed heat as she recalled the awkward incident. She reached up self-consciously to find that her hair had tumbled down out of its bun. What would the earl think? He must think she was a careless hoyden. Not only was she wandering in the upper hallways, reserved for the gentry and their guests, but she had tumbledown hair as well.

"Are you unhurt?" Anna asked, her brow furrowing. "Where did you fall?"

"In the hallway," Penelope said, looking down. "The bottle is broken," she added. That made her feel terribly guilty.

"You yourself said that there were two. So, there is no harm done," Anna insisted gently. "Now, sit and rest. You need not rush downstairs to prepare another straight away. He is sleeping quite soundly," she added.

Penelope nodded. "I should sit for a moment," she agreed. The dizziness lingered, though she couldn't tell whether it was the result of the blow to her head or simply the aftershock of the moment.

"Rest. I can prepare the bottle," Anna told her firmly. She gestured to the baby. "Of all the work you do, I am quite certain that preparing the bottle is not the hardest part. And my mistress is occupied in the ballroom," she added, one brow raised. "So, I will not be needed for a while."

"Is there to be a ball?" Penelope asked, glad to focus on something else besides the pain in her head and the embarrassing incident.

"Tomorrow, I believe. Guests will be arriving today and tomorrow. Or, so my mistress plans," Anna added, grinning. "She has been rather busy all week, which can only be good from my point of view."

Penelope giggled. Anna took her work seriously, that was clear, but not so seriously that she was averse to joking about her employers, which was a pleasant change. Penelope herself had enough bad experience in her recent past to find nothing amusing.

"That is good," she agreed. Anna stood up.

"Now, I will go and prepare that bottle. I hope I shall be able to do so in the correct manner." She frowned.

"I am certain you shall," Penelope said. "If you rinse it with hot water and warm the milk, all should be well. Thank you, Anna," she added, her heart full of appreciation.

"It is no trouble," Anna replied. "If you truly want to thank me, you can help me with the laundry. Wretched opera gloves," she added, her face crinkling in mock disapproval. "Trying to find them all after a batch of washing is a job for someone far more patient than I am."

Penelope laughed.

Anna shut the door behind her, and Penelope heard her steps retreat. She leaned back and closed her eyes. She was exhausted. It was not just the shock, or the pain in her head. It was the interaction with the duke that had drained her.

He is so confusing, she thought, heart pounding. The way he looked at her, staring into her eyes, left her wondering what he thought of her. It was not like any stare she had ever seen before. It was not censure in his eyes, or judgment. But nor was it any sort of lewdness or lechery, and that was the only other thing that she expected from a wealthy employer who believed themselves above the law.

The look he gave her was almost amazement, or fascination. Like the look in her own eyes if she saw a dragonfly or some particularly beautiful creation of Nature.

"Don't be silly," she told herself aloud, very firmly. That made absolutely no sense whatsoever. *The way that I hit my head has addled my brains,* she told herself, feeling at once annoyed and, for some strange reason, oddly warm inside. She pushed the warmth away.

"Your hair is a mess," she told herself aloud, going to the looking glass that hung on the wall and tidying it swiftly. It had fallen loose from its neat bun, and the thick, glossy brown curls hung to her shoulders. She pinned it up swiftly, her cheeks flaring again.

She studied her reflection. She did not need any kind of trouble with her employers. That was precisely why she had lost her job at Hatfield House. She did not need to face that sort of trouble again.

She shivered, recalling the fear and horror of that. As if he could feel her emotions, Thomas began to stir in his sleep, making small moans of distress.

"Shh. Shh, little fellow. Nothing is amiss," Penelope murmured. She stared out of the window as she comforted the child, watching the birds in the pale blue morning sky. They were flying merrily; no trace of the storm left to affect them.

"We can go outside for a walk," she told the baby, who was starting to wake, his eyelids fluttering. "I think you might enjoy that." Some fresh air and sunshine were exactly what they needed.

"Here it is!" Anna called, appearing at the doorway to the servants' corridor.

"Thank you, Anna," Penelope replied with real relief. "And just when I needed it. Thank you," she repeated, taking the bottle. It was warm, but not too hot. She held it carefully, waiting for Thomas to wake more fully.

"No trouble," Anna replied.

"If you need any help with the laundry..." Penelope began. Anna's face lit up.

"I will come and fetch you. You can leave Mrs Aldham to look after the baby. She already said she'd do it for half an hour or so if you need it," Anna added persuasively.

Penelope smiled. "I'd be happy to help you."

"Truly?" Anna clapped her hands delightedly. "That would be grand. I will fetch you tomorrow afternoon."

Penelope smiled. "I would be glad to help," she repeated. Her heart lifted. Anna had helped her so much—she truly would be happy to help her with the laundry.

She fed Thomas and then dressed him warmly, donned her own dark pelisse and bonnet and carried him, wrapped in a shawl, out into the garden.

A slight breeze blew, and she hugged Thomas tight against her, holding him until they reached a bench in the sun.

"What a lovely garden," she murmured to the child, holding him on her lap. He seemed to enjoy the sunshine too, cooing happily and lifting his hand as a butterfly flitted overhead.

"You like it, I think," she said softly to the baby, bending to fluff his downy blond hair. She frowned. Little Thomas was a mystery. He truly looked nothing like the earl. She recalled those severe features—that thin, handsome face, the sweetly romantic long eyelashes and that frosty stare of cloud-grey eyes. There was no trace of him in the cheerful, soft face of the happy baby.

A motion drew her eye, and she looked to see a man was walking in the distance—tall, with broad shoulders. Her heart thudded. Almost certainly it was the earl. She sat up straighter, cheeks flaring.

What does he think of me? she asked herself. Did he think she was incompetent? Untrustworthy? Or was that admiration she had seen in his eyes?

"Stop being so silly," she chided herself firmly. Whatever he thought did not matter. Provided she could work at his home, live in the servants' quarters and be fed and earn a wage, nothing mattered at all. She was a servant in his household. He was a noble. What else he thought of her did not matter.

All the same, I do still wish that I could know, she thought with a blush, recalling the intensity of his gaze. That stare made no sense, and she could not help puzzling about what it meant and wishing that she could guess the answer.

Chapter 5

"You're a fool," Peter muttered to himself harshly as he stalked across the lawn towards the stable. "A quite incurable fool."

He could not shake the feeling of shame that enveloped him every time he thought of the new maid and the brief interaction in the hallway. Not only had he walked into her and interfered with her carrying out of her duties—the broken milk bottle on the floor made his cheeks flare with embarrassed heat whenever he thought of it—but he'd hurt her.

It was neither fact, though, that made his cheeks flare with shame. It was the feelings that she had stirred in him—things he had thought he had forgotten how to feel.

If it were desire, he thought in annoyance, it would be simple. Desire was something that he could excuse, since it was something that his body could not help but experience occasionally. He was still young, and the woman was young and not unattractive. He would simply have avoided her and tried to focus on things he enjoyed, like riding and collecting exotic plants for his greenhouse.

But this was not just desire. It was something else. Admiration was part of it—not only for her dedication to her job, but for her fearlessness where he was concerned. And something else. An interest, a fascination. Those green eyes drew him in, making him want to talk to her, to find out about her.

"Nonsense," he rebuked himself. His father would have taken him to task for such folly.

The thought made his throat tighten, his heart aching with a pain that he thought he had forgotten. When he was sixteen, he had become fascinated with a young woman in the village. She had been briefly employed at the house as a seamstress and had her own seamstress shop in the village. She was the daughter of the schoolmaster and both beautiful and well-spoken. She was two years his senior. That was not, of course, the reason why his father had objected. He had said it was entirely inappropriate for an earl's son to ride into the village just to take arbitrary trips to the village seamstress's shop. People, he had said, were going to talk. They had already begun to talk, and the poor young lady's reputation was ruined. She had disappeared from the village, and Peter had been beyond distressed.

"What a fool I was," he murmured, stepping behind the stable for a moment, not wanting to risk any of the staff coming upon him in a debilitating moment of regret and grief. He could recall the young lady's face so clearly—her name was Amy Winters, and she had been tall, slim, fair-haired and beautiful, with a neat, oval face and brown eyes that were almost chestnut brown in tone. He had admired her beyond anyone that he had ever met.

He had managed to find out what had happened after considerable dedication and the assistance of his manservant, Mr Highgate. The young lady had wed a prosperous farmer and moved to Dorchester. He had no idea if she truly was happy, but Mr Highgate had reported so. He hoped beyond what he could express that it was true.

His infatuation with Amy Winters had come close to ruining her. His love only brought harm. His parents were both dead, his cousin and Eliza... he pushed the thought away.

He drew in a shaky breath. He could not afford to let himself become interested in another person. Especially not one who was, like Miss Winters, so much below his station. It would not only harm him—and, as Millicent assured him, their status in society was tenuous enough—but it would harm her. He had to ignore it. It was only right.

He walked round to the front of the stable and went in. Mr Leeson, the stable master, was there, talking with the stable hand. Peter nodded in acknowledgement of their greeting.

"Saddle Wildfire, please," he instructed the youth, Benjamin, who looked after the horses.

"Yes, my lord," the young man replied at once and hurried off to do so.

Peter remained with the stable master, feeling somewhat awkward. He had nothing particular to say—no instructions, no idle conversation. His mind was elsewhere, too preoccupied to focus on anything around him. He had hoped for company on this ride, but George had suddenly recalled some overlooked business that needed attending and had rushed off to see to it, leaving Peter to ride alone.

Fortunately, Benjamin was quick with his work, and only five minutes later, he reappeared.

"Wildfire is saddled, my lord."

"Thank you," Peter replied. "Good day," he added, nodding to the stable-master. He took Wildfire's reins and led him from his stall. Wildfire—a dark red-brown thoroughbred—whinnied a greeting, and Peter mounted up swiftly in the yard, leaning back and putting his heels down. Riding was something he did on a reflex—thanks to lessons that had begun when he was only four years old. Perhaps it was that, he reflected as he rode out, that made it so comfortable; something that he sought out when he needed to relax. Perhaps, he thought with a smile as Wildfire neighed again, it was also the company of his special horse.

"Easy, old chap," he said lightly, patting the stallion's neck. Wildfire had been his horse for the last five years and they had an easy, comfortable relationship. He trusted Wildfire. It felt good, since he trusted nobody else. *George, perhaps,* he thought as he gazed out over the landscape, the easy rhythm of Wildfire walking up an incline to the forest making his mind free to wander. But nobody else.

He leaned a little forward as they reached the top of the hill, giving Wildfire the instruction that he could speed up. Wildfire began to canter, clearly enjoying the chance to relieve some of his pent-up energy. They sped along the path through the forest.

The estate was bordered by woodland on three sides; some of which was the property of his family and some of which was not. The boundaries were clearly marked, but Peter trusted the locals and, since he was not an avid hunter himself, keeping a hawk's eye on the game on his own land was not interesting to him.

Millicent would be scandalised by my laxity, he thought with a slight smile. As he rode, the tension in his shoulders and the uncomfortable ache in his belly eased and he could find the events of the morning amusing. Millicent's insistence on Lady Adeline was less humorous, however, and his stomach twisted nauseously again as he recalled that soon the guests would be arriving.

He rode through the woods, taking a path that he did not often use that led upwards again, up a hill that would overlook the village. An unused verderer's cottage was on one side of the path; a relic of a time when his father had managed the estate and the woods had been carefully maintained, stocked with game for hunting. Oak trees lined the path, their leaves a rich summery green against the blue sky. Larks sang overhead. The scent of the loam of the forest floor was in his nostrils and he started to relax as he rode upwards.

The hill overlooked the valley where Brentdale Manor lay, along with the distant village which had been the oldest part of the earldom over which his family presided. The landscape was peaceful, smoke rising over the village. People were probably beginning to prepare their midday meal; he realised as the church bells rang the eleventh hour.

The earldom had never seemed more of a responsibility than it did now. He looked away, not wanting to think about the land and tenants and all the things that weighed on his shoulders. For just a few hours, he mused, it would be pleasant to be an ordinary man, with no heavy duties on his shoulders, and without the watchful eye of high society as a presence that judged him without even needing to see him.

"A pox on this party," he murmured, turning to ride down.

The added tension that his sister's planning brought to the house was not making anything easier. He tensed as he saw coaches on the road as he and Wildfire hurried down the path towards the manor. He let Wildfire dictate the pace, clinging on with his knees as his horse elected to gallop. The hours of lessons meant that he did not need to feel unsettled, no matter what happened. His horse had bolted with him enough times for him to know that, for the most part, he and Wildfire could manage even that frightening possibility.

He rode to the stable.

"Please see that he receives warm bran and a good rub," he told the young stable hand. The youth inclined his head respectfully.

"I will do it directly, my lord," he replied, and hurried off.

Peter strode towards the house, his heart sinking. There was a coach waiting in front of the door. He glanced at the insignia and his spirits lifted. The slightly unusual badge of a blackbird perched on what looked like a thorny tree was one he knew well. It was his aunt; Aunt Marcia. And, he thought with a smile, his cousin Sophia.

"My lord," the butler greeted him as he walked briskly up the steps. "Guests have begun to arrive. Your sister the marchioness requested that they be directed upstairs. I have brought tea and refreshments to the drawing room."

"You did well," Peter answered. He nodded to the fellow in thanks, passed him his hat and riding coat and strode up the stairs.

The sound of voices reached him as he strode up towards the drawing room. Millicent was there, and Edmund, her husband. He thought George might be there too, and then he heard his aunt, just as he reached the entrance to the room.

"Peter! My dear nephew! Wherever have you been hiding?"

"Aunt," Peter declared, opening his arms just in time for a fragrant and surprisingly strong hug. "Wonderful to see you."

"You cannot have grown, but I had forgotten how tall you are," Aunt Marcia declared, tipping back her head to look up at him. "Hugh would be more than proud."

Peter tensed. Hugh, his father, was Aunt's brother. He always felt a little uncomfortable at mentions of his father. His own relationship with his father had been complicated. He both loved, respected and feared him, and his passing eight years before had made his feelings no easier to understand. He was grateful that he and his father had managed to make peace before he had passed away, but there were still many things that he wished he could have understood.

"It's grand to see you," Peter repeated gently. "And Sophia. An honour to see you," he added, turning to his cousin.

Sophia, who was tall, with a soft oval face, big blue eyes and thick honey-coloured hair, beamed shyly at him and looked down at the floor.

"Cousin Peter. How pleasant to see you," she murmured, dropping a curtsey. "I trust you are well?"

"Yes. Thank you," Peter replied, smiling at his cousin. She looked like a young, softer version of her mother, who had an angular face and an astute gaze that missed little. Aunt's hair was white, touched with a few dark grey strands, and pulled back into an elegant chignon. She wore a pale grey gown and had blue eyes like her daughter. His cousin wore a blue muslin dress that complimented her own blue gaze.

"I hope you had a pleasant ride," Aunt Marcia commented. "One should be outdoors in this weather. It is very fine. And one should take advantage of clear skies here, not so?" She smiled at him.

"Yes. Quite so."

"We do have more than our share of storms here," Sophia reminded him with a grin. She giggled. "I did get such a fright yesterday night. It was so loud, the thunder! I was quite terrified."

Aunt Marcia looked fondly at her daughter. "The mantel in the drawing room did rattle now and again," she agreed. "Was it as bad here?" she asked Peter.

"I don't think the furniture rattled," he replied with a smile. "But the roof in the west wing does leak. The nursery had to be moved to the Green Room," he added.

"Oh, Aunt does not want to hear about tedious estate details," Millicent began. "The roof barely leaks. Not so?" she added, shooting him a piercing glare. She was clearly embarrassed that Aunt knew about the roof. Peter cleared his throat, unsure what to say.

"The nursery? How does the new maid fare?" Aunt asked, one brow raised. "I understand she is a talented maid for looking after children."

"Oh?" Peter blinked in surprise. "Well, I thought she was competent. Moving the nursery showed some dedication to her work," he replied, his cheeks flaring uncomfortably. Even talking about her made him feel warm and slightly embarrassed, though he could not say why exactly.

"Quite so," his aunt said with a nod. "I employ her sister. I found out yesterday. And so far, she seems very competent." She turned to Sophia, who nodded, smiling.

"She is a very good ladies' maid," she agreed. "Unfortunately, we could not bring her with us. Millicent said that her maid will arrange my hair, though." She smiled at Millicent, who smiled back, though she looked tense.

"I must go down and greet our guests as they arrive," Millicent said to Peter. "Perhaps you will remain here?" Her grin could not hide her evident discomfort. She clearly wanted to go downstairs and welcome the arriving guests.

Peter nodded. He felt guilty, seeing her tension. She had put a great deal of work into organising the party, and etiquette was so important to her that a slight lapse would almost make her lose consciousness.

"Of course," he agreed softly. He glanced at Edmund, her husband. Edmund bowed smoothly. His dark brown hair showed grey at the temples, his smooth, oval face seeming tranquil.

"I should go with Millicent," he said, offering Peter a bland smile. "A united front, eh? First rule of warfare."

Peter lifted one shoulder. He wanted to reply that it was a party, not a war, but there was no point in arguing with Edmund. The fellow was smoothly affable to everyone and, even though his dark brown eyes would narrow at the slightest perceived insult, he made a point of being friendly. Peter could do no less, though he could not warm to the fellow no matter how hard he tried. His family had all been charmed by Edmund, who had been a colonel in the Hussars. Peter, however, could not like him, finding his manners too smooth and bland for comfort.

"Come and sit down, do," Aunt Marcia said, patting his hand in a caring way. Peter smiled.

"Thank you, Aunt," he replied warmly.

"I want to hear all about the garden. And the stable!" Sophia replied, clapping her hands. She was twenty, Peter recalled, though sometimes she seemed much younger. He had always been fond of his youngest cousin.

"There is not much to relate, in terms of the garden, I am afraid," Peter replied honestly. "In London, I managed to collect absolutely nothing aside from some seeds from a flowering creeper." He gave her a shamefaced look.

His cousin giggled. "I hope it is a pretty one, then."

Peter nodded. "It is very pretty," he assured her. "And when it flowers, I shall invite you to come and see it."

"Thank you, cousin! That would be grand. I do love flowers!" She clasped her hands in delight, a rapturous grin on her face.

Peter leaned back, relaxing in the easy company of his aunt and youngest cousin. With Millicent and Edmund downstairs and no longer in the room to cast awkwardness and judgment into each corner, it was easy to feel comfortable and even to look forward to the upcoming ball.

As he sat sipping his tea and listening to their news from the estate, his mind wandered to the new maid. Her sister worked for Aunt Marcia. He had not thought to wonder about her family, or even if she had any siblings. He frowned as her face came vividly to his mind. He thought far too often about her and he pushed the thought aside, not wanting to lose himself in wondering where she was and what she might be doing at that very moment.

Chapter 6

"It's windy out here," Anna called out, her voice carrying across the empty space around the washing-line, buffeted by the wind.

Penelope giggled. "Yes, it is," she agreed, laughing as she reached up to remove the pegs that held a big bedsheet. The linen billowed out, cracking in the breeze and almost smacking her. She laughed in delight and lifted it from where it hung on the line above her head, then carried the crisply-scented linen to Anna, to fold it.

"This is actually rather enjoyable," Anna said with a grin as they stood folding the sheet. It was not particularly easy, since the wind kept on buffeting it, making them shriek as they almost dropped it. But it was fun. Penelope smiled warmly.

"It is," she agreed. She drew a deep breath. It reminded her painfully of home, where she and Emily did the laundry together. On a fine day, they would have gone out to fetch it in exactly the same way. When they were younger, they played dress-up in the clean curtains, running around the lawn pretending to be ladies going to a ball.

"I am of a mind to seek your help every week," Anna said teasingly.

"Gladly," Penelope agreed.

She took the folded sheet and put it in the big, flat basket they had brought with them to carry the laundry, and they resumed collecting bedclothes and petticoats from the line.

The sunshine was warm, beating down on her face. She wore a white linen uniform, which made the hot weather slightly easier to bear. With the breeze that ruffled her hair and billowed the laundry, it was very pleasant outside.

"I should bring Thomas out here," she mused to herself. Anna was fetching clothing off the line higher up and did not hear her. Penelope looked around the garden. It was a fine, warm summer day. Perhaps she could find a blanket and bring the little one out to lie in the shade. She could read to him from a book. He needed company and fretted whenever she was out of his sight. He might enjoy a simple excursion and a chance to sleep in the fresh air and warmth.

"There! Now, we just have to take it inside and sort through it. I should do that bit. I do not want to keep you from your duties," she said quickly. She lifted the big basket, supporting it on her hip.

"I can help for a few minutes," Penelope assured her. She had asked an older woman on the staff to sit with Thomas while she helped, and the other maid had been more than happy to do it. She smiled to herself. Thomas was sleeping peacefully. He seemed happier when she was happy. Grandmother was right, she mused, walking behind Anna as they went back towards the house.

"Now, we should go to the laundry room and sort this into piles," Anna told her as they walked through the door that led into a warren of servants' corridors. The bottom floor of the house was entirely dedicated to service, with the kitchen, the butler's office, the laundry and pantry and several storerooms. The gentry and nobility never went down there. Penelope followed Anna down the hallway, feeling interested and a little tense. She hardly ever went downstairs where the other servants often carried out most of their work. She and Anna spent most of their time on the upper floors, where the nobles lived, and that made some members of the house's staff treat them a little resentfully. Penelope looked in through open doors as they passed them, wanting to know more about what was downstairs.

"Here we are," Anna declared, pushing open a door. "The laundry room."

Penelope looked around. A long table dominated the room, where linen could be folded and pressed with a clothes iron. There was a sideboard along the one wall, and beside it stood a big wooden tub with a washboard leaning beside it, a mangle and another table. The air smelled of a mix of lavender and carbolic. It made her eyes water if she breathed too deeply. A fireplace was beside the table, where water could be heated for the big tub. The air was very warm in the room, which was also lit with a few big windows.

"We need to sort through the laundry so that it can be taken to the correct rooms later," Anna explained, putting the basket on the big long table and straightening up.

"Where must I put the sheets?" Penelope asked.

"Those are for my mistress. Let us put them here," Anna suggested, indicating a place on the table. Penelope lifted the folded sheets and put them where she had shown her.

"And those?" She pointed at the jumble of washing in the basket, which consisted of some slips and petticoats, some smaller items of bedlinen, silk socks and satin gloves.

"Mostly, those belong to my mistress as well," Anna explained. "Though I think some are from other ladies of the household. Whatever I do not recognise, I will put into another pile for one of the other lady's maids to look through." She began taking the smaller items out of the basket, sorting through them easily and quickly.

"There's a great deal to learn about being a lady's maid," Penelope commented. Emily was so young. She wondered how she fared. She could style hair better than anyone that Penelope knew, but there seemed to be so many skills one needed to have. An even, easy temperament was certainly also needed. Emily was easily the most easygoing person Penelope knew. She was actually quite well-suited for the job, she realised as she helped Anna with her tasks.

"Not really," Anna commented mildly. "Mostly, it is no more complicated than looking after oneself might be. One also has to do one's own laundry, style one's hair and draw a bath occasionally." She chuckled. "Of course, one needs to be ready to face difficult people sometimes." She made a wry face.

Penelope nodded. "Certainly." She had not done more than see Lady Penrith from a distance, but she did not like the look of her. She had neat, chiseled features and a small, neat mouth that made her otherwise pretty face seem disapproving and unkind.

She resembles the earl, but only in looks, she mused. She blushed. She could not stop thinking about him. Their brief exchange in the garden often came to her mind, and she recalled it regularly, the words playing through her thoughts as she worked on her tasks.

"There! Now, I just need to check again that I have not missed anything, and then I will take this to the bedchamber for my lady this evening. Thank you so much," she added, reaching for Penelope's hand to squeeze in appreciation. "I am so grateful."

"It was nothing, truly," Penelope replied warmly. "Thank you for helping me too."

"Friends help each other," Anna reminded her, grinning.

Penelope smiled back and she was still smiling as she walked lightly down the long hallway towards the exit to the garden. It felt lovely to have already found someone she liked so much on the staff.

She walked lightly past the kitchen, hurrying as she heard voices. The housekeeper was a delightful older woman, always kind and helpful, but the cook was not quite as friendly, and Penelope did not want to face any unpleasantness. She hurried past and opened the door. The warmth outside hit her like a physical thing. She paused in the shade by the kitchen door, fanning herself. It was high summer, and even with the breeze, it was hot.

The kitchen garden was cooler, shaded from the direct sunshine. She walked through it, enjoying the shade. The air smelled cool and loamy; the garden beds lined with rows of fresh vegetables. They had a small vegetable plot at her home, and Penelope smiled, remembering working in the garden with Emily and with her mother. They did not have as much space, and their vegetables did not seem to grow as well, but it had been enjoyable. She breathed in, her heart aching with the memories of their mother.

The gate that led out of the kitchen garden led onto the lawn, and from there, it was possible to walk leftwards and go around the back of the manor to where the servants' entrance was. Penelope walked down the path, grateful for the shade of a tall hedge, hurrying to get indoors where it was a little cooler, and back to Thomas, who might have woken.

She tensed, hearing footsteps. Servants occasionally passed this way—errands to the stable or other duties sometimes required them to use the back entrance. However, it was not impossible that one might bump into members of the nobility taking an afternoon stroll, and she tensed. She was not sure how she would react. She straightened her back, planning simply to curtsey in acknowledgement and keep walking. The footsteps were closer and she stopped, then looked up.

"My lord," she murmured, dropping a low curtsey. The earl was hurrying towards the path, moving towards her across the lawn. He saw her, and, to her amazement, he smiled.

"Miss Matthews," he greeted her. He stared at her for a moment, and her cheeks reddened with warmth. His grey eyes were not unfriendly, and there was that strange look in them that she did not understand. It was almost interested. She looked hastily at her toes, her heart thudding.

"I apologise. I was hurrying back, and..." she began, but he interrupted her.

"I was looking for the stable-master," he began. "We need to find accommodation for the guests' horses."

"He was in the kitchen, I think, my lord," Penelope told him, recalling that one of the voices she heard had been a man's voice, and it had sounded a little like him.

"Thank you," the earl said with a grin.

Penelope smiled. "My pleasure," she said wryly.

He chuckled. Penelope held his gaze. For a second, it felt as though they were not an earl and a member of his household staff, but two equals; two people who understood each other well. His grey eyes were warm and amused, staring into her own. She looked back; her lip lifted in a playful smile.

The earl seemed to shake himself visibly, as though he had been asleep, deep in a dream, and awoken. He tilted his head. "I must hurry," he said briskly.

"Of course. Good day, my lord," Penelope replied, dropping another curtsey.

"Good day," he murmured, hurrying past.

Penelope drifted across the lawn towards the servants' door, feeling as though she was floating. It was strangely unreal, the interaction so confusing and so strange that her mind focused on nothing else. She opened the door and stepped in, standing in the hallway while the events that had just happened flitted through her active mind, trying to make sense out of it.

"There is no sense to it," she murmured aloud as she wandered, still thinking deeply, up the hallway towards the stairs. The earl and his smile, how he gazed into her eyes with that interested glance; how he smiled with her as though they shared a secret, or as though she was an equal. It made no sense whatsoever. *And yet,* she mused, a small smile on her lips, *it was beautiful.*

She hummed to herself as she drifted up the servants' stairs towards the new nursery, her mind full of the earl's handsome face and that warm, wonderful smile.

Chapter 7

"Look! There is Lady Winthrop's coach."

Peter, standing in the entranceway with Millicent and Edmund, tried not to show how singularly unenthusiastic he felt about that. It was six o'clock in the evening, he was tired and hungry, and regardless of both, he would far rather have been doing almost anything than standing in the doorway to welcome their guests.

"Here they are," Millicent hissed as the coach door opened. Peter, in a navy-blue tailcoat that strained across his wide shoulders and charcoal trousers, straightened his posture, feeling uncomfortable. His shirt-collar felt itchy and hot and he wished he could go upstairs and escape the wretched party. It was another two hours before the ball would begin, and he longed to escape and take some tea and rest before he was required to socialize again.

Lord Winthrop alighted from the coach. Slightly older than their own father would have been, he had white hair and was tall and thickset. He reached up to the coach and assisted his wife—a slim older woman with greying dark brown hair, wearing a dark ocher gown—and then his daughter, Lady Adeline. She wore a dark blue pelisse and a bonnet in matching blue, offset with a grey feather plume. Her black hair just showed under the bonnet, in contrast with her pale skin.

The coachman jumped down, staggering a little with the impact. He wobbled a little close to Lady Adeline, who recoiled with an expression of distaste on her face, as though the man was a source of contamination. She was a beautiful woman, with a long, slim face, a neat nose, red-lipped mouth and exquisite dark brown eyes; almost black like her hair. Her glare at the servant made her seem almost ugly.

"How dare you, sirrah!" she snapped at the coachman. "Comport yourself."

Peter bit his lip, anger rising within him. It was not the poor man's fault. He was clearly exhausted, barely able to lift the heavy luggage down from the top of the coach. He had done nothing, merely stepped back a little close to her. Her lack of any sort of compassion at once surprised him and left him terribly weary. He had seen such things all too often in London, and they upset him a great deal.

He turned to Millicent, but she was looking at the guests, a big, not entirely sincere smile on her face.

"Good evening!" she declared as they walked up the steps, dropping a curtsey and beaming the slightly brittle smile.

"Good evening," Lady Winthrop greeted her, dropping her own curtsey. Peter bowed low; first to her and then to Lady Adeline, who dropped a brief curtsey, straightening up and fixing him with those magnificent eyes.

"Good evening, my lord," she said softly, lowering her gaze modestly again.

"Good evening," Peter replied. She truly was lovely, and part of him was almost surprised that a look that would have made anyone in London practically swoon left him entirely unaffected. It was the way she had looked at the coachman. He could not forget that, beautiful as she was, she had no apparent tenderness in her soul.

"Thank you for inviting us to your house party, Millicent," Lady Winthrop said, addressing his sister. Her smile was as big and as insincere as his own sister's smile seemed.

"Why, of course!" Millicent replied gushingly. "We simply *had* to include you. And dear Adeline is the talk of London!" She beamed at Adeline, who dropped her a curtsey, her eyes not entirely friendly.

"Good evening, Lady Penrith," she greeted Millicent.

Millicent dropped a curtsey, though even she seemed a little chilled by the brief and not exactly warm acknowledgement. Lord Winthrop made a good-natured comment about the fine weather, which helped a little to restore the earlier affability. Lord and Lady Winthrop and Lady Adeline drifted into the house. The butler went out to instruct their servants where to take the luggage. Peter turned away, still feeling a little angry about Lady Adeline's distaste towards the coachman. The fellow would be given a proper meal in the kitchen and a chance to rest. Provision had already been made for the extra staff who would be staying during the house party.

Thoughts of the staff brought a vivid image of Miss Matthews to Peter's mind. Their brief meeting in the garden near the kitchens had not really left his thoughts all afternoon. Recalling her smile made his sister's preparations and welcoming the guests more bearable.

"Ah! Lord and Lady Knightsbridge!" Millicent greeted some more arriving guests, dropping a graceful curtsey.

Peter bowed, and the guest came forward and chatted a little while their servants unpacked their luggage from the coach.

"We are very excited about your ball this evening," Lady Knightsbridge told Millicent, her brown eyes bright in her lined face.

"Thank you, dear Gertrude."

Peter allowed his mind to drift again as the guests walked past him towards the stairs. Miss Matthews' green-eyed stare filled his thoughts, that strange look—so amused and so understanding—filling his mind.

She was someone interesting, someone different.

"That should be almost everyone," Millicent murmured. Peter turned to look at her, his heart twisting. She was seven years his senior, but she looked much older in that moment. Her face was lined in ways he had not noticed before, and her gaze was tired as though she had not slept for more than one night.

"We should go and have some tea," he suggested softly. The guests would need more than an hour to settle in, relax and change their clothing, and the ball was only due to begin at eight o'clock. They themselves had easily more than an hour before they would need to start thinking about getting dressed. Millicent looked like she needed some food and tea, and he was practically dreaming of a chance to sit down and relax before the guests arrived.

"I must oversee the last few preparations," Millicent said, her voice almost a whisper of tiredness.

"You must come and rest," Peter said firmly. He shot a hard look at Edmund. The fellow should have been taking better care of Millicent. Why was he not the one insisting that she should drink some tea and eat something?

"The servants can do all that," Edmund said affably, and just a little patronizingly, to Millicent.

Peter tensed. The fellow always managed to say something that wore on his nerves. He pushed the thought aside. All that mattered was that Millicent took some rest and that he, too, had a moment's respite from the evening's proceedings.

"I suppose I should eat a little something. Dinner will be very late tonight," Millicent murmured.

Peter nodded. "Good idea, sister," he said supportively. No matter how terribly he might resent her dragging him into the horrible house-party, he did not want to see her suffering or wearing herself out. She was his sister, after all.

He walked up the stairs with Millicent and Edmund to the drawing room.

After relaxing for an hour, Peter withdrew to his chamber. Spending any time at all with Edmund grated on his nerves, and, as a result, tea had not been as enjoyable as he had wished.

"You have the evening off," Peter told his manservant, Mr Radford, who was still tidying when he arrived in the room.

"My lord!" Radford exclaimed with surprise. "Thank you," he added. He hurried out of the room.

Peter sighed. While some people might have wanted the assistance of a manservant to choose their clothing or at least to tie their cravat, he found it far less tedious to do it himself. He opened his wardrobe and selected a dark blue velvet tailcoat and knee-breeches in navy blue. The selection was fairly random, but when he put them aside on the chair together, they did not seem to clash, and so he decided that was a fair choice.

As he dressed and paused to tie his cravat in the looking-glass, he could not help but wonder how he might have felt if Miss Matthews would see him.

That is a ridiculous way to think, he told himself, blushing, as he tied the cravat. It would have taken much longer to choose his clothes. He would have wanted to look his best.

The thought made him blink in surprise, his grey eyes staring into their reflection confusedly. He had known her perhaps five minutes and he already cared if she thought well of him.

"You're a ridiculous fool," he told himself aloud, but it did not stop him from smiling as he recalled that gentle green gaze and that strange, half-amused, understanding look.

He put on a pair of shoes and strode to the door, trying to push the thoughts away as he walked down to the ball. Imagining her and recalling their conversations was not helpful.

Not when there was no hope of speaking with her about anything beyond the confines of their prescribed roles.

***

"Brother! Just on time." Millicent, looking relieved, made space for him beside her at the top of the stairs leading down into the ballroom. Edmund stood with her, smiling the same mild, disinterested smile that always seemed to be on his face. Peter went to stand beside Millicent, nodding in acknowledgement towards Edmund.

"Plenty of guests, eh?" Edmund asked in a mild, inquiring tone.

"Yes," Peter commented. He did not want to be drawn into conversation with Edmund. He looked at Millicent. "The ballroom looks splendid," he told her sincerely. The marble tiles shone, their high polish making them seem as smooth as an ice-skating pond under the light of a hundred candles. Millicent looked decidedly tense, her dark blue gown making her face seem pale and wary. She smiled.

"Thank you, brother! Thank you! One does one's best. I do hope the guests will find it likewise appealing."

"Of course, they shall," Peter reassured her.

Edmund's smirk did not waver. Peter shot him a sharp look. It ought to have been Edmund himself offering Millicent his support, yet time and again, he seemed more inclined to unsettle her than to encourage her. The realisation only deepened Peter's dislike.

"Ah! Lady Dalwood," Millicent greeted a guest. "Lord Dalwood! And Lord Matthew! Welcome," she said, smiling at the guests who appeared at the door. An elderly lady in a pale grey gown, a gentleman in a blue tailcoat that was of a fashion from a good few years ago, and a young man with blonde hair and a slightly awkward smile; Peter bowed and smiled in welcome at them all.

The guests chatted for a moment or two, then drifted down into the ballroom. More guests appeared almost instantly.

"Lord Ainsfield. A pleasure to see you here," Millicent greeted another guest.

Peter bowed and chatted and smiled and tried his best to be sociable, but he was feeling exhausted and drained already. The bright lights of the glittering chandeliers in the entranceway and in the ballroom strained his eyes and the loud chatter hurt his head.

"Lady Winthrop! Lord Winthrop! And Lady Adeline!" Millicent enthused.

Peter bowed low, straightening up to find himself looking straight into the dark brown eyes of Lady Adeline. She smiled, that lovely, mysterious grin that had half of London clamoring to dance with her.

"Good evening, my lady," he murmured. He wished he could warm to her, but somehow, for all her loveliness, he could not find her beautiful.

Her parents chatted with Millicent at some length, and then all of them descended into the ballroom. Peter was starting to feel lightheaded, his vision swimming as he stood.

"Not much longer," Millicent hissed, clearly aware of his discomfort. "The guests are almost all arrived now."

"Good." Peter could not hide his exhausted tone.

Two more guests arrived. Then the butler was closing the door, and Millicent grinned at him.

"Now we may enjoy the evening," she told him, her hazel-brown eyes sparkling with merriment. Peter tried to smile back. His sister apparently enjoyed balls, but he hated them. "And don't forget, Peter. You did say you would spend some time dancing with Lady Adeline... do try."

Peter looked down. He did not want to show his sister that her comment annoyed him. She was tense enough, doing her best to enjoy herself despite her exhaustion. But her comment did annoy him; mostly because he had not agreed to any such thing.

He walked down the stairs into the ballroom.

"Ah! Peter! How grand. It has been years," Lord Winthrop drawled.

Peter lifted a shoulder. "Not years, surely," he commented. He recalled the family being often at the house before he went to Cambridge. But that, he supposed, was several years ago. It felt like perhaps a year ago, at most two. He ran a weary hand down his face.

"Why! It certainly is years," Lord Winthrop said, laughing. "Adeline was still in the schoolroom."

"Not in the schoolroom, dear," Lady Winthrop protested mildly. "See what a fine young lady she has become?" she asked Peter. Peter nodded.

"Lady Adeline is a fine young lady," he echoed. Lady Adeline was standing a few inches away and his cheeks burned, his voice fading as he looked at his shoes. He hated high society, he hated balls, and he hated having to say things he did not wish to say. If it was possible to become invisible, he would have wished to do so.

"Why! How gallant," Lady Winthrop said with a grin. "Surely, Adeline, even your heart must be moved."

Peter looked at Lady Adeline as she grinned; a mix of shyness and amusement in her dark eyes.

"Moved enough, perhaps," she replied coyly.

Peter sighed. Three pairs of eyes were looking at him expectantly, and the musicians were starting to tune up. Somewhere, he knew, Millicent was watching and waiting. He had to do what was expected.

"Might I have your hand for the next dance?" Peter asked automatically.

"Perhaps you might," Lady Adeline teased. She unfolded her dance card, which was fastened to her wrist, and perused it. "Indeed! You may."

Peter bowed. "Thank you, my lady," he murmured. It was the polite way to respond. He took her hand, the silk of her glove seeming cool against his fingers, and they walked through the crowded room towards the dance floor.

They stood among the couples gathered there. Peter glanced across the ballroom. Millicent was talking to some guests, her dark blue gown resplendent in a sea of paler gowns belonging to the debutantes and other young ladies, for whom pastel shades were more fashionable. She was not looking at him, and he hoped she would see what he was doing. If he danced with Lady Adeline once, perhaps Millicent would relent for the rest of the three weeks.

The orchestra began to play a waltz. Peter sighed inaudibly. He had never enjoyed the waltz—though he was good at it, and able to execute the steps well, he did not enjoy the inescapable intimacy of the turns, when a dancer might press right up against their partner. It was for that reason that the waltz was considered scandalous and not performed at every ball, and it was also for that reason that he tended to avoid doing it. He did not like any sort of intimacy—even touching hands—to be forced on him without his seeking it.

As he stepped into the dance with Lady Adeline, he recalled walking into Miss Matthews. Reaching out to take her hand had been so natural, and the feeling of her fingers in his was warm and soft. He had not felt strange holding her hand—rather, it had felt good and right.

Stop it, he commanded himself, annoyed. His mind had already strayed to her green eyes. He could not afford to let himself think like that—she was a member of his staff, and that was what she should remain, for the reputation and rationality of them both.

"Fine music," Lady Adeline murmured as they twirled around a corner. Her pale blue muslin skirt brushed against his calves, clad in their silk stock. He tensed.

"Very fine," he agreed. His voice was cold and formal, and part of him, seeing her eyes narrow just a little, wished he did not feel that way.

She is beautiful. She deserves to dance with someone who appreciates her, he thought guiltily. He straightened up, trying to focus. He was not a bad dancer—not as good as she was, but not bad by any means. He brought his attention to the steps, trying to do the dance justice.

"It's almost salacious, this dance," she said with a grin, as their bodies pressed close together, stepping neatly around a corner. Peter winced.

"I suppose that is why it is so controversial," he commented. Her face was tense, and he knew that was not the answer she wanted.

I cannot flirt, he wanted to shout. *I do not know how, and besides, I do not wish to.* He did not like the meaningless pleasantries of society, and he did not like saying things simply because it was what one should say. If he expressed anything—affection, anger, care—it was because he meant it. There was no room in his heart for other things.

"There are many dancers here," Lady Adeline commented as they stepped around a pair who had almost halted in a corner. "One finds oneself quite crowded here."

"Quite so," Peter murmured. He knew that he should comment differently, since her posture changed, her hand stiffening in his and her back—where his hand rested on her shoulder-blade—becoming more rigid. He felt helpless and useless.

The waltz slowed, the cadence changing and becoming grander. It was the concluding few bars, and Peter was glad when they halted. He bowed.

Lady Adeline curtseyed. Her curtsey, like her dancing, would have graced St. Edmund's Palace. She was a model of societal elegance.

"Thank you for the dance," he murmured. He knew it was the right thing to say. She smiled.

"Of course. Thank you, my lord." She lifted her head, her dark eyes holding his for a moment.

Peter escorted her to the refreshments, then excused himself, saying that he needed to take the air.

He walked out to the terrace. There were a few other people there, murmuring conversation and laughing. The sound of the music drifted on the cool air. Peter went to the railing, his back to the few people standing outside nearer to the door. He longed for quiet and for a space to be by himself.

As he leaned on the railing, staring out into the dark night, his mind wandered to Miss Matthews. She was uncomplicated, and he could not help but long for someone as uncomplicated to appear at the ball. He recalled her green eyes and he wondered what she was doing right at that moment.

Chapter 8

The distant strains of music drifted up through the window. Penelope stood at the windowpane, staring out at the night. Her lips lifted as she heard a particularly lovely, lilting waltz drift in. Her imagination filled with images of women in beautiful spangled ballgowns and men in velvet knee-breeches and high-necked shirts, dancing on a marble floor under a glittering chandelier. She grinned to herself, shutting her eyes and letting her mind linger there. There were dozens of good things to eat on sumptuously-decked trestle-tables, she imagined, and a quartet in black tailcoats played the lovely music.

Thomas let out a wail, and she brought her attention swiftly back from the beautiful tune.

"Oh! You poor dear," she murmured, lifting the baby up out of the cradle. Guilt made her flush—her momentary reverie had made her forget about little Thomas. He was red-faced and seemed fretful. "Shh. Hush, now. Are you wet?"

She checked the cloth diaper that he wore, but it was as dry as when she had wrapped it carefully around him after his bath an hour ago. She walked with him to the window, patting his back and making soothing sounds. The music calmed her own soul, and she stood in the cool night air with the baby, listening to the distant refrain.

The little child in her arms seemed calmer—perhaps because of the music, or perhaps because of her own response to it. Whatever the reason, while she stood there with him in her arms, he seemed to become drowsier. His eyelids drooped, and she stroked his hair, rocking him where she held him cradled to her chest.

He was not sleeping, but he was not distressed either, and Penelope stood at the window and rocked him, gazing into the nighttime treetops.

The manor was surrounded by beautiful gardens on all sides, and some tall trees grew near the eastern wing so that the Green Room looked out onto the tops of some trees. The lawn seemed very far below, and she could hear the music clearly. Light from the ballroom spilled from long windows onto the distant grass, and if she leaned forward and watched, she could see the shadows of the people inside the ballroom moving across the bars of light.

Her mind wandered again to the ballroom downstairs, trying to imagine what it might be like to be there. She had only ever experienced dances in her village, and she had both enjoyed those and found them terrifying. Being surrounded by admiring young village men had been quite frightening, since she and Emily were usually visited only by Papa's parishioners who were older and certainly not there to cast admiring glances at anyone.

Her mind strayed to an image of the earl, and she grinned and heat flooded her as she tried to imagine what he looked like in the ballroom. Did he wear knee-breeches and a tailcoat and a frothy white silk cravat? The thought made her want to giggle, as if she were a young girl overhearing gossip in the servants' hall. He was handsome. Would he be more handsome in such finery?

"Penelope," she scolded herself, grinning even more. It was entirely improper to think of him like that. And yet, part of her felt happy when she did, like a child who stole tartlets from the kitchen, savouring them all the more for being forbidden.

She gazed down at Thomas, who appeared to be slumbering. His face still seemed a little red, and his brow was crinkled in a frown that suggested that, though he looked peaceful, the pain or whatever troubled him was still present. She cradled him closer and moved across the room to the chair by the fire. As soon as she sat down in the warmth, he began to waken and whimper again.

"Shh," she murmured gently, stroking his brow. It felt a little hotter than usual. She frowned. He could not have a fever, could he? She pressed her lips to his brow and winced. His skin felt a little hotter than she would expect it to.

A pitcher of cold, clean water stood on the nightstand, along with a porcelain bowl in which one might rinse one's hands and face, or bathe a fretting, hot baby. Penelope frowned, then dipped a clean handkerchief into the cold water and laid the cold cloth on the baby's brow instead.

His relief was apparent, and she frowned. He did seem to have a small fever. She laid him carefully in the cradle with the wet cloth on his brow, then fetched a wooden stool and came to sit beside him, holding his small, warm hand in her own.

He seemed much calmer with the wet, cold cloth, and she prepared another cold handkerchief, ready to swap them when the one that she had already used became too warm.

A song strayed into her thoughts, and she sat singing it, holding his hand, until she needed to change the handkerchief. He seemed much calmer, and his small fretful noises had been replaced with smooth, even breathing. He was almost asleep.

She put a fresh, cold handkerchief on his brow, and he fell slowly into a fitful slumber. Penelope leaned back, her body slumping with her relief.

While the baby slept, her mind drifted to the possible causes of his fever. It could be something as simple as teething—though he was surely old enough to have all his milk teeth by now—or something far more concerning, a true illness.

"If you are still fevered tomorrow, then I shall send for the physician," she promised the baby. How did one even send for the physician? She could not ride to the village herself, since she had no horse and she could not ride. Presumably one of the staff would ride out to fetch him, but who should she ask? She frowned.

A knock sounded at the door, distracting her from her thoughts. She stood up and hurried over.

"Shh," she cautioned as she opened it.

"Penelope!" Anna greeted, a big grin on her slender features. "You must be starving to death up here," she whispered dramatically.

"No," Penelope murmured. She stepped aside to allow Anna to walk in. Anna was not wearing her uniform, Penelope noticed, but a dark red dress that suited her a great deal. She had a plate in her hands, covered with a ceramic bowl to preserve the heat of whatever was on the plate. "No, I'm not starving. It's grand to see you," she added as she gestured to Anna to take a seat at the small table.

"Well, I thought you might be. So, I collected some things. Look. We had such a fine supper! The gentlefolk are having a grand meal, and there seems to be a great deal left over." She lifted the lid of the bowl to show some cuts of meat in gravy and some potatoes. Penelope's mouth watered as the savoury smell hit her.

"Anna! You are so kind," she murmured, tears forming in her eyes. She blinked them away. After the cruelty she had endured from her former employer, kindness felt like a gift to be treasured.

"No tears! It is only some meat," Anna said with a grin. "We've even had better at home, I daresay. Papa knew a farmer, and in return for teaching his children their letters, he always made sure we never wanted for meat. And good meat, too—not like some of what you find in London, which has walked halfway across the country before it reaches your plate." She wrinkled her nose in distaste.

"Well, it looks wonderful," Penelope replied, the sight and aroma of the meal stirring her appetite. She looked around for a knife and fork, and Anna grinned again.

"You are fortunate. I deduced that you would need them." She was carrying a small cloth bag, and she drew out a knife and fork wrapped in a napkin.

Penelope giggled. "This is a feast," she murmured, not able to wait a second longer. She cut a slice of the meat and lifted it to her lips. It was soft and perfectly cooked, the rich, strong juices running down her throat and the taste so intense that her mouth watered.

"I'm so glad you like it," Anna said with a grin. "There was so much that some people had more than one plateful. It would have been a crime not to keep some for you."

"Thank you," Penelope murmured, meaning every word.

"It's nothing, truly," Anna said warmly.

They sat silently while Penelope ate. Strains of music drifted through the window. She smiled to herself.

"It sounds like a wonderful ball down there," she murmured as she leaned back, her plate empty.

Anna nodded. "Oh! How grand it must be to attend. I wish we could conceal ourselves in there, just to see what is happening."

Penelope giggled, the thought filling her with delight. "Imagine if someone caught us," she commented.

Anna made a face. "Yes. Much safer just to attend the village dance."

"Is there a village dance?" Penelope asked, interestedly.

"Yes! It's the day after tomorrow. You simply have to attend!" Anna said with a grin. "I am going. The village fair is first, and in the evening, there is a dance. Mrs Halldon said that we might all have an hour or two off that day, both to visit the fair and to attend the dance. I can barely wait!"

Penelope's heart lifted. It would be wonderful to attend a fair. She had not been to one in years. Perhaps there might even be something she could purchase as a gift for Emily and Papa, for when she could call on them. Her heart sank. It might be many months before that.

"We shall wear proper clothes, not our uniforms," Anna commented. "I have some things. Have you?"

Penelope tilted her head. She had brought so few items of clothing—just two dresses, one of which might be suitable for a fair. Most days, she wore either her black uniform or the lighter white summer uniform, depending on the weather. Beyond her duties at the manor, there was little occasion to wear anything else.

"I have a dress," she replied.

"I have some dresses my mistress gave me," Anna replied. "They are old dresses of hers, and they are not quite long enough for me—I had to let down the hems, but mostly they fit." She giggled.

Penelope smiled. "I would love to see them," she replied. "They must be very fine."

"This is one," Anna told her proudly, indicating the dark red dress. It had long sleeves and was made from a thick, velvety cloth. "It is one of my favourites. The hem is quite worn, but I love it." She gestured to the hem, which did, indeed, have some pulls and even some holes.

"It is a lovely colour for you," Penelope commented sincerely.

"Thank you. Blue is your colour, I think," Anna commented, tilting her head to study Penelope. "Or green. Yes! Your eyes are such a lovely colour. You have to try a green dress on. I have one that would suit you very well indeed."

Penelope smiled. She and Emily had never been able to afford whatever fabric they chose, limited to what was practical. Papa did not receive a large stipend from his congregation, and they never had extra money for anything special. Penelope had never even thought about what might suit her.

"I would like to," Penelope murmured.

"We will attend the village dance together," Anna said firmly. "I am sure that one of the maids can be persuaded to sit with little Thomas. Not everyone will wish to go," she added slowly, clearly thinking about the problem.

"I will only be able to go if it is possible for him to be without me for an hour," Penelope reminded her gently. There were some things that she would only trust herself to do, and caring for a sick baby was one of them. It was her job, and she would not let another person do it for her while she was elsewhere—it would be a great unfairness.

"Of course," Anna agreed. "It will be such a grand day! I can barely wait."

Penelope giggled. "I am excited too."

They were both silent for a moment, imagining the dance and the evening's events.

"There must be lots of handsome men in this village," Anna declared thoughtfully.

"Anna!" Penelope giggled, cheeks reddening with delighted embarrassment at the idea.

"Well? Men in Devonshire are handsome. So, there will certainly be a few handsome ones there." She was laughing, and Penelope chuckled warmly.

"We shall see," she murmured, turning to check on the baby. He was still sleeping. The cloth on his brow was warm, and she went to the pitcher of water to soak it again, laying a cold cloth on his brow.

"I will be given time off duty at eight o'clock in the evening for the dance," Anna told Penelope. "My mistress will be at an evening party and will not need a maid for an hour or two."

"Grand!" Penelope nodded. "If I can go, I will come and find you."

"I will wait for you in the kitchen garden," Anna promised.

"Then I will come down as soon as I can to tell you if I can or cannot attend the fair." Penelope smiled warmly.

"Grand. I can hardly wait," Anna replied, pushing back her chair. She lifted the plate, and Penelope helped to tidy the table.

"Thank you, Anna. Thank you so much for the supper. It was so thoughtful and kind of you." She had not been aware of quite how hungry she was until she ate.

"It was nothing," Anna said warmly. She went to the door, and Penelope opened it for her, closing it after she had waved at her friend as she headed down the servants' corridor to the kitchen. She went to stand by the window, staring out.

The music was still drifting up from the ballroom, and Penelope shut her eyes for a moment, trying to imagine what it was like down there. Did the earl dance? It was hard to imagine that he liked dancing—he seemed so formal and serious. She smiled.

I know nothing of him, she reminded herself impatiently, *and yet I wonder so much.*

"You're silly," she told herself firmly. She knew that she would be excited about the dance if a man like him were to attend. She would want to borrow that green dress so that she could look her best.

She was smiling as she went to sit by the cradle, thoughts of the earl bringing a grin to her lips.

Chapter 9

Penelope straightened up from bending over the cradle in the corner of the nursery. The sky was a rich, early evening blue, the sunshine golden on the treetops. She sighed, smiling warmly as she gazed out at the evening. In his cradle, Thomas slept peacefully, his eyes, with their long golden lashes, closed and making him look like a small angel.

A knock sounded at the door, making her tense and hurry across to open it.

"Thomas is..." she began, her voice a whisper. She grinned as she recognised her guest. "Anna! What a surprise."

"It's time to go to the village dance," Anna reminded her, eyes twinkling. "Come on! You said you'd ask Mrs Aldham to sit with him."

"I have," Penelope agreed. "I need to go and fetch her. Could you please watch him for a moment? He is sleeping." Her heart thudded with excitement, even though she felt a stab of guilt about leaving the child even for two hours. He had fretted that morning, his brow a little warmer than it ought to be, but a dose of herbal tea—one her grandmother had used—had helped him, and he seemed to sleep easily, his brow as cool as it ought to be.

"I'd be delighted to," Anna replied, going to the chair by the cradle. "Don't be long," she added, whispering to avoid disturbing Thomas.

"I will be as quick as I can," Penelope promised and hurried out.

Mrs Aldham was in her chamber, resting before the task of preparing dinner for the house-party guests began. She smiled at Penelope as she paused in the doorway to tug on her shoes.

"It's a fine thing to see young people enjoying themselves." Her face brightened with a big grin.

"Thank you, Mrs Aldham," Penelope said sincerely as she walked down the hallway to the nursery with her. "I appreciate your help so much."

"It's no trouble. I do like babies," Mrs Aldham replied, her gaze tender as she looked over at the cradle. "And you shan't be long," she reminded Penelope.

"No. Just an hour. Two at the most," Penelope promised. They had been given leave by Mrs Hallden to take two hours during the day and two hours in the evening, if they could be spared from their duties.

"I will see you at ten o'clock. Enjoy the evening," Mrs Aldham said warmly.

"Thank you," Penelope replied. She gazed down at little Thomas, filling her thoughts with him. It would be strange not to sit with him while he slept. She was becoming accustomed to the evenings with him, even only after a week of service. There was a deep peace in tending him, in their comfortable daily routines.

"Come on!" Anna called, a big grin on her face as they shut the door and hurried towards the servants' quarters upstairs. "We have to get dressed first."

Penelope rushed after her. They reached Anna's room. It was on the top floor with the other servants' rooms. Penelope's room was next to the nursery so that Thomas could sleep beside her bed. When Penelope stepped into Anna's chamber, she noticed that it was a little bigger than her own and that it received a little more sunshine. While, as a nanny, Penelope was quite high ranked among the staff, a lady's maid just slightly outranked her. Emily was a lady's maid, and that thought made Penelope happy. Perhaps Emily's room was even nicer.

"Here," Anna said, opening the door to the small wardrobe made of unvarnished pine boards. "I will wear the blue gown, and there is a green one for you." She reached in and took a dress out. Penelope stared.

The gown was made of a light fabric—she thought muslin, but in the shaded part of the room where she stood, it was difficult to see. It was the colour of moss, a rich, strong green. The skirt fell from a fashionably high waist with a waistband in what looked like a rich yellow-ocher velvet. The sleeves were puffs of gauzy fabric edged with the same yellow ocher.

"It's beautiful," she murmured, feeling almost scared to take it. Anna grinned.

"I hope so. I find the blue one a little nicer, but I think the green will be magnificent with your eyes," she added, taking a dark blue gown out of the wardrobe.

Penelope gazed at it. The gown was also made of a soft, gauzy fabric, the waist encircled with silk in a darker blue than the gown. The sleeves were puff sleeves, edged with the same dark blue as the waist. The colour was intense, sapphire blue, and that alone made it stunning.

"It is also beautiful."

Anna chuckled. "If we can't have a ball, we can at least outdress those who do."

Penelope laughed with delight. Anna gestured to the door.

"Go on! Hurry! We need to be ready by eight o'clock."

Penelope chuckled and hurried to her own chamber downstairs. She struggled with the buttons on the back of the uniform and then tugged on the gown over her shift. She stopped and stared at her reflection. Her hair had come loose while she fought to get her own gown off, and it tumbled about her face. Her skin seemed paler and clearer, her green eyes wide in her long, slim face. It was on her eyes that she focused: in the green dress, they seemed big and luminous.

"Is that me?"

She giggled. Anna would laugh to see her reaction

She twirled in front of the mirror, the gown swirling softly around her bare ankles. It felt wonderful. The chimes from the church informed her that there were fifteen minutes before eight, and she raced to complete her hairstyle. *Emily would have done it better*, she reflected with a wry grin as she rolled her hair into a bun and tied it with a green ribbon. The ribbon was a dusky olive colour. It did not really match the gown, but it was good enough. She tugged on her white outdoor boots to complete the outfit.

Then she hurried upstairs again towards Anna's room.

"Penelope?" Anna called as she hurried up the hallway in almost the same moment. She paused, standing abruptly still. Her eyes widened. "Penelope! You look magnificent!"

Penelope blushed. "No, you do," she assured Anna, flapping her hand in Anna's direction. Anna blushed.

"Oh, not really," she said, though spots of colour appeared on her pale cheeks. With her long neck and tall, regal bearing, she looked the epitome of a lady. How ironic it was, Penelope thought, biting her lip, that Anna was the lady's maid. She looked so elegant and noble.

"Hurry!" Anna called as they walked briskly down the servants' corridor and to the lower entrance. They had arranged for a carter to take his hay-cart to the village, with the collier set to bring them back to the manor upon delivering the coal. It was a task ordinarily carried out in the early hours of the morning, but he had agreed—just this once—to make the journey in the dead of night.

Giggling, they ran down to the entrance and threw open the door.

"Where is he?" Anna asked, frowning. She stood in her blue muslin gown, resplendent against the dark green lawn. Penelope shrugged.

"I will look at the front of the house," she suggested. "Will you check at the kitchen?"

"Of course," Anna replied at once. She hurried off around the side of the house while Penelope took the path that led to the lawn. Her brow creased, her heart thudding as she ran.

There was no cart waiting for them at the side gate that the carters typically used to enter the manor grounds, and he most certainly would not wait on the gravel drive where the coaches of guests would draw up.

"Where is he?" she muttered to herself. Anna would be so upset if they could not go, and she would be too. Her frown deepened, and she turned, hurrying back towards the kitchen.

The path that led from the lawn to the kitchen curved around the front of the house, and she slowed her steps, lest other servants—or even the earl himself—might be using it. Her cheeks reddened as she recalled meeting the earl on the path just a few days ago. She walked as cautiously as she could towards where the carts usually drew up to deposit their wares at the kitchens or cellar.

As she reached the corner, she heard voices. She tensed. Anna was talking to someone. The person, whoever they were, was a man—she heard the rich, warm sound of deep laughter. Trust Anna to flirt with the carter. She imagined him as a strapping, blonde Devonshire man, and that thought made her want to chuckle. She neared the bushes. As she reached them, she tensed. Anna's voice had stopped and the man was answering. His voice was low and unaccented, the tone rich and cultured. It was not the carter at all. No carter spoke in such refined, noble tones. She peered through the bushes, heart thudding and her cheeks lifting in a grin.

The person to whom Anna was talking was dressed in a dark grey tailcoat and dark trousers. He had a high-necked shirt and his hair was chestnut brown. He was tall and had a long oval face, and she thought his eyes were brown, but he was standing too far away to see, his posture relaxed and casual. He was smiling at Anna. His smile seemed appreciative.

Not a carter. But a noble. Anna! Penelope grinned warmly, a delighted tingle of excitement on her friend's behalf rising in her.

"... I hope that your transportation arrives soon," the man was saying as Anna lifted her hand in a cheery wave.

"Thank you! As do I," she called. She turned and walked down the path. Then she ran around the corner, and Penelope hastily turned around to face her so that she would not see she had been spied upon.

"Penelope! There you are!" Anna exclaimed, pressing her palm to her chest as if she was having trouble breathing. "Grand. We should check by the stable," she added, drawing a gasp into her lungs.

Penelope grinned. "Of course," she replied. "We should check directly." She paused, wondering if Anna was going to tell her about the mystery noble.

"Yes. Yes," Anna replied, though she sounded distinctly distracted. They hurried towards the stable.

"There he is!" Penelope exclaimed in delight, spotting the carter waiting under a tree, his horse cropping the grass near the stable-yard. "Did someone tell you that he was here?" she added, frowning curiously at Anna.

Anna lifted her shoulder in a shrug. "Oh, someone. Yes. A man." She went red.

Penelope giggled. "A man?" she teased. "Oh! Well. That is something."

"Yes. Yes, he was," Anna replied, her grin radiant and her cheeks flaring bright red.

"Anna!" Penelope giggled, shrieking in delight.

They were both laughing as they ran up to the cart, greeting the carter with relieved smiles.

"Please get in, ladies," the carter—who was tall and blond, just like Penelope had guessed—suggested shyly.

Anna clambered into the back, reaching for Penelope's hand. She laughed, and they half-tumbled over in the wide back of the cart that smelled of sawdust. The carter laughed and clambered up into his seat, and they headed off towards the village.

"The dance is on the village green," Anna told Penelope as the cart rolled nearer to the village. They could see the outline of a church against the sky, which was turning a dusky blue with evening.

"Grand," Penelope replied, wincing as the cart jolted on the country road. Despite the discomfort, it was exciting, and she was laughing happily as she and Anna clambered out by the church.

"Thank you for your help, Tom," Anna told the carter. "And my best wishes to your mother."

"Thank you, miss," the carter replied. "She will appreciate that."

Anna and Penelope waved as the carter turned his cart and then they hurried across to the village green.

Penelope tensed, her heart thumping with shyness as she approached the crowded lawn. People of all ages were there, from children who seemed not much older than twelve to grandmothers and grandfathers. All were wearing their Sunday best, and the sound of chatter and laughter calmed her a little, despite her tension. The faces turned towards them were all friendly, and she soon started to relax.

A trestle table was set out at the side of the village green, and on it there were some sandwiches and other things, presided over by an elderly lady who seemed to be selling refreshments. Anna approached.

"Two sandwiches and lemonade, please," she requested, digging for coins in a reticule that Penelope had not noticed she was carrying. Penelope blushed.

"I shouldn't let you buy me..." she began, but Anna interrupted.

"I want to. Next time, you buy the sandwiches," she stated.

They both laughed, and Penelope's spirits soared as she tucked into the jam and bread. Sweet and delicious, it restored her energy. Soon, she was standing laughing with Anna, enjoying the freedom and relaxation. Anna's eyes moved to a spot just behind her, and Penelope turned to see what she was looking at, then went bright red. There were three young men of around their age standing under a tree, and they were staring straight at her and Anna.

"One of them is coming here," Anna hissed. "Try and look natural!"

Anna reached up and tucked a stray hair behind one ear. Penelope wanted to giggle at her obvious discomfort. She took a steadying breath, her heart thudding in her chest.

"Miss?" The young man—who was tall, with broad shoulders and rich honey-brown hair—stammered. "Are you... Do you have someone to dance with?" He inclined his head politely.

Anna—to whom he had addressed the comment, though his gaze darted to Penelope, including her in the question—lifted a shoulder.

"We have not," she replied.

"Oh!" The young man's brown gaze widened in a way that made Penelope bite back a grin. If he had not been sure they did not have someone to dance with, why had he asked? she wondered. Young men were confusing sometimes. "Oh. Well... Stewart and I... um... we were wondering if you young ladies would... would..." he looked awkwardly towards his friends, as though pleading with one of them to assist him.

"We would be pleased to dance with you," Anna replied boldly, showing compassion for the stuttering young man.

Penelope blushed. She did not want to dance—she felt terribly shy and awkward—but Anna was walking towards the men, and there was music already drifting across the green, and her heart leapt with a strange, unexpected mixture of anticipation and awkwardness as the tall, dark-haired man—Stewart, she presumed—walked across to her and took her hand in his. His hand was big and callused as it enfolded hers. His grip was a little tight, and she could not help but think of the earl and how he had tenderly but firmly held her hand and helped her up when she had fallen. The touch of this tall young man was nothing like that. While it was not rough or cruel, it had a feeling of forcefulness and briskness about it that the earl's had entirely lacked.

She looked up into the young man's eyes. They were a warm hazel brown with deep lines at the corners, despite his youth, from staring into the sunlight. She could not guess what his job might be, but he had broad forearms packed with wiry muscle that showed where he had rolled his sleeves back in the heat, and he clearly spent long days out of doors.

"I'm fond of a jig," he commented as his hand moved to her waist. Penelope tensed. She did not like the feeling of his closeness when she had never spoken to him before.

"Jigs can be enjoyable," she said awkwardly.

He laughed as though she had said something amusing, and then the music truly began and there was no space or time or even the possibility for talking, since the crowd around them—and the music—was so lively and so deafening that talk was simply not audible anymore.

He is not a bad dancer, Penelope thought, trying to be reasonable. He seemed friendly, too, and a little shy; smiling at her as he gazed into her eyes and then looking sharply down or across the green as though whatever he saw there had surprised him.

They danced a jig, and Penelope drew in a shaky breath as the music slowed and stopped. She was exhausted. It was a lively dance, demanding a lot of footwork, and she had not danced in years. The young man bowed shyly. She curtseyed and tried to take a breath.

"Thank you," the young man stammered. "It was... grand." He reddened, and Penelope's heart twisted.

"Thank you for the dance," she replied gently. She did not know what else to say.

"If you ever need a farrier," the man added, not looking at her as he spoke hesitantly. "You can ask for Stewart Murdoch." He smiled broadly.

"I will be sure to do so," Penelope replied politely.

"Thank you, miss," he repeated and looked around shyly, then hurried to where his friend stood under the tree where they had first spotted him.

Penelope stood on the green for a moment, surrounded by dancers, trying to clear her surprised, weary mind. Steward Murdoch. A farrier. She realised that she had not told him her name, and her frown deepened.

Somehow, I simply did not warm to him, she thought. She could not have said what it was she did not like—he was friendly, affable and handsome. But somehow, there was something. Something that the earl had, she thought, going bright red.

It was not breeding or class—she would not usually have cared, and besides, though he was shy and a little rough around the edges, Stewart Murdoch was polite and pleasant. Many nobles were anything but polite and pleasant. It was not that.

It was the look in the earl's eyes, Penelope thought, going red. He had such a ready, keen mind and it shone out of his gaze. His warmth was undeniable, drawing her to him with an ease that was impossible to ignore.

"Penelope!" Anna walked through the crowd towards the edge of the green, and Penelope waved to her, coming over to join her. Anna leaned back, seeming exhausted. She was smiling. "A fine dance," she declared.

"It was very fine," Penelope replied. She did not sound entirely convinced, and she was not sure that Anna sounded any more so.

They went to where they had set aside their lemonade and drank and chatted and laughed. Somewhere, someone was cooking meat over an open fire, and the savoury-smelling smoke drifted across the green. People moved in the direction of the meal, and Anna and Penelope danced two more dances, then ate some bread and cheese and then, after one concluding dance, hurried off to find the collier. He had said that he would meet them at half-past nine opposite the church.

"Ahoy!" Anna yelled, waving theatrically as they ran up. It was dark, the collier and his cart a silhouette against the dark blue of the night sky. "Here we are!"

"Come on, girls! It's late," the collier called.

"Sorry," Anna said apologetically and clambered up to the front seat of the cart. They could not ride in the back, since it was full of coal. Penelope clambered up beside her, and then the collier lifted the reins and they set off.

The regular jolting of the cart was wearying, and Penelope's eyelids drooped. She fought to stay awake as the cart moved through the darkened countryside back up towards the manor.

"Thank you!" Anna yelled as they clambered down. They were close to the kitchen and they ran for the door.

"Thank you!" Penelope called. She ran lightly down the path with Anna, who threw open the door that led to the kitchen corridor. Penelope leaned against the wall as they took off their outdoor boots. It was much warmer in the hallway than it was on the cart, and she let out a long sigh, shivering as she realised just how cold she'd been.

"Whew! That was grand," Anna murmured as she drifted up the hallway.

"It was," Penelope agreed. "Very fine. Thank you for everything," she added honestly, looking into her friend's hazel-brown eyes.

"It was nothing. I had a splendid evening. Thank you as well, then, since it would not have been half as enjoyable without you." She smiled warmly at Penelope.

"Good night," Penelope called as they hurried to their chambers. She paused in the doorway of her own. It was almost ten o'clock at night, but she had to go downstairs to check on Thomas and to relieve Mrs Aldham of her duties. She glanced down at her dress. She could change into her uniform first, but she decided not to. It was late and she would use the servants' stairs. Nobody would see her.

She hurried downstairs towards the nursery.

Thoughts of the earl filled her mind as she drifted up the hallway towards the room. His face entered her thoughts all the more if she tried to ignore it. She could not stop herself from imagining what it might have been like if he had been at the village dance instead of the men she'd danced with. In her imagination, the Earl's grey eyes watched her thoughtfully with that warm, dry humour sparkling in their depths. She could not help but smile at the thought; delicious warmth spreading through her. *He is an interesting man*, she thought, cheeks burning, and it was impossible not to compare the men on the village green with him. He had affected her more profoundly than they did and, no matter how hard she tried, she could not think about anybody else.

Chapter 10

Peter walked as quietly as he could down the hallway, escaping the crowded drawing room. His sister's house party held the manor in its grasp and the drawing room was packed with guests, chatting and laughing and playing cards after dinner. Peter felt stifled, though his high-necked shirt and dark blue tailcoat added only a little to the oppressive feeling. It was solely because of the guests. He hated feeling hemmed in by too many people.

The library was downstairs on the immediate left of the staircase, and Peter walked swiftly down and to his left. The silence enveloped him the moment he stepped in and relief washed through him. He turned to shut the door and give himself some peace.

"Nephew? A moment, if I may."

Peter tensed. He recognised his Aunt Marcia's voice instantly. He turned to find her in the hallway.

"Yes, Aunt?" he asked as politely as he could under the circumstances. He genuinely liked Aunt Marcia, but he had hoped to escape and have a moment or two for himself and he schooled his face to neutrality.

"Sorry, Peter. I know you are seeking some silence. I do not blame you. I think I will retire early myself. The noise of so many people is something I am no longer accustomed to." She made a wry face.

"Did you wish to speak to me about something, Aunt?" Peter inquired, feeling curious. Aunt Marcia was not one to engage in idle chatter. If she had gone out of her way to seek him in the library, she undoubtedly had a purpose.

"Yes, Peter. I did. I wished to ask you about your new maid. Is she suitable for the position?" She raised one white, well-shaped eyebrow.

"The new maid?" Peter blinked in surprise. Of all the topics he had imagined she might discuss, the new maid was certainly not one of them. "She seems to be, yes. How did you know of her?" he asked, his desire to know overriding his concern that it might be rude to ask.

"Oh, only because I recommended her," Aunt said lightly. "Her younger sister is in employment in my household. She seems a competent young lady."

"You *recommended* her?" Peter asked, the news amazing him.

"Yes. I trust that it was no disservice to do so," Aunt said swiftly, looking worried. "Is she truly skilled in her employment?" She bit her lip.

"Indeed, she is. I have been very impressed by her," Peter replied briskly. "She seems very competent, and I was surprised and pleased when she moved the location of the nursery, for example. She said the west wing was too drafty and damp, and I, for one, have to agree with her. The east and south wings of the house are far more supportive of the health." He blinked in surprise as he spoke. He truly had been impressed, but it was only as he described the incident to his aunt that he realised how impressed he had been. He blushed, realising he was praising her quite excessively.

"That was a good notion," Aunt replied approvingly. Her blue eyes sparkled. "So, she seems quite competent?" she inquired again.

"Yes. Yes, most competent," Peter replied, repeating his praise from earlier. "Why do you ask, Aunt?" he added, frowning a little. If she had recommended her, surely that should mean that Aunt had some faith in the young woman and her skills. News of her competence should be unsurprising.

"Only this. The poor young woman was badly maligned by her previous employer. I took it upon myself to inquire, and a quite different story emerged. I believe that the young lady is entirely innocent of the allegations of her former employer, who I believe made them because of her own insecurity. But I wanted to be sure. One can never be sure nowadays. So many people are untrustworthy." She shook her head, her mouth setting into a thin line. "True integrity is rare everywhere."

"That is true," Peter replied, nodding slowly. He often thought the same when forced to navigate the world of high society. The people he encountered at such gatherings seemed devoid of sincerity, their words and mannerisms carefully curated to maintain a fragile illusion of decorum. It was all an elaborate performance—one where everyone played a part and no one spoke or acted with true feeling.

Peter was bewildered and resentful whenever he thought of it. Why did they all insist on such artifice? Surely, openness and honesty would be far simpler.

"Quite so. Exactly," Aunt murmured, nodding her head.

Peter frowned. "You said allegations had been made," he began, confused. "What manner of allegations? What is she alleged to have done?" His heart twisted with worry.

"Her former employer was a countess, married to a singularly difficult and unpleasant man," Aunt began with a sigh. "Unfortunately, either the man truly was a little too interested in Miss Matthews, or the countess believed him to be, because she no longer wished to have Miss Matthews on her staff. She fabricated an elaborate story to ensure her dismissal. She accused the poor young woman of stealing money. I do not for a second believe that she did it. Emily is scrupulously honest." She looked up at Peter with a hard stare.

"Emily is Miss Matthews' sister?" he inquired.

"Yes. And Sophia is inordinately fond of her already. The two of them struck up a grand friendship. Sophia often has money lying around in her bedchamber—she isn't very careful with it, and inordinately generous as well. A dear." She smiled indulgently. "But not so much as a cent has gone missing despite the temptation it must offer to a poor young woman like Emily." She sighed.

"I believe that one must examine all tales with caution," Peter said in as noncommittal a way as he could. He was absolutely sure that Miss Matthews was no thief. Yet she was beautiful, and beauty had a way of clouding judgment, of making a man see only what he wished to see. Not that, he thought with a small smile, they could blind his aunt. He was not sure that anything could blind his aunt to people's bad characters. She was astute and seemed to have noticed absolutely everything.

"Well, I should return to the drawing room. Sophia asked me if I would play a round of bridge with her. I am grateful we do not wager on cards, for between her skillful play and her generous soul, I do not know whether she or I would be the first to be beggared by the sport." She chuckled.

Peter smiled. He was very fond of his cousin, who was generous to a fault, as Aunt said. One of his fondest memories was of when Sophia had lent him money when they were both children and they had gorged themselves on gingerbread in the village bakery. Aunt had sent their nurse to fetch them, and they received a thorough scolding, but were unrepentant. He still recalled the day with fondness.

"Thank you, Aunt, for telling me," Peter murmured. His aunt held his gaze. Her blue eyes were surprisingly firm as she looked into his.

"She's a good young woman," she told him briskly. "A good young woman."

Peter nodded. "I am sure she is, Aunt," he said a little bemusedly. "It is my policy never to believe the stories spread by others. I shall judge her merit for myself."

"Wise words," his aunt said, nodding. Peter smiled. His aunt was truly wise, so it was a compliment.

"Thank you, Aunt," he said gently. He watched as she turned in the doorway, heading back out with her characteristic graceful posture. He stood in the library, the sound of the fire crackling behind him the only noise in the silent space.

After fifteen minutes by the fireside with an old favourite book, a creeping sense of guilt began to take hold. His sister had gone to great lengths to arrange the house party, and yet here he was, avoiding it entirely. She would be hurt if he made no effort at all to mingle with the guests.

With a resigned sigh, he closed the book and rose to his feet. Fatigue blurred his vision, though it could hardly be later than ten o'clock. The guests would no doubt remain awake for several more hours, engaged in cards and conversation.

Bracing himself, he stepped out to join them.

As he went up the stairs, he paused. There was a light flickering in the eastern wing, and he guessed that it was near the new nursery. He drew a breath and headed in that direction, feeling curious. The talk of the new maid had made him wonder about her; about how she performed her duties and whether he should really be as trustworthy as he was.

Odd, but I never doubted her. He let out a sigh. Perhaps he was foolish. Perhaps all it took to make all of his caution dissipate was beautiful eyes.

He walked up the hallway towards the nursery. As he reached the door, he paused. Someone was in there. There was a lamp burning, and he could hear someone—a woman—talking to Thomas.

He stepped in through the door. And stopped.

Miss Matthews whirled round. She was standing by the fire, a frown on her brow. She was dressed in a vivid green gown, and her long brown hair was coming loose from the ribbon that tied it back. Her mouth opened in surprise.

"My lord!" she exclaimed.

He grinned. He could not help it. In that moment, she did not look like a maid at all. In the beautiful green dress, she could have been a guest at any ball he had ever attended. His heart soared. He inclined his head.

"I am sorry to have startled you, miss," he said softly, the smile still on his lips. "But I saw a light. I was curious. Forgive me for intruding." He inclined his head again in apology.

"No... no need to be sorry," she stammered. Her gaze held his, and it seemed frightened. His heart started to pound. He longed to reach out to her, to take her hand and comfort her. She looked so scared and alone. Her green eyes looked very big on her pale face, the firelight making the contrast even more intense.

"I startled you. I should allow you to do your work," he murmured, stepping back towards the door. It occurred to him to wonder, briefly, if she always wore plain clothes in the evening rather than her uniform. Not that it mattered—the uniform was there mainly because others expected it and because the housekeeper, Mrs Hallden, said it was cleaner and that it gave the servants pride in their work. He could not have cared less if she turned up casually dressed every day.

"No," she said swiftly. "I mean... I am grateful you are here, my lord. I need someone to fetch the physician. Thomas is not well."

"Not well?" Peter's heart thudded with fear. It was something he was terrified of, since discovering he was the baby's guardian. "In what sense is he unwell?" he demanded, concern tightening his tone. He could not fail Thomas. He had failed Charles and Eliza in every other way. He had to take care of their child.

"He has a fever," she stammered. "I am sorry. I have done my best. I noticed a slight fever, but it seemed to have broken. I made a preparation for him that my grandmother used to make for us. But I am worried. I would like the physician to see him." He could hear the strength in her tone, though he suspected it was hard fought-for.

"Of course. Of course," Peter nodded. He drew in a deep breath, trying to be calm. Miss Matthews knew what she was doing. She had already prepared something. All he had to do was to send for someone to fetch the physician. "I will have him sent for immediately."

"Thank you, my lord," Miss Matthews called. Peter hurried into the hallway.

"Send for the physician," he demanded as soon as the stable hand could be awoken. He was the best rider at the manor and the only member of staff besides the stable-master who regularly rode. "Take whichever horse you deem best suited for the task."

"Thank you, my lord," the youth said respectfully.

"And please take whatever you need from the kitchen to victual yourself when you return," Peter added, seeing how weary the boy looked.

"Cor! Thank you, my lord," the youth replied. He hurried outside.

Peter returned to the upstairs hallway, pacing outside the door. After a few minutes, he could not wait a second longer, and he knocked at the door to the nursery. The door opened.

"My lord," Miss Matthews greeted him. As he looked at her more closely, he could see the grey prints of exhaustion under her striking green eyes. His heart twisted in sympathy.

"I have sent for the physician," he told her gently.

"Thank you," Miss Matthews replied. She looked relieved, her shoulders lowering instantly, her posture relaxing.

"You should rest," Peter commented awkwardly as he watched her go to the cradle. She was holding a glass nursing bottle. He recalled having ordered two in London when he became aware that the child still needed milk. He watched as she gently lifted the baby and fed him whatever was in the bottle. Little Thomas fussed and refused at first, but then he seemed to calm as she wiped his brow, and began to drink.

"Hush, now," she murmured gently. Her voice was the only sound in the room. She went to sit down in the only chair in the room, resting the baby against her shoulder and rocking him. Peter's heart twisted. It was a beautiful scene and he looked away, almost shy to witness that care and tenderness.

"Is he very ill?" Peter asked. A fist of fear was gripping his heart. He could not lose the child. He would never be able to forgive himself. He would always think he should have done something differently. He knelt down beside the chair so that she did not have to tip her head back to look at him. Her eyes widened.

"He is... I cannot say, my lord," she stammered. "He seems not to be too terribly afflicted, and yet his brow is overly warm, and if I put him on his back to sleep, he begins to fret. He has no other signs of illness, just this high fever." She looked up at him, brow furrowed.

"I wish I could help." Peter gazed down at the small baby, a sense of helplessness settling over him. A part of him felt utterly useless—perhaps he would be of more practical benefit if he simply joined his sister in playing cards. But that was impossible.

Little Thomas was his responsibility. He had hired Miss Matthews to tend to him, but the actual weight of being the boy's guardian was on his shoulders. If aught happened to Thomas, it would be only him to blame.

"He is resting now," Miss Matthews said softly. She rested her hand on the baby's body. He appeared to be sleeping.

"You have done well," Peter murmured.

Her gaze held his. She looked surprised and almost distrustful, as though she did not know whether to believe him.

"Thank you, my lord," she murmured.

"There is nothing to thank me for," Peter replied softly.

He drew in a breath as her beautiful green eyes held his.

"I thank you for the fact that you trust me," she said quietly.

Peter stared. He wanted to say that nothing other than trusting her would have occurred to him from when he met her. But at that moment someone knocked on the door.

"My lord?" A male voice called. "The physician is here."

"Send him in," Peter said swiftly.

The physician, Doctor Ainsworth, was a tall, greying man with a slim face and a slight frame. He always looked troubled. The butler stepped back and ushered him into the room.

"Good evening, my lord," Doctor Ainsworth murmured. "Might I see the patient?"

"He is there," Peter replied, gesturing to Miss Matthews, who was holding the baby in her arms.

The physician gently lifted the baby from her embrace, and the little child became fretful immediately, thrashing and whimpering. Peter winced. Miss Matthews gazed at the baby with care.

"I will allow the physician to do his work," Peter said, gesturing to the door. "But when he is gone, I shall return. I wish to hear his assessment." He added the last for his own satisfaction, though he was not entirely sure why he felt compelled to come back.

Miss Matthews gazed at him. "Thank you," she said softly. Her posture relaxed a little.

Peter smiled at her, wishing he could give her some assurance. Then he hurried out into the hallway, shutting the door and walking up the hallway to his chamber to wait. He sat down on an upholstered chair, mind whirling with thoughts and images. Care for the baby and worry for him were uppermost, but among the images were thoughts of Miss Matthews with her wide green eyes and that beautiful, wary face. He could not get her out of his thoughts, even if he tried to.

Chapter 11

Peter walked restlessly back to the nursery, unable to wait a second more. He had waited for what felt like an age, though only ten minutes had passed on the clock on the mantelpiece. The waiting was impossible.

The drawing room seemed quiet as he hurried past. News of the baby's illness must have been carried to Millicent and the others, and the evening party seemed to have dispersed. He registered the silence without giving it too much thought and then hurried to the nursery.

The door was shut, but he pushed it open. He had to know whatever was happening. He saw the physician standing before Miss Matthews, a grave expression on his face.

"He is in the grips of a high fever," the physician explained ponderously to Miss Matthews, who was leaning on the chair-back, looking almost too tired to stand up. "This is a very serious condition. I hope you are aware of this," he added, levelling her with a dark stare.

"Of course, she is," Peter interrupted, anger rising in his throat. "Tell us what to do about it," he added.

The physician shot Peter an angry look. "I was about to," he said pompously.

Peter looked at him, frustration and worry making him barely able to contain his anger. Somebody had to be able to do something to help the child.

"I suspect that the child's ears are afflicted," the physician explained. "He frets when he is placed on his back, which is a sign that there is an infection there." He paused, as if for dramatic effect. When nothing was forthcoming, he continued. "I have prescribed oil of garlic to address the infection. It is to be administered three times a day."

Peter let out a sigh of relief. "And will it cure him?" he demanded.

The physician sighed. "I have done all I can," he replied. In that moment, he looked old and tired.

Peter nodded, exhausted. Even through his rage and fear, he knew that was true. He took a deep breath. The condition sounded dangerous. He looked at Miss Matthews, silently imploring her for help. He could not let Thomas die. He could not. But what could he do?

"Send a rider to my house tomorrow morning to collect the treatment," the physician told them as he went to the door. "I will prepare it and have it ready."

"Thank you," Peter managed to say. He did not like the man, finding him surly, self-important and generally unappealing. But he had to admit that he relied on him in such moments.

The physician left the room, the soft click of the door shutting behind him the only noise in the quiet space.

Miss Matthews stood by the cradle. Her shoulders drooped; her posture making it plain how exhausted she was. Peter's heart ached for her. She went to the pitcher of water and fetched a wet cloth, which she laid on the child's brow. Her touch was tender and gentle. The gentle gesture made him draw a sharp breath. She was not simply doing a job—she cared for Thomas, and that was evident in every line of her. He went to stand by the cradle.

The little baby was resting, but his small face was contorted even in sleep, his brow furrowed as if even in the realm of dreams he was not at ease. Peter looked away. The little face was a thousand accusations—Charles' accusations from beyond the grave. Was Charles angry because he had lost his life? Did he feel that it was Peter's fault, as he himself did? Peter could not say. Guilt haunted him, and that guilt meant that he felt entirely helpless.

"How does he fare?" Peter asked. The room was steeped in the deep hush of the night, a silence so complete it felt almost tangible. His senses swam, dulled by the strange, weighty fog of sleepless hours.

He turned his gaze to Miss Matthews. Though she looked every bit as weary as he felt, there was still an air of quiet capability about her, steady and unwavering.

"He is resting now. When he wakes, I will try to feed him. He needs to keep up his strength."

Peter watched as she checked the cloth on the infant's brow, then straightened, going to a door he had barely noticed in the wall. It must lead to the servants' corridor. She was still wearing the beautiful green dress, her lovely dark brown hair loose around her shoulders. She looked so beautiful as she turned at the doorway, so vulnerable. Yet she stood straight-backed, radiating a strength that offered him hope.

"I need to go and prepare his bottle. Might you stay to watch him? I fear nobody else is awake," she murmured.

Peter nodded. "Of course, I will," he replied at once.

"Thank you." She looked at him with weary relief, then opened the door and shut it behind her.

When she had left the room, Peter paced to the window. With her present, it was possible to feel confident, to be sure that the cure would work and that the boy would recover. With her downstairs, worry gnawed at him.

The child was so small, so frail. It seemed impossible to understand how he could withstand a sickness.

"Please, let this pass," he murmured, a quiet plea slipping from his lips.

After Charles' passing, Peter had lost all sense of faith—for months, he had been consumed by grief and anger, searching for someone to blame. Though his burden was one he placed upon himself, the weight of it had made him lash out, even at forces beyond his control.

With time, he had regained some perspective, but he seldom allowed himself such moments of reflection. Yet now, in this moment, he felt the need to hope—for something, anything—to guide them through.

His voice seemed to unsettle the baby, who began to stir. Peter walked to the cradle as the child cried out fearfully. He gazed down at the child, who twitched as if he was about to wake. Peter tensed. He had held the baby only once, when Charles and Eliza were alive. From the moment that Thomas had arrived at the townhouse, Peter had avoided contact with him, the guilt and sorrow overwhelming him whenever he looked at the infant. Now, he gazed down at him, helplessness making him want to scream, to run away. He did not know what to do. He could do nothing.

The child's hazel eyes opened, and he began to fret, whimpering. Peter's heart twisted, and the urge to run from his own helplessness warred with the desire to help.

"Shh. Shh," he murmured, trying to do as Miss Matthews did. It did not seem to work. As Peter looked around, desperately wishing that someone—anyone—would come in, the door opened.

"I have the bottle. Is he awake?" Miss Matthews asked.

"He's awake, and crying," Peter told her, relief soaring in his chest. She could deal with it—she knew how. He watched as she bent down and lifted the child to her chest, cradling him in her arms.

"Shh. Hush, now. Easy, little one," she murmured. The baby seemed to calm as she sat down with him in the chair, his small head resting on her shoulder, her hand mopping his brow with a cool cloth. Peter watched as she half-stood, struggling to get up. Without thinking, he rushed over, lifted the glass bottle from the table and handed it to her.

"Thank you," she replied softly. She gazed up at him for a moment. He smiled back.

"Of course," he said gently.

He watched as she fed the baby. He sucked readily this time, seeming thirsty. As he did, he seemed to grow calmer. He still fussed, even when he had drunk his fill, but the fussing seemed less when he was held in Miss Matthews' arms.

"He seems restful," Peter said softly.

"I think he feels more at ease," Miss Matthews whispered back, leaning back a little so that the baby could lie comfortably.

"He was so fretful, and now he is almost asleep," Peter murmured. "Thank you." His heart was full of gratitude. She was competent and skilled where he felt like a fool.

"I did nothing, my lord," she said softly.

"You have done a great deal," Peter told her firmly.

Her gaze held his. She was so tired, but he saw surprise in the depths of her stare. It sent a flicker of joy through him.

"Thank you," she said.

They were quiet. Peter stood beside her where she sat in the upholstered chair with the baby.

"Sleep, little baby," she began to sing, the tune lilting and simple. Peter's heart contracted. It was a beautiful tune. Her voice was neither bad nor exceptional, a little flat here and there, but melodious nonetheless, and in the deep silence of the night, it was truly lovely.

He stood where he was, afraid to move lest she stop singing. Her eyes were closed, and she rocked the child as if she, too, was about to sleep. Her grip on the baby was as firm as ever, holding him safe.

Peter watched, afraid to breathe. It was so beautiful.

This is not simply a maid, performing a task, he thought. *This is a dedicated woman, caring for a child who she loves.* His heart filled with warmth.

Miss Matthews stopped rocking as the baby quieted, and he thought for a moment that she had fallen asleep too. He frowned as his eye settled on the clock. It was almost one o'clock in the morning. He blinked wearily.

Neither Miss Matthews nor the baby stirred, and Peter settled on the stool by the cradle, keeping watch over them. Miss Matthews leaned against the back of the chair, her head tipped back, her dark brown hair loose around her shoulders. The baby was gripped in her arms, her embrace seeming to remain firm even as she slept.

Peter's heart ached, watching them. There, in that scene, was all the tenderness that he had never known, all the love and closeness that he had craved. The only person in his life to whom he had been truly close was his cousin, Charles. Mama had passed away when he was little more than a baby, and his father had been cold and distant. He had never known love and care such as he saw now.

He sat guard over them. He did not know how long he sat there, nor whether he slept.

After some time, he stirred. He opened his eyes. Pale dawn light showed at the window. It was the clock chiming that had woken him. It chimed the sixth hour. He blinked and sat up straight. Had he truly slept in the chair for half the night? He tried to stand up and winced. His foot had gone numb and his back ached. He sat down and then stood again a moment later, his foot throbbing and tingling.

He glanced across at Miss Matthews. She was fast asleep. The baby slept in her arms. Whether he had slept all night, Peter had no idea. He gazed down at them, his heart twisting. Miss Matthews was so pale, the light from the window making her seem even paler and painting highlights the colour of coffee in her hair. She looked small and frail, even the fine lines around her eyes smoothed out in sleep. He looked around for a blanket to cover her with, but there was nothing in the small room. His heart filled with tenderness that almost hurt; it was so intense as she stirred, eyelids fluttering.

Peter stepped back hastily so that she would not be startled. Her eyes blinked shut and then open. She looked around the room and slowly woke. He held his breath as her gaze moved across him and then focused.

"My lord! You... you're still here." Her voice was surprised. He tilted his head.

"I fell asleep," he told her, his mouth quirking into a grin. "I don't think I ever slept in a chair before." He winced at his sore foot.

She stretched. In her arms, the baby stirred, and she lifted him, wincing as she stood up. She carried the child to the cradle and settled him in it, propping his head on a small pillow. He woke and turned over, making a small noise of discomfort. He still seemed sleepy, though, and Miss Matthews looked up at Peter.

"I'm sorry," she began, but he shook his head.

"No need to be," he said gently. "You did not tell me to fall asleep." He smiled. "I did that by myself."

She grinned a tired grin. "I suppose," she admitted.

His smile widened. In that moment, they were not master and servant, but two people who had faced a challenge together. His heart lifted as she stared into his eyes.

"I should prepare a bottle for the baby," she began, turning to the chair where the bottle still lay on a small table beside it.

"I can wait for you," Peter began. As he walked towards the cradle, a knock sounded at the door. He tensed.

"Peter?" an authoritative voice said outside. "He cannot be here," it added, and Peter recognised his sister, Millicent.

"My lady, he..." the butler's voice began. Peter tensed. His gaze darted to Miss Matthews. She had gone white. He understood why. To anyone's eyes who did not understand that he had been watching over her and the baby, it would look terribly incriminating. A master and a maid having spent the night in the same room looked appalling for them both. He drew in a breath to explain. As he did, Millicent opened the door and walked in.

"Brother?" She stared at him for a moment, taking in the evening jacket and trousers and then turning to Miss Matthews, who stood with the bottle in her hands and rigid fear in her manner. "How does the baby fare?" she asked Miss Matthews, crossing the floor and going over to him. She gazed down into the cradle, her expression more or less neutral as she looked down at the sleeping child.

"He is a little better, my lady," Miss Matthews replied. "And I hope he will heal the faster for the remedy the physician has recommended." Her voice was neutral, and Peter admired her strength.

"Good. Good. I am sure he will heal," Millicent said, her tone brisk. She turned to Peter. Her expression changed to surprise as she studied him, then her eyes narrowed. "You need to dress for breakfast," she told him firmly. "Our guests will begin to wake at seven o'clock. I have a morning tea planned, and then the music evening tonight. Do not forget that Lady Adeline will perform," she added with another hard look in his direction. "She is a most excellent pianist."

"I'm sure she is," Peter murmured, not sure what to say. He reddened. His sister mentioning her made him feel deeply embarrassed, and he glanced at Miss Matthews. She was busying herself with the baby, lifting him out of the cradle. He turned to his sister. "I will come directly," he murmured. With her stare boring into him, he crossed the room to join Miss Matthews. "I will send a rider for the medicine. Thank you for your care of Thomas." He kept his voice neutral.

"Of course, my lord. Thank you," she murmured. She did not lift her gaze to him. He swallowed, feeling the loss of their earlier ease together.

He turned and went to the door where Millicent was waiting. As he went out into the hallway and shut the door behind him, she turned to him with a hard look.

"Your devotion to the baby is strong," she said evenly. "But do not overdo it." Her gaze bored into him.

Peter looked away, feeling angry and annoyed. Was she suggesting that he had done more than simply watch over the baby? He had no idea.

"He is recovering. That is of the greatest importance," he said tightly.

"Yes. Yes, it is," Millicent replied. She did not turn around, and he followed her to the breakfast room. The church clock was chiming a quarter to seven as he stumbled to his room, exhausted, to change into coat and trousers suitable for the day. As he wearily leaned back against the wall, his thoughts drifted to Miss Matthews—her quiet courage, her unwavering strength, and the delicate fragility beneath it all. Most of all, he thought of her gentle, tender care for the little boy.

He smiled, his heart aching with warmth.

As he dressed and splashed water on his face, he winced at the weariness etched into his reflection. His thoughts turned to Miss Matthews—her tireless devotion, her quiet strength. He hoped he might find a moment to excuse himself from the guests, not only to inquire after the baby's health but hers as well.

Chapter 12

Penelope sat down in the big chair in the nursery. Her feet ached. Her back hurt. Her head was foggy with the need to sleep. She gazed tiredly around the room. The curtains were open, showing a bright blue late-afternoon sky. The treetops were painted with rich golden light. A fire burned in the grate though it was not particularly cold in the room. She had lit it for Thomas's comfort, and for her own. The lack of sleep made her feel cold. And yet, as she rested, her gaze moving to where Thomas slept peacefully in his cradle, her heart was filled with contentment and joy. He was safe. He was sleeping. Her world was, in that moment, one of complete contentment.

Her eye moved to the stool against the wall where the earl must have slept. Her heart twisted even as an amused smile lifted the corners of her lips. He was not a small man—slim, but muscled. How had he slept on such a small seat for such a long time? She frowned as the recollection of his sister's arrival drifted into her thoughts. The lady had not been rude or accusing towards her, and yet how could his sister fail to wonder what had happened that night? Penelope's cheeks burned with shame.

Please, she thought fearfully, *do not let her think such ill of me*.

If the earl's sister thought what it was altogether too easy to think, then perhaps she would be dismissed. Papa needed every cent—both for medication and for coal for the winter as well as for everyday expenses. She shut her eyes for a moment, willing herself to stay strong, hoping for some stroke of fortune.

When she opened her eyes, Thomas was stirring in his cradle. He had slept for almost an hour. She sighed in relief. She had administered the first dose of the garlic oil at seven o'clock in the morning, dabbing a little on her fingertip and placing it carefully into his ear. By four o'clock in the afternoon, the baby seemed less fretful, as though the ear was slightly less painful already. He was still fevered, but the fever was not as bad as it had been the previous day, and the cold cloth she placed on his head seemed to bring him relief.

She glanced at the window. The summer's heat was cooling outside. Perhaps a storm would blow in later. It was a good opportunity to take the baby outdoors, and the sunny garden beckoned to her. She stood and went to the door, taking her shawl from where she had placed it on the chair. Her stiff black uniform rustled as she moved. After the beautiful muslin gown, it felt hot and a little stifling.

"Here, little one," she murmured, replacing the cool cloth on his brow with a fresher, cooler one, and lifting him up. "Shall we go outdoors?"

The baby murmured fretfully. While he usually responded with babbling or the occasional coherent word, the fever seemed to have taken all his strength, reducing him to mere wails or murmurings.

"You'll be happier in the fresh air," Penelope murmured, lifting him and wrapping him in a blanket, then cradling him against her shoulder. She planned to find a warm—but not hot—place for them to sit on the lawn somewhere. Several guests had drifted around the garden for part of the morning—she had noticed ladies in bright dresses wandering about the grounds, and gentlemen in somber jackets and trousers. She had paid them no attention, and they seemed to be otherwise occupied during the afternoon, for she had seen nobody out on the lawn for a few hours.

She walked down the stairs and out of the side door.

The garden was warm, the air scented with fresh grass. She breathed in deeply. It felt wonderful to feel the warmth on her skin and the slight breeze ruffling her hair. After the stuffy, stifling indoors, it was a true pleasure and she walked across the lawn towards some shady trees, revelling in the clean air and the soft, fragrant scents around her.

"Here, little one," she murmured, settling on the lawn near some tall conifers and spreading the blanket out. She rested the baby in the dappled shade and sat beside him in the sun. A bonnet shielded her face from the direct rays—a precaution against freckles, just as Emily had always advised.

Emily always paid more attention to fashion and matters of beauty than Penelope ever had. The job of a lady's maid was a good match, and Penelope smiled, thinking of her sister and hoping that she fared well.

Her gaze widened as she spotted movement on the lawns. Some ladies had appeared on the front lawn and were wandering down the path. She could see brightly-coloured day dresses and some in pastel shades or white, as young ladies often preferred. Her gaze narrowed, spotting an elderly lady in a blueish grey gown, a young lady with blonde hair partly covered by a bonnet walking beside her. The young lady had a friendly, open smile, and the two were laughing at something that one of them must have commented. With them was another older woman in a dark red dress and a young woman in white, whose black curls showed under a white bonnet. The black-haired woman had a pale, oval face, and even from that distance away, she seemed quite lovely. Penelope stared at the other lady, praying that it was not the earl's sister, but when she turned, she did not look like her, even across the distance of perhaps twenty yards.

The sound of chatter, light and pleasant, drifted across the lawn as the ladies walked along the path. They did not come close, and Penelope watched them until they had moved beyond the hedge that appeared to screen a water garden or an arbour from the sight of the house. She sighed and leaned back, closing her eyes.

Worries of what the earl's sister would think mingled in her mind with recollections from the night. The earl had been so caring, so tender. He was so handsome, so kind. When he had thanked her and stared into her eyes, her heart had filled with something—some strong emotion that she could not name. When he bent close to her, she had longed for something. She had wanted him to kiss her.

"You're a fool," she said aloud, though her voice sounded warm to her ears. Part of her was distressed, while part of her was bathing in a sea of delight. The earl was like no other man she had ever met. Every memory of him—of the night—was precious. When she recalled the dance that she had attended—it seemed like an age ago, though it was not even a day—she could not help but think that no other man had the appeal that he had.

She leaned back against the tree, grinning to herself. She was a fool. A ridiculous, wild dreamer. He was an earl, and she was a maid; there could be nothing more between them. And yet, there was tenderness in his stare when he looked at her.

"I don't know," she said aloud, distress evident in her tone. Thomas, who had been sitting on the blanket quite calmly, turned and looked at her, his little face creasing.

Penelope drew in a breath, trying to contain her own confused feelings. The child was even more sensitive than most babies his age, noticing the slightest fluctuation in her tone and moods. She wondered again what had happened to him.

"It's all well, little one. Shall we go somewhere cooler? Perhaps you'd like to sit by the fountain?" she asked him brightly. The brightness in her tone seemed to calm him a little, and he stopped whimpering, looking at her confusedly.

They crossed the grass, heading back down towards the house.

Sunshine poured onto the lawn, and the trees painted the margins of it with a cool blueish-green shade. Tall conifers and spreading oak trees surrounded the manor grounds, part of a large forest that she guessed was attached to the estate. The scent of flowers drifted across to Penelope, making her breathe deeper. The garden around the manor was big and it seemed beautiful. She longed to explore it, but she did not have the opportunity to do so. Only the area close to the manor was familiar to her, and she knew that, between the front lawn and the path that led to the kitchen, was a small ornamental fountain. There was a bench beside it, and she headed in that direction, hoping that the splashes and the reflected sunshine would amuse the child.

"Good afternoon," a woman's voice greeted her as she walked across the lawn. Penelope jumped, then turned around and grinned.

"Anna!" she exclaimed, delightedly, seeing the tall, slim lady's maid there.

Her friend laughed and smiled back. Her auburn hair was partly loose about her face, straying from under the black bonnet she wore. Her uniform was black, like Penelope's. Her expression was brightly happy.

"Are you taking a walk?" Anna asked her happily. She glanced at Thomas, and her brow creased, her expression serious. "How does little Thomas fare? I heard that he was unwell." She peered at the little boy, who frowned back, brow crinkling.

"He fares much better, thank you," Penelope replied. Her heart thudded. Anna was the lady's maid to the earl's sister. Had she heard anything about the apparently scandalous goings-on that night? She tensed, unsure if she even wanted to know the answer to that question. "Did your employer, Lady Penrith, mention that he was ill?" she asked carefully, her stomach knotted.

"No. The butler was in a state, hurrying about to send for the stable hand to ride to the village last night. We all heard him, and everyone was concerned about the little fellow. Weren't we?" she asked, grinning at Thomas. Thomas smiled back, lips moving in nonsense syllables that seemed to convey delight.

"Oh," Penelope murmured. Perhaps Lady Penrith had sworn the butler to secrecy to protect the earl's reputation, since Anna—and presumably the rest of the staff—did not appear to have heard any rumours. She breathed out, feeling relieved. At least for the moment, that worry was lifted from her. She glanced at Thomas, who was gazing wide-eyed at Anna. "He likes you," she commented.

Anna's eyes brightened.

"I like him," she replied, eliciting a grin from the child, who seemed to understand. Penelope smiled down at him.

"Shall we go and sit by the fountain with Anna, eh?" she asked him. "Have you some time?" she inquired of her friend as they strolled across the lawn.

"I have," Anna replied. "Though at five o'clock, I need to help my mistress dress for the soiree this evening." She made a wry face.

"Soiree?" Penelope asked. She had heard of such things but had never so much as walked past a building where one was being held. Curiosity made her hunger for details.

Anna nodded. "Ladies showing off their skills on the pianoforte, mostly, or poetry readings." She lifted a shoulder. "Not sure which is more tedious. Have you ever played the pianoforte?" she added casually.

Penelope grinned. "There was one at the vicarage," she answered. "Papa could play a little. He used to play hymns sometimes, though Mrs Penning played them for the service. Papa always said he would have felt silly performing the hymns." She smiled, her heart twisting at the thought of her family.

"I played a little. Papa fancied the idea of me being a companion for a fine lady. I think being a lady's maid suits me better," Anna answered. "I have my time to myself for most of the day. At least here in the countryside, I do. And that suits me well, since I can take fine walks with my friend and enjoy the sunshine."

Penelope giggled. "This is pleasant," she agreed, as they walked to the fountain.

Thomas was restless, thrashing his little arms. Penelope laid out the blanket by the fountain, sitting him on it. He cooed in delight, watching the water, and crawled off to stick his hand in the pond. Penelope and Anna watched him indulgently as he splashed. He seemed to feel better, though his forehead still felt a little warm. Penelope smiled, amazed by how children could ignore pain and fever if they were truly enjoying themselves.

"Did you sleep much?" Anna asked. Penelope shrugged.

"A little," she said guardedly. She was still not sure if Anna had heard any rumours. "Thomas fell asleep at around one o'clock in the morning."

"Good," Anna replied sympathetically. She gazed across the lawn. More people were walking from the house to the path. One was a tall gentleman in a charcoal tailcoat. Anna's hazel eyes widened as she saw him, her posture straightening.

"Who is that?" Penelope asked, trying to sound like she was not really interested. Anna's reaction intrigued her.

"That is... nobody. Um, a viscount. The earl's cousin, I believe. Lord Chelmsford." Anna lifted a shoulder as though the viscount was nobody important. Penelope smiled.

"And who is he?" she inquired playfully. Anna flapped a hand at her.

"Perdition take you!" She grinned in delight. "He is nobody. I just talked to him. Once. Twice. He is an interesting man. He likes gardens. And travelling." Her cheeks were bright red.

"Oh." Penelope said and grinned back. Anna flapped her hand again, aiming a slap at Penelope's wrist. Penelope giggled in delight, shuffling back across the grass away from her. Anna made to chase her, and they both collapsed in giggles. Penelope sat up, checking on Thomas, who was watching them and laughing. She dabbed at her eyes. It reminded her sharply of playing with Emily, teasing one another. Her heart ached. She longed to hear from her sister.

"I should go," Anna said after a moment, gesturing at the manor. "My lady will be ringing the bell for me soon, and I don't dare to be out of the house when she needs me." She made a wry face, getting up slowly off the grass.

"I will stay here for a while," Penelope replied. Thomas was happy, watching the fountain and the butterflies that skimmed over the lawn. He seemed more relaxed than he had been for days.

"Enjoy it," Anna said with another grimace. Penelope laughed.

"I hope to see you soon," she replied as Anna walked across the lawn.

"I should be able to take dinner in the kitchen tonight," Anna replied. "My lady will be at the soiree all evening."

Penelope watched her walk across the lawn, waving a friendly salutation as she went. Penelope waved back and then leaned back, the sunshine warm on her face. Anna's delight in the viscount amused her, but it also made her think about her own wild, unprecedented attraction to the earl. Maybe she was not so crazy after all. Maybe it was not mad to dream of someone, at least, even if they were so far removed from her.

"Don't be silly," she told herself firmly and stood, going across the lawn to Thomas, who was crawling to the pond again. It was getting cold, the shade already moving towards the pond, and he should stay warm, if not overly hot.

She swiftly pushed aside her thoughts of the earl and lifted the baby onto her knee. As she held him close, her mind drifted—half occupied with thoughts of writing to Emily, half wondering about the soirée, and, despite herself, what the earl might be doing.

Chapter 13

"My lord? I crave your pardon for the disturbance, but..." Mrs Hallden, the housekeeper, whispered urgently to Peter where he stood by the door of the drawing room.

Peter turned to the door with barely concealed annoyance. He was exhausted, uneasy, and burdened with worry—and to make matters worse, his sister had been pestering him all day. Her efforts to steer him toward Lady Adeline had only intensified. Millicent seemed determined not to grant him a moment's peace, forever materialising at his side, urging him into walks or drawing him into conversation.

"What is it, Mrs Hallden?" Peter asked, a little impatient.

"Sorry, my lord. But a rider has arrived. He said he came all the way from London." Her dark brown eyes were wide in her dignified, lined face. Peter raised a brow.

"London?" he asked. That would be serious news, whatever and whoever it was. Some message from the warehouse there, perhaps, which was a large source of the estate's income. Perhaps some communication from Mr Dalfort, his solicitor. Or perhaps... he pushed away any other thoughts. The third option was too unlikely.

"Yes, my lord. He awaits you in the hallway. What should I tell him?"

"Tell him I will come directly. I'll meet with him in my study. But I can only spare a few minutes," he added, gazing around the room. The guests were mingling over a sumptuous tea, and soon they would sit down for the evening's performances. It was six o'clock, and the air of the room was loud with the sound of lively chatter and laughter. He spotted Millicent and went over to excuse himself as Mrs Hallden hurried to fetch the visitor.

"Brother! The performances... you are going to miss them! What am I supposed to tell the guests?" Millicent objected as he told her. He sighed.

"You can begin without me. I promise I shan't be long," he told her hurriedly. He walked to the door before she could begin any further objections.

"Brother..." she began, but he was already by the refreshments table, and she could not very well rush after him. She sighed, and his heart twisted with a stab of guilt as he hurried to the door.

The hallway was empty, and he strode briskly to his study. Nobody was waiting for him and he lit the oil-lamps to give some light in the darkening evening, then sat down and waited for his visitor to arrive.

"Enter," he called at the sound of someone knocking. The door opened and the butler appeared, a man with him. Peter tensed. He recognised the man, though he had last seen him six months ago. His stomach twisted with concern. He had imagined the case closed.

"My lord," Mr Irving greeted Peter. He bowed low. He was a decade or so Peter's senior, with greying brown hair and a blunt, unremarkable face. Yet his eyes—sharp and keen—had always struck Peter as those of a man both intelligent and levelheaded. It was for this reason that he had chosen Irving for the task.

His work lay in investigating crimes, and Peter had employed him to look into Charles's death. It was the one action he felt he could take to ease his own grief, however futile the effort seemed.

After six months, he had ceased expecting any new developments. The highwayman and his accomplices had vanished without a trace, their presence on that particular road a singular event—never seen before, never reported since. It was strange. Too strange.

"Irving. State your news," Peter said briskly.

Mr Irving cleared his throat. He faced Peter directly, back straight, though he could not quite look him in the eye.

"My lord, this is not easy news to convey. But I will do so," he added briskly. "The men who attacked the coach that night were not highwaymen."

"What?" Peter demanded. His heart skipped a beat, sending a sudden pain through his chest. He put his hand up, pressing the pain. He gaped at Mr Irving.

Mr Irving cleared his throat. "I am sorry, my lord. But we managed to find a night watchman who had seen something of the attack. He ran to fetch help, but by the time he reached the coach, the occupants were already..." he looked down. "The man was able to furnish me with a description of the three men. Through careful investigation and questioning the locals, I was able to determine their identities. They are not highwaymen. They are mercenaries."

"What?" Peter shouted. This was too bizarre.

"They were mercenaries, my lord. Of late, with the wars quieting, they have turned to other pursuits—harassing rivals, sabotaging businesses. And killing for hire."

"No." Peter's thoughts reeled. It was not an accident. It was not a terrible misunderstanding. It was murder. A heavy silence gripped the room.

"But..." Peter began, grasping for reason, for something that might anchor him to sanity.

"We could not find any trace of the men, my lord," the investigator explained. "They left London soon after the task was performed. I believe that they have taken ship to another land. If it is possible to find them in England, I will question them. But I do not think that we can rely on their being here. Nobody knows anything about why they were hired."

"Why would anyone kill Charles?" Peter breathed. It made no sense whatsoever. He was well-liked in the *ton* and by his tenants and farmers alike. He was a kind, honest, friendly man who had never hurt anyone. It was impossible to imagine that he had enemies. His heart ached and he stood. He was going to lose his self-control and he did not want a stranger to see it.

"Nobody knows, my lord," Mr Irving said gently. "I am doing my best to investigate. If need be, I will inquire at the docks to determine if and when the men may have sailed from England."

"Do it," Peter demanded, going towards the door. "Do whatever you can, Irving. You have all the funds you require. If more is needed, write to my solicitor—he will see to it."

Irving raised a brow. "Thank you, my lord," he murmured. "I regret having to bring such grave news."

"Keep on with your work. I need to know all that I can." Peter blustered, stepping into the hallway. "Refresh yourself as you need. If you require to remain here for the night, request that Mrs Hallden arrange the accommodation and stabling."

"Thank you, my lord," Mr Irving replied, bowing low.

Peter hurried away. His mind was numb, leaving him only that ridiculous box of pleasantries that filled it whenever he was too exhausted to think. He walked to his chamber. He could not rejoin the evening's entertainments. Not yet.

"It can't be," he whispered in the closed, silent space of his chamber. He paced the space, desperation and horror making it impossible to stand still. If Charles and Eliza had been murdered, why? Who could possibly have hired those mercenaries? Who could have known that he was going home from the opera that night? And who could have known that he would not be in his usual barouche, but in the Landau, the one with the Brentdale crest on the side?

An ugly thought struck him. He gripped the table, horror flooding his mind.

"It wasn't him. It was me."

The coach was the Brentdale coach. It displayed Peter's crest. Not Charles'. Nobody looking for Charles would have known to shoot the occupants of that coach. If Charles had been the target, they would have been looking out for the small, expensive barouche. Not the unwieldy Landau, and certainly not one with the wrong insignia.

He exhaled sharply; his breath unsteady.

It was too possible, too likely. The target had never been Charles in the first place. It was him. Someone had shot Charles by mistake—he and Eliza had died in Peter's stead.

"No."

The thought was horrible, shattering something inside him as cruelly as a gunshot broke glass. He sat down by the fireplace, too exhausted and shocked to remain on his feet. His mind was empty, a dull fog of horror swirling through it, blanking out thought.

"Peter? Peter!" A knock sounded at the door, a man's voice—one he knew—calling him.

"George?" Peter managed to ask. "What is it?"

"Peter? Are you quite well?" George demanded, sounding worried. "Your sister said you'd be only a few minutes, and it has been half an hour. Are you ill?"

Peter groaned. He wished he was actually sick. He did not want to see anyone or talk to anyone. He did not want to do anything. His world was a place of numb, impossible shock.

"Peter?" George demanded from outside the door when there was no reply. "Let me in, for Perdition's sake. I'm worried sick."

Peter tried to call out to him, but he felt too tired and weak. "Come in," he managed.

George pushed the door open and burst in. When he saw Peter, he sat down heavily at the writing desk.

"By the blazes! What happened to you?" George inquired. His own gentle face was a picture of shock. "Are you ill? We should summon a physician. You're paler than a phantom, old fellow."

Peter shook his head. "I'm not ill," he said, though even to his own ears he did not sound convincing. "I just... I can't, George. I just had some bad news, and I cannot face anyone now." He covered his eyes. His head actually was sore, and he felt cold.

"Easy, old fellow," George said gently. "It cannot be that bad, whatever it was." His expression was kind and caring. Peter stared into his eyes. He wished that George's kindness could redeem him. But if George truly understood what had happened, even he—steadfast and compassionate as he was—would see him for what he was. The one to blame.

"It is bad, George," Peter replied. "So bad that I cannot bring myself to relate it."

George sighed. "When you and I both failed history at Cambridge, you said that nothing is as bad as one thinks. That we could write the exam again.

And we did. And we managed it the second time. So, you were right in thinking that."

Peter sighed. "It's not so simple, George. I wish it was. It is not something I can fix. It's something I did months ago. Something that I wish beyond anything that I could undo." He covered his face with his hands. It should have been him. If he had simply kept the Landau at the townhouse, perhaps it would have been. Perhaps Charles and Eliza would be alive, and the little baby would not be suffering as he did without his parents.

George said nothing, and Peter bit his lip, fighting the urge to cry. He had not cried for a long time. Even when Father had passed away, just two years before, he had not cried. He had cried for Charles and Eliza, but that had been different—an unbearable shock. He stood up and went to the window.

George remained quiet, and Peter drew in a breath. The weight of his unspoken story was pressing on him. Mayhap if he told George, it would lighten the burden.

"Charles and Eliza were not killed in a robbery, like we believed that they were," Peter began. George had barely known Charles—both were Peter's cousins, but Charles had been the son of Father's younger sister, and George was the son of Mama's brother. "The men who shot them were hired killers. I do not know who hired them." He let out his breath in a sigh.

"Hired *killers*?" George stared at him. His brown eyes seemed huge.

Peter nodded. The next part he could barely relate. "They were clearly paid to shoot whoever was riding in the Brentdale coach. That means that they were trying to kill me that night. Not Charles and Eliza." His heart twisted. He was crying and he had ceased to care what anyone thought of him for it.

"Now, old fellow, you cannot know that," George cautioned him. "It is nothing more than speculation."

"It has to be so, George," Peter argued. "Nobody, not even Charles, knew that he was going to take the Brentdale coach that night. It was a decision made at the last moment because Eliza felt unwell. Charles thought the bigger, steadier coach would be more pleasant for her." His heart ached.

George was quiet for a moment. Then he cleared his throat. "It still does not have to be so," he said carefully. "If someone was waiting to kill Charles, do you not think it is possible that there was also someone paid to spy on him? I am sure they would have checked which coach Charles was going to be in before they planned anything."

Peter let out a weary breath. "No. Unless they were spying on me in my study with Charles, they would never have known. Charles asked me privately if he might borrow the coach, just an hour before the opera."

George sighed. "I do not know, Peter," he said after a moment. "All I know is that it cannot be your fault. You did not hire the killers. You did not instruct them. And if you could have done anything to prevent Charles's passing, you would have." He shook his head sadly.

"I know," Peter said quietly, though George's words did comfort him greatly. "But I still feel this terrible weight of guilt." His heart ached. He was sure he would never stop wondering if he could have saved them.

"You have no need to," George said gently. "Charles would not want you to. I only met the fellow once, but I know that he was the sort of person who believed that he was the master of his own fate." He smiled sadly.

Peter's heart twisted. "He would have said that," he agreed. The words reminded him so strongly of Charles. He was a quiet man but a strong one. One who would certainly have insisted that his fate was only in his own hands. He would not have wanted Peter to take all the responsibility. George was right.

"Well, then. You cannot continue believing that it is all your fault," George said in a gentle tone. "Stop blaming yourself and come and have some diversion. The pianoforte element to the evening is almost concluded," he added with a wry smile.

Peter sighed. "I cannot, George. You go and enjoy yourself. I cannot go and talk to people. I am in no state for it." He looked away, feeling guilty about that too. His sister would be upset. She had worked so hard, and all she had wanted was for him to see Lady Adeline perform her piece.

"No, of course not, old chap," George agreed. "I will tell Millicent that you are indisposed."

"Thank you. I appreciate it more than I can say, George." He meant every word. He could not face Millicent, and yet he could not bear to think of her being angry with him. George's help was precious indeed.

"No bother, old chap," George said kindly. "If you change your mind and need the physician, for goodness' sake, send for the fellow," he added with an exasperated chuckle.

Peter smiled back. "I will. I promise," he said gently. He did not want to make George worry.

George smiled a weary and relieved smile. "Good. Goodnight, old chap," George said as he turned in the doorway.

"Goodnight," Peter called.

He remained on the chair, too tired to move, as the door shut behind George and his cousin's footsteps echoed down the hallway. He let his gaze wander to the fireplace. A thousand images moved through the flames—things he did not wish to think about. Coaches on lonely roads. Gunfire. Babies with fever.

He stood up. One thing he could do was check on Thomas. If something happened to the child, too, he would truly never forgive himself. He went to the door and walked as quietly as he could down the hallway. Distant sounds of talking and amusement drifted from the drawing room, and Peter sighed in relief. The guests were having a marvelous time, it seemed. Millicent would be happy. His burden of guilt lightened a little.

He walked as quietly as he could up to the nursery, where the half-open door showed a crack of light. He paused on the threshold. He did not wish to disturb. He peered through the door to see if there was anything amiss.

Miss Matthews was sitting with the baby in her arms, rocking him as she fed him. He appeared a little better—no crying, no red face. No discomfort, if he was any judge at all. It was a normal scene, if a beautiful one. He slumped in relief. He gazed through for a moment longer, trying to decide whether or not to disturb her and the baby. After a second more, he walked away silently.

He went to his chamber and shut the door. The weight on his shoulders eased just a little further as he recalled the previous night. He had done all he could for Thomas. And it seemed like the little child felt better. He sighed. Even if all he had done to help was to hire Miss Matthews in the first place—or agree to her being hired—then he had done a good thing. He smiled to himself. She truly was a blessing.

As he sat down, exhausted, by the fire, an image of her in that green dress drifted into his mind, and he had to smile, recalling how beautiful she had looked. His feelings for her usually unsettled him—something dangerous and tempting at once—and he knew he had to resist. But for the moment—just for the next few hours—they were a safe refuge. He could allow himself their comfort, just this once.

Chapter 14

"My lord? The newspapers?" The butler asked from the door, interrupting Peter's silence. He was sitting at the breakfast table, sipping a cup of tea and staring out of the window. The day was misty and quiet, the birds singing in the trees. It was seven o'clock in the morning, but the strange, diffuse light made it seem much earlier. None of the guests were yet awake. Peter shook his head in answer to the butler's question.

"No, thank you. Put them there," he added, gesturing to the long, slender table that ran almost the length of one wall. "Perhaps one of the guests will wish to read them."

"Very good, my lord," the butler replied, and put the folded newspapers down, then went out of the room.

Peter leaned back, shutting his eyes. He had slept, but it had not been a refreshing sleep and he had awoken early, thoughts of the investigator's news tormenting him. He felt restless and drained at once. It was a mood where he needed silence and time to think. He pushed back his chair and stood.

"I will go riding," he told the butler as he walked past him in the hallway. "If anybody inquires as to where I am, please inform them of this."

"Yes, my lord," the butler replied, bowing low.

Peter inclined his head in acknowledgement and hurried down the hallway to his bedchamber.

He changed into his buckskin riding breeches and chose a riding jacket made of a thick, warm velvet. The weather was chillier than it had been, and the smell of rain was heavy in the air. It was, Peter reflected as he tugged on knee-high boots, not the best day for a ride. But he could not bear to sit with the noisy, cheerful guests and try to exchange pleasantries. It would be torture when he had so much to think about.

He walked down to the stable.

"Saddle my horse," he commanded of the stable hand.

"Yes, my lord." The young man hurried to do the task, and Peter had to admire how quick he was, because in a little over five minutes, his horse was bridled and saddled and waiting for him.

Peter thanked the youth and mounted up in the stable-yard, then rode out and up across the back part of the garden and into the forest.

A path led from the manor gardens directly up into the woodland and he rode along it, the tall trees on either side shading him still further from the pale, diffuse light and making another layer of mystery and darkness around him. He rode on, his own mood low and tense. His horse could feel his tension, his ears swivelling and his back shivering with the need to move or to flee.

"Easy, boy," Peter assured his horse, but he knew that it was not a great deal of help. His horse was restless because he was restless and nothing was going to change that.

He rode on.

The forest route that he had chosen led up towards the ridge and down through the trees. He had chosen it more or less at random, and he did not pay attention to where they were going. He was comfortable on horseback, and he did not need to concentrate, using the time to think about the news and try to come to terms with it.

"Charles, I wish you were here," he said aloud in the silent woodland. It was the first time since Charles's death that Peter had addressed him directly. Even when he was furious with Charles for dying and leaving him to face all his challenges alone, he had never railed against him. The leaves overhead rustled, and somewhere, a bird sang.

The path descended sharply, heading towards the river. Peter leaned back, slowing his stallion, who seemed eager to move. When they reached the water's edge, he noted that, at this time of year, the river was not particularly wide but remained swift and strong. Rather than attempt a crossing, he turned back toward the bridge.

As they emerged from the forest, rain began to fall—a fine drizzle, cool against his hands where they gripped the reins, misting his face and settling lightly in his hair. It was only a drizzle, nothing to seek shelter from, and the thought of retreating indoors—of facing the guests, engaging in empty pleasantries—left him with a vague sense of unease.

He had no desire for forced conversation. Far better to remain out here, where the air was fresh and unburdened by expectation.

The rain intensified, growing heavier with each passing moment. At first, the distant rush of the river had been the dominant sound, but now the downpour drummed against the earth, cascading in relentless sheets. His horse snorted, ears flicking back and forth, shaking its head with unease. Peter leaned a little forward, turning the reins so that his horse turned left.

"Come on, old chap," he said gently. "Let's go home."

His horse understood the words, it seemed, for he turned around and returned up the path at a quick pace.

They rode at a canter down the path, the rain sluicing into Peter's face and streaming down his clothes and stinging his eyes. He let out a yell—a raw, wild yell that was grief and anguish and rage and all the emotions that he could never usually voice. His horse, hearing the noise, began to run even faster.

For a moment, the world was a wild tumult of rain and hoofbeats and speed and untamed freedom. Peter leaned forward, urging his horse on, the rain so intense that he could barely see or hear. In the complete madness of their run was the freedom that he had craved, the cleansing and absolution that he had sought. His mind was no longer focused on worry or guilt, but only on surviving. The rain washed him clean, body and soul.

They were going down the hill, back down towards the river. His horse slowed and then reared, and Peter yelled aloud, surprise and anger mixing as he was thrown backwards. He gripped with his knees and held onto the reins, gritting his teeth.

His horse landed with all four feet back on the ground and stood, snorting and shaking. Peter sighed.

"Easy, boy," he managed to say, though he, too, was shaking, and it wasn't entirely because of the cold. The shock of almost falling had brought him back from the wild freedom of their run. He looked around, wondering what had caused his horse to rear. His eyes widened in disbelief.

"Madam? What are you doing here?"

A woman was standing beside the path. Her face was pale and she was sobbing in fright. The rain sluiced down her face, her thick brown hair soaking and plastered to her skin. She looked up, and Peter gasped.

"Miss Matthews!" He exclaimed. Her eyes were a vivid, wild green. Her hair was dark brown. Her skin was pale and her face a long, slim oval. It was her. It was undeniably her. He dismounted at once.

"My... my lord," she stammered. Her teeth were chattering. She wore a white gown and it was soaked through. "I'm sorry. I do not know if we are allowed here, but I was collecting herbs," she began to explain. Peter swore.

"Perdition's sake, miss. Sorry," he added, blushing. "But you'll catch your death of a fever here. Whatever are you thinking? I do not care if you use the forest. Now come and stand under those trees," he demanded, gesturing towards the forest.

Miss Matthews turned and walked to where he had pointed without speaking. Peter led his horse, patting the stallion's neck appreciatively. If he had not stopped at once, perhaps Peter would not have seen Miss Matthews and ridden into her.

"Here," Peter said, more gently. "The forest protects us here."

The trees in the clearing by the track were densely packed and they kept off a great deal—if not all—of the rain. Peter straightened, taking a deep breath. His horse shook and the droplets flew, hitting him and Miss Matthews. He laughed aloud.

"Easy, boy," he commented, grinning. His horse made a snuffling, snorting noise and stamped. Peter laughed again.

"He's a fine horse," Miss Matthews commented shyly.

"He is," Peter agreed warmly. "The best companion." He patted the strong, dark neck. His horse snorted and lowered his head, focusing on the forest floor and searching for something edible. Peter smiled.

Miss Matthews smiled too. She was shivering and the white uniform clung to her. Peter winced and looked away. While the fabric was not see-through, when soaking and clinging, it left little to the imagination. He bit his lip, desire flooding him for the first time in years.

"You must be so cold," he murmured.

"N—no," she tried to say, teeth chattering.

Peter sighed. "I am unconvinced," he replied.

Miss Matthews chuckled. She was shivering terribly, and Peter looked around. The rain was still falling, but it seemed a little less heavy than it had been even a minute before. He looked at Miss Matthews.

"We need to get you back to the house," he told her firmly. "I do not know if you fear horses, but if so, you must set that aside for now. You need to ride with me if we are to reach a warm place in good time."

Miss Matthews stared at him. Her jaw dropped, and he sighed again.

"I cannot let you spend a minute longer in this rain," he told her firmly. "Either you ride alone to the manor on my horse, or we ride together. It is not far and I am sure he can carry us both over the short distance. But walking will take too long. You are already too cold," he added, looking at her with worry. Her lips were blueish and she was shivering wildly.

"But... my lord, I..." she stammered.

He shook his head. "Yes, I am aware of propriety, Miss Matthews, and normally I would respect it. But this is a serious matter. Fevers can kill, as I am sure you know. And you are already in serious danger of getting one."

Miss Matthews said nothing, just looked at him with those big, beautiful eyes. Her thick, dark hair hung in wet strands around her shoulders, plastered to her head and neck. He resisted the urge to brush it away. He gestured to the horse.

"If I may?" he asked, gesturing to her. She looked at him in surprise, her lips parting in a small, shocked "O". She nodded, and without waiting for further agreement, he reached out and lifted her up onto the saddle. Her long dress clung to her legs wetly. He looked away, giving her a moment to arrange it more decorously. An unfamiliar tension pulled at him, one he resolutely pushed aside.

"Now, if you do not mind," he said softly, "I will ride behind."

He drew a deep breath. She gazed at him, fear mixing with trust. Then she sneezed.

Peter chuckled. "I take that as proof of my argument," he said, and she grinned. He laughed and stepped lightly up, swinging his left leg over. She sat up straight, and he reached forward and took the reins, trying to maintain as light a touch on her body as possible.

"Grip the front part of the saddle," he instructed her. "It will be easier to hold on that way."

She did as he had instructed, and he leaned back, gently easing his horse to a walk. They could not manage more than a trot with their combined weight on his back—the horse was also tired and chilled by the icy rain. But it was still faster than going on foot.

"Did you walk for long in the forest?" he asked as they rode back along the path by the river.

"No," she said after a moment. "I came here to fetch herbs. Mallow root. It is good for infections of the throat and ears. My grandmother used to give it to us when we were children," Miss Matthews explained.

"It sounds as though she was well-versed in the use of medicinal plants," Peter commented, impressed.

He could hear the smile in Miss Matthews's voice, a lightness in her tone as she replied.

"She was."

"Did she live with your family?" he asked.

"She did, for a while. Then she returned to her own village," Miss Matthews explained.

"You must have been sad when she returned home."

"I was," Miss Matthews replied softly.

Peter closed his grey eyes for a moment. The rain had lessened a little, and the forest was quieter than before. The sound of the horse's hoofs was able to be heard as much as the rain was. Water trickled down his face, but not in the icy torrent of before. He tried to imagine Miss Matthews's life and found that he could not.

He opened his eyes, leaning back a little as the horse went downhill. They were almost at the manor and he straightened up, letting the horse regain his speed as they reached the firm ground.

"It is not long, now, before we are in the stable," Peter commented. "I must insist that you go straight indoors. You may order a warm bath to be drawn," he added, feeling her shivering. "And whatever else you need to become warm."

"My lord, I..." she stammered. They had reached the stables and he stopped, jumping down. He looked up into her face, seeing confusion there.

"After all that you have done for us," he said quietly, "the least I can do is to ensure that you do not suffer a fever. Take whatever you need from the kitchen. And I am certain another maid can watch over young Thomas for an hour until you are warm and dry."

"Thank you," she stammered. Her gaze held his, a mix of hesitance and something gentle. He reached up to help her down, looking away as he set her on her feet so that she might arrange her skirts more modestly.

He looked up as she looked at him. He drew a deep breath. Her gaze was no longer scared but seemed interested, inquiring.

"You are cold too, my lord," she murmured.

He shrugged. "Then I am cold," he said, his lip lifting in a grin. "I will have to do something about that when I return indoors."

She laughed. "Do take care, my lord," she murmured. Her gaze was caring. His heart ached.

"Make sure that you stay warm," he told her a little abruptly, turning to lead his horse into the stable. "And take care," he added more softly. "We are often caught by storms in the summer." He turned and held her gaze. Her own mesmerising green eyes stared back, gentle and warm.

"Yes, my lord."

She hesitated as he led the horse away, but by the time he had removed his dear stallion's saddle and bridle, rubbed him down and ordered the stable hand to feed him warm bran and rub his legs, she had gone inside.

Of course she has left—you told her to, he reminded himself as he strode back to the house in the drizzling rain. All the same, his heart ached and he could not stop thinking about her beauty, her quiet wisdom and those unforgettable green eyes.

Chapter 15

"Look at how soaked through you are! You'll catch your death of a fever!" The cook exclaimed as Penelope stepped as quietly and carefully as she could into the hallway alongside the kitchen. Her cheeks reddened. She had wanted nobody to notice her. Her dress clung to her, and her bonnet hung down her back, her hair a mess.

What had the earl thought? She wondered, heat rising to her cheeks. Thoughts of him pressed in—his eyes, his voice, the way he had steadied her— and suddenly, nothing else seemed to exist. The memory of his presence behind her on the horse returned with startling clarity, the solid warmth of him, the way he had held the reins with effortless control. Her blush deepened, spreading like fire across her skin.

"Are you well?" the cook's demanding voice asked pointedly.

"I'm quite well," Penelope stammered, her teeth chattering. In a warm, dry hallway, it seemed as though her body could no longer withstand the cold. She was freezing. Her body shivered and she curled her fingers into fists, her fingertips tingling with cold.

"No, you are not," the cook countered. "Go upstairs and change out of those wet things at once! How did you come to get soaked so early in the day?" she demanded.

"I was in the forest." Penelope bit her lip, looking down. It was not really a good explanation, but the cook shrugged.

"Upstairs with you!".

Penelope turned in the doorway, her courage almost failing her. As she paused there, she willed herself to say something.

"May I have a bath drawn?" she asked in a small voice.

"Why, in Perdition's name, would you have a bath drawn?" the cook exclaimed. It was not the place of the staff to order baths—the pitcher of water on the nightstand was sufficient to wash off, and one could wash one's entire body piecemeal with the cold water. To ask for an entire bath was the height of pretension. Penelope's cheeks flushed red, but she managed to reply in an almost-whisper.

"The earl said I could ask for a bath."

"The earl! I..." the cook gaped at her, but then shrugged. "Well, then. A bath it is." Her tone was flat and cold, shutting Penelope out. Penelope winced, turning away. Some of the staff hated her already, simply because of her special status in the household and her unaccented speech. Anna had reassured her that she had faced the same challenge, which offered some comfort. At the very least, she was not alone in it.

Penelope walked to the stairs as briskly as she could. She went to her small bedchamber that adjoined the nursery, and shut the door. She was shaking so much that she could barely undress, but she managed to unbutton most of the buttons and slip out of the uniform. Her shift, worn under the uniform, was soaking wet too and she left that on for the moment. She hung the dripping uniform up, wincing at the mess it made on the floor. As she tried to dry her hair with a flannel, which was hard, because she was shaking and she could barely hold the towel, someone knocked on the door.

"Miss Matthews?"

"Yes?" Penelope called, back tensed and hands clenched. She was wearing her dripping-wet shift. It was a small voice, which she recognised as that of the scullery maid, replied.

"The bath, Miss Matthews. I brought it. Water's coming now."

Penelope closed her eyes, relief flooding her. "Thank you!" she called back. She ran to open the door. The girl—a small, skinny young woman of perhaps fifteen years old with red hair and a foreign accent—dragged the heavy wooden tub, and Penelope lifted the end.

"Let me help," she insisted gently. The girl gazed up at her in surprise as if she had not expected anyone to help her.

"Thank you, Miss."

"Thank you," Penelope said gently. She held the girl's eye, and her gaze widened, again in apparent surprise. Then, the girl turned and walked into the hallway. At the door, she paused.

"Miss?" She asked softly. "Can I use the water?"

"When I'm finished?" Penelope gaped as the girl nodded enthusiastically.

"Yes, miss. It must be terribly fine to have a bath."

Penelope winced. Her own family had been poor, but she and Emily had taken regular baths.

She nodded, and the girl's delight made her heart ache. She turned away, not wanting to show her sorrow.

A minute or two later, an older woman turned up at the door with two buckets of steaming hot water, and then Mrs Aldham came with a bucket of cold water.

"Here you are, miss," she said with a grin. "Enjoy it."

Penelope thanked them and shut the door behind them.

The water was deliciously warm and she slipped into it, shutting her eyes and leaning back. Her toes burned in the warmth, but she made herself stay in it, moving from the sudden shock of the hot water to a drifting, soothing pleasure. It felt so good and she lay back, letting her mind drift.

The earl's face drifted into her thoughts. His grey eyes, filled with concern and care, stared into her own. His face was close to hers and she felt the same shivering, confusing, wonderful feeling that had passed through her on being so close to him. She longed for him to press those firm, thin lips to her own. Her body flushed at the thought, and she shook her head at herself. She was foolish. And yet, it was undeniable how much she longed for it.

She lay in the bath for a long time—or what felt like a long time, with her thoughts drifting and her body soaking in the warmth—and then slipped out. There was a towel among her things and she dried herself off, then changed into a fresh shift and the black uniform, wrapping the towel around her hair to dry it. She went to find the scullery maid and then, while the girl soaked in the tub, she went in to relieve Anna, who had taken charge of the baby while she was out walking.

"Penelope! There you are! Oh, goodness... you're soaking wet!" Anna exclaimed. The baby—who was awake—made a small fretful noise and Penelope ran to him, lifting him out of the cradle and holding him close.

"My hair, yes, is wet. But I had a bath when I came indoors. Oh, Anna! It has been such a strange day. Thank you so much for sitting with little Thomas. I cannot thank you enough." She held the baby close. He was making softer, less distressed noises, and she rocked him, humming a tune under her breath. He seemed to relax.

"He's much happier since you returned," Anna said with a grin. "Little fellow was fretful. Weren't you, little boy?" she asked him. He gazed at her with big, round eyes. Anna giggled. "You had a strange day?" she asked, frowning.

"Does he need a bottle?" Penelope asked. The baby was making small repeated syllables as he gazed up at her.

"I don't think he is hungry," Anna replied. "You said you had a strange day?" she prompted again.

Penelope blushed. "So strange!" she confided. "I do not wish to detain you, though. You must have work to do."

"Only the laundry," Anna replied. "And you can help with that." She grinned. "I have plenty of time. What was so strange about the day?" Anna demanded. Penelope smiled. They settled in chairs beside the fireplace. Thomas drowsed contentedly on Penelope's knee, seemingly pleased that he and she were reunited.

"Nothing," she began, then looked at Anna. "I saw the earl," she confided. "In the forest. He was worried about me. It was pouring with rain. He brought me back to the manor." She did not relate the part about the horse. That was too intimate. Anna would probably laugh. She did not feel ready to be teased about it. It was something deeply meaningful to her, something she wished to think about for a long time.

"The earl brought you back!" Anna stared at her, a delighted grin on your face.

"Yes. He said he was worried that I would catch a fever," Penelope told her. She focused on the baby in her arms as she did so, stroking his head in a way that she knew soothed him. When she risked looking up, Anna was smiling.

"How wonderful!" she said. "Penelope! This fellow is not indifferent!" She grinned at Penelope, whose cheeks heated in a blush.

"Oh, I think we cannot say that..." she demurred, but Anna laughed.

"Penelope! Of course, he is not indifferent. One does not escort someone back to the manor in the rain out of indifference. You silly goose." She added caringly.

Penelope laughed. "Mayhap," she agreed.

"Not mayhap," Anna countered.

They both laughed.

Anna sat for a moment or two longer, chatting about the morning and the doings of little Thomas. Then she stood, a worried expression on her face.

"I must hurry to the laundry—goodness knows it has little enough time to dry as it is." She went to the doorway.

"I will help you to collect it later," Penelope promised.

"Good. Thank you!" Anna called and hurried away.

Penelope sat with Thomas until he slept. She could not take him outdoors, so she sat and sang to him. Then she went to the corner to fetch the mending that she had set aside to do on just such an occasion. The sound of footsteps outside the door made her tense and she went to it, opening it hurriedly. It was rare to hear anyone in that part of the building and she was not expecting visitors. Stiff with a mix of anger and fear—since it seemed that nobody who intended any good would pause outside the door without so much as calling out—she threw open the door.

"My lord!" she exclaimed. The earl was standing outside the door. He gazed at her, eyes round.

"Miss Matthews," he greeted her, inclining his head. The astonishment was swiftly covered with a polite expression. "I apologise. I was about to knock."

"I apologise too," Penelope said swiftly. "I thought you were a burglar."

"You did?" His lip lifted with laughter. Penelope giggled.

"Pray accept my apology. I did."

He laughed aloud. "I accept," he said gently. His expression became caring as he looked at her. "You are warm?" he asked.

She inclined her head in agreement.

Her cheeks were burning, her heart pounding in her chest, and she could not think. His presence overwhelmed her, filling her with so many feelings—surprise, joy, delight, apprehension, confusion. She looked away, her soul soaring.

"Forgive me for the intrusion," he said gently. "I had to come to see how Thomas fares. Is he well?" he asked. His grey eyes were filled with concern. She nodded.

"He is a great deal better. He had the fourth dose of the medicine this morning, before I went out to search in the forest. His ear seems less painful. He can sleep on his back if I prop a pillow under his head. And his fever is less intense." She did not quite look at him as she spoke because if she did, then she could not concentrate on what she had to say. She would stare at his eyes, and her mind would suddenly be empty of anything except for him and the confusing mix of feelings he called up.

"Good. Good," he nodded, seeming relieved. He gazed at little Thomas with such tenderness that her heart ached. She wished she knew more about him and the child. His worry and care made her wonder if this was not, in fact, his child after all. It seemed like the only logical explanation for his deep and sincere concern.

"Something is troubling you, my lord," she murmured. She could see the deep frown on his brow and the way his mouth turned down.

He shook his head. "No. Nothing..." he began, then drew a deep breath. "May I tell you something in confidence?" he asked softly.

Her eyes widened. "Of course, my lord," she said at once. Her heart skipped, and she forgot, for a moment, to take a breath. He wanted to confide in her? It seemed impossible.

"You see..." he paused. "My cousin, Charles, was very dear to me. Like a brother. He passed away a few months ago. We believed it was a robbery; that he and his wife were shot by ruffians attempting to steal their valuables."

"How horrid," Penelope breathed. She could imagine nothing worse. She had a dear sister and even imagining losing her, and in such a horrible way, brought tears to her eyes.

"It was," the earl said grimly. "But yesterday, I learned news that is even more horrid. It was not a robbery at all. It seems to have been murder." He breathed out, shoulders slumping. His brow knotted with worry.

"Murder." Penelope gaped at him disbelievingly. "But, why? Who?" she could not help asking. A man as good as the earl—and she could only imagine that his cousin was good too, like him—surely had no enemies who might hate him so much?

The earl sighed again. His wide, grey eyes were sorrowful. "We cannot understand it either," he replied. He bit his lip as if he was about to say something but was unsure of how to say it. Then he shook his head. "I should not burden you with such worries," he replied quietly. His gaze held hers. "But somehow, it lightens my burden to talk to you." His voice was soft, sending shivers through her.

Penelope gazed at him. "I am honoured that you told me."

He looked into her eyes and she stared back, her body tingling as he leaned forward. Her breath caught in her throat, and those cool grey eyes widened, for an instant a shiver of desire moving down her back. She was sure he was about to press those thin lips to hers.

He blinked and seemed to shake himself as if regaining awareness of where he was. He stepped back.

"I must go," he said quietly. "I have meetings to attend to." His cheeks were flushed.

Penelope gazed at him, her heart racing. He inclined his head and stepped back.

"Good day, Miss Matthews."

"Good day, my lord."

She watched as he went to the door and stepped out. She stood in the middle of the nursery, unable to move.

The door closed, and she heard his footsteps. She still could not move. Her heart was thudding in her chest and she lifted her hand to it, a small smile lifting her lips. She felt dazed and amazed.

Blushing furiously, she went to the cradle to check on the baby, though her thoughts were in disarray. Delight and confusion battled within her, sending her heart soaring even as she struggled to steady herself.

Chapter 16

"Brother? Might you pass the butter?" Millicent asked brightly. "And do try to mingle with the guests a little?" she added in a quieter tone, only for his ears. "I have no entertainments planned for today, but it would still be courteous to join the guests for a walk."

Peter passed Millicent the butter and attempted not to show how irritated he was by her other, quieter request. He had already explained that some bad news had left him needing solitude. Could she not have some actual heartfelt compassion for him instead of trying to fix what she believed to be broken?

"Thank you," Millicent murmured, opening the butter-dish and buttering a slice of toast. Her husband Edmund sat beside her, nodding as he read the newspaper, apparently not paying anyone any attention. Peter's irritation grew. The fellow annoyed him at the best of times, but when he already felt raw and exposed, the last thing he needed was Edmund, grinning fatuously at some amusing column in the *Gazette*.

Peter looked down at his plate, removing his linen napkin from his knee.

"Excuse me, sister. Excuse me, Edmund," he murmured, standing. "I have some pressing business to attend to." He went towards the door.

"Peter, do try to be punctual?" Millicent asked, pouring some tea as she spoke. "I have no entertainments planned, as I said, but morning tea is at ten o'clock." She raised a brow, and Peter nodded, holding back the annoyed comment he was tempted to make.

"I will try to be on time," he managed to say. He kept his voice even and light. Then he turned and walked, as quickly as he could, to the garden.

The cool morning air was pleasant on his skin and he breathed out as he walked, feeling the tension of the morning ease. He had woken early and had hoped to avoid sharing the breakfast room with anyone. He had too much on his mind, and he desperately needed time to think about it.

His steps led him towards the rose garden. He breathed deeply, smelling the sweet, drowsy scent in the air. One of his mother's passions had been flowers, and he had inherited that love, collecting plants from all over the world in the Brentdale greenhouses and gardens.

He walked through the archway and found himself among the bushes. Roses of all colours bloomed in profusion, planted in the eastern corner of the manor grounds to benefit from the gentle morning sun. Red, white, pink and yellow, their blossoms unfurled in the soft morning air, breathing out their generous fragrance. Peter's shoulders relaxed and he walked towards a bench in the corner, settling himself there.

He shut his eyes. As often happened, his thoughts drifted to Miss Matthews. He bit his lip. He had come so close to kissing her. He thought of that moment when he stood opposite her, her soft lips just a few inches from his own. He had needed every ounce of his strength to step away. His heart ached just thinking about her.

A sound drifted across the garden. He tensed. It was a woman's voice, talking. Perhaps some of the guests were out taking a morning turn about the grounds. He stiffened, easing back into the shadows. He did not want to see them.

"...easy, little fellow," the voice was saying, the words drifting clearly to him in the cool, still air. He frowned. He recognised that voice. It was Miss Matthews.

He stood, intrigued. Was she sitting on the lawn with little Thomas? His curiosity drew him towards the gate again, then left. As he stepped around a corner, he tensed.

Miss Matthews was a few yards away.

She was sitting on a square of lawn near a fountain. Low rose bushes grew close, framing the scene on her left. On her right, an arch of briar roses nodded their gentle blooms in the morning breeze. Miss Matthews sat on a blanket. She was wearing her white uniform, her long hair arranged in a low chignon. Thomas lay on the blanket, kicking his feet happily in the cool air and laughing. Miss Matthews was smiling, an expression of tenderness on her face that hit his heart like a gunshot. He breathed out, the scene so beautiful that it twisted his heart almost painfully.

He tried not to move, not wanting to disturb them. He was perhaps four or five yards away, his back to the box-hedge, and if either of them looked up, they would spot him immediately. He did not want to intrude. He stepped backwards slowly. His foot found a twig and cracked it. Miss Matthews looked up.

"My lord!" she exclaimed.

Peter went red. "Beg your pardon, Miss Matthews," he managed to say. "I did not know you were here. I had no intention to interrupt or intrude." He took another step back, heart pounding. He wanted so badly to speak with her, and yet part of him was just too shy. Her lips parted in a moue of surprise.

"You are not intruding, my lord. It is your garden, after all." Her brow raised. He smiled.

"It is the garden of all those who are in residence at the manor," he said, relaxing. "It is pleasing to see someone who appreciates it." He stepped forward. He stopped a few paces from the blanket where Thomas played happily.

She smiled. "I think he appreciates the outdoors in general," she commented, nodding at the child, who had rolled from his back to his front and crawled to the edge of the blanket, where he began to tug the grass with chubby fists.

"He certainly seems to. Though the head gardener will not thank me if little Thomas pulls up the entire lawn." He chuckled as the child pulled out a handful of grass and scattered it around, laughing happily as if it was a fine game.

Miss Matthews laughed. "He would need a great deal of time to pull it all up with such little hands."

Peter guffawed. "Indeed."

Miss Matthews grinned up at him, and he realised that he had knelt down instinctively, crouching on the grass beside the child. Little Thomas continued to pull up the grass, then handed a bunch to Peter. His gaze was open, eyes friendly. Peter bit his lip.

"Thank you, little Thomas," he managed to say. His throat was tight with emotion. It was the first time the child had interacted with him in any way at all. He took the grass and closed his fist around it.

Little Thomas took another handful and passed it to Miss Matthews.

"Oh! A bouquet!" Miss Matthews exclaimed, grinning at the child, who laughed. "Thank you, Thomas! It's grand."

The child chuckled, seeming to understand her. He pulled out another handful for her and presented it with a toothy grin. Miss Matthews laughed.

"Oh, no, little fellow! At this rate, you'll have the lawn dug up." She laughed and lifted him into the air, making him shriek and giggle. Peter laughed too as Miss Matthews put the child down for a moment, then stood and lifted him again, carrying him towards the fountain.

Peter followed them. Miss Matthews set the child down on his short legs beside the fountain, and the small boy toddled towards it and then began to splash his hands into the water, sending drops sparkling in the morning sun. Peter watched, his heart too full for words as his cousin's son and heir frolicked in the morning garden.

Charles would be happy, he thought silently. A bird trilled somewhere, as if in answer.

Peter looked down; his eyes misty.

"Thank you," he said softly to Miss Matthews, who had settled on a stone bench a few paces from the carved fountain. "I have not seen him so happy ever, I believe." His heart ached. In London, Thomas had been fretful and impossible to settle, crying until Peter had thought the sound would break his heart. In the first week in the countryside, too, the child had been miserable and restless.

Miss Matthews looked up at Peter, her green eyes gentle.

"I did nothing," she said in a quiet tone. "You fetched the physician."

Peter swallowed. He had not meant to thank her for helping the child recover from his illness, but, since he did feel the urge to thank her for that as well, he did not counter what she had said.

"He has healed well," he commented, watching the child throw sticks into the water, seemingly fascinated by the fact that they were not sinking.

"He has. It was even faster than I expected," Miss Matthews replied, her gaze drifting briefly from the child to Peter's face. "Your prompt action helped us a great deal, I think. Another day of that fever, and he could have been hurt."

Peter shrugged. "It was nothing," he said uneasily. He looked away. The roses around them were all flowering, some rare pink blooms unfurling shyly in the sunshine. Peter pointed to them. "Those were planted in my mother's time," he commented. "She was the one who really established the collection here."

Miss Matthews glanced over at them. "They are beautiful," she murmured, standing. "And the scent in the air is remarkable." She breathed deeply. With her eyes shut, a grin on her face, she looked so beautiful that Peter drew a deep breath.

"Mama loved the rose garden," Peter told her when she had opened her eyes. "They were her favourite flowers. I have added some bushes to the collection, but I have to admit that the exotic plants are more intriguing to me." He inclined his head towards the greenhouse that leaned up against the manor on its western side, invisible from the rose garden with its high hedges on all sides.

Miss Matthews came to stand closer. Peter tensed. This close, he could smell the lavender scent of her hair and clothing, mingling with the fresh blooms. The scent made his heart race.

"What sort of plants do you collect?" she asked, sounding interested.

Peter shrugged, his heart lifting. Very few people—besides his cousins George and Sophia—were interested. "Various ones. The Spanish colonies in the Americas, particularly those near the tropics, are home to a wealth of fascinating plant species—bromeliads, orchids, creepers. I have a few of each. They are not easy to cultivate, but with careful tending in the greenhouse, one can manage." He smiled shyly. Plants were an interest that he had only indulged following his father's death. His father had not approved when he had expressed the interest as a youth, saying that it was a foolish hobby for a grown man. Peter had felt ashamed, but his aunt's approval had emboldened him to keep going, despite his father's distaste. The collection at Brentdale was quite impressive, built up mainly from samples and seeds from Kew Gardens in London.

"I wish I could see them," Miss Matthews murmured. "I can scarcely imagine such far-off places. What do you think it is like there?" she asked, her face turned up to look at him, eyes wide and dreamy.

Peter grinned. "Hot, I expect," he said with a laugh. "The plants seem to like it when it's very warm and humid. I imagine acres and acres of dense vegetation—jungle, I suppose." He shut his eyes for a moment, imagining vast forests. "And lots of beautiful flowers and birds." He sighed. He had borrowed books from the best libraries in England, featuring colour illustrations of many of the plants—and some of the animals. Before she asked him, however, he had never tried to imagine the landscape and what it might be like. He found himself gazing into the distance, imagining a world of lush trees and magical birds, a forest teeming with life.

"How lovely," Miss Matthews breathed. "Would you ever imagine going there?"

"Oh, goodness, no," Peter said with a chuckle. "There are monstrous alligators. I don't think I would like an alligator. Nor would my horse," he added with a grin. "No, I am happier to have the plants than to go there to visit the jungle myself."

Miss Matthews gazed up at him, her eyes wide with interest. "Alligators?" she asked, jaw dropping.

"Monstrous reptiles, as long as that flowerbed." He shrugged. "Or so the explorers say. Obviously, I have never seen one for myself." He grinned again. She laughed.

"I think I would not want to," she replied, giggling.

He nodded. "We are of like mind, Miss Matthews," he answered warmly.

Her giggle was as bright as the water splashing in the fountain.

Miss Matthews was gazing at Thomas, and Peter watched as the boy sat down on the lawn, his stare intent on something in the grass. A snail was moving there, and the little child was fascinated by it. Miss Matthews went over to him, and Peter walked closer; his heart full. He had never watched a child exploring the world before, and it was beautiful to see.

He is as fascinated by that snail as I am by exotic plants, he thought with a grin. The snail was every bit as strange to the little boy as the exotic animal life of the Americas was for them.

"Better not to touch it," Miss Matthews told the boy gently as he reached out. "You could hurt it. It's very delicate." She picked up the shell and carried the creature carefully to a shaded corner of the garden. Peter watched her, heart aching. She was gentle and beautiful, and he admired her.

Voices drifted over the lawn and he tensed. There were people coming. Miss Matthews had not heard them and she came over to stand with him and Thomas.

"Have you any herbs..." she began. Peter assumed she wanted to know if he had collected any herbs—that was an interest of hers, he knew—but before she could speak, people entered the garden. They were standing near one of the gates, and Peter tensed.

Millicent was there, with Lady Winthrop and Lady Adeline. They were all staring at him.

Peter reddened. He was standing close to Miss Matthews, and he saw Millicent's gaze move to her and then to him, shock replaced instantly by a polite mask. She smiled at Peter, ignoring Miss Matthews and little Thomas utterly. The small child had run to Miss Matthews, and she bent and picked him up, holding him on her hip.

"Peter! Why! What a surprise! I had not thought to find you here. Beautiful blooms, are they not?" She beamed at Peter, then turned to Lady Adeline. "You find flowers fascinating, do you not, Adeline?" she prompted.

"Most fascinating," Adeline murmured. She turned to smile at Peter.

Peter did his best to smile back, but his heart was full of confusion. He glanced at Miss Matthews, but she was looking at the child, her posture tense and her discomfort evident to him.

"Peter! You must show Adeline those fine red roses. The ones right over there? In the south bed?" Millicent gestured pointedly to the other side of the garden. Peter scowled. She was trying to get him away from Miss Matthews. It was obvious. He could not say anything to her in front of the guests and he stood unspeaking, trying to overcome his anger.

As he tried to reply, two more ladies appeared. He relaxed, seeing his aunt and cousin. Aunt smiled at him.

"Peter! How fortunate—we have found the perfect guide. You can show us the best roses," she announced, seeming to notice his tension and bustling over to stand with him. "Sophia is particularly fond of them."

"I love all flowers," Sophia gushed. "And you have so many beautiful ones! Show us the best ones, Peter—do!" she demanded.

Peter's gaze moved to Millicent, who was looking at Aunt Adeline and Sophia with apparent anger. Lady Winthrop and Lady Adeline looked angry, too. Peter smiled at his aunt, relieved beyond measure that she had rescued him from Millicent and her blatant attempt to make him walk elsewhere, away from Miss Matthews and the child.

"I would be glad to," he replied.

He walked with his aunt and cousin to the gate, with Millicent, Lady Adeline and Lady Winthrop walking close behind. He glanced over to the fountain.

Miss Matthews was folding up the blanket, the little boy running on the grass in the dappled sunshine as she did so. His heart ached. He turned to watch them. He wished that he could have stayed there with them.

"Are these new, Peter?" His aunt asked. Peter looked at the blooms she was indicating, shaking his head.

"No. They have been there a few years," he replied. He tried to focus as Sophia asked him a question, but his mind kept drifting, filled with recollections of Miss Matthews.

He watched her walk through the gate, out of the garden, and he longed to see her again soon and perhaps to show her the exotic plants in the big greenhouse. Her interest intrigued him as much as her joy and laughter, and there was something about her—a quiet mystery—that drew him in.

More than anything, he longed for another chance to speak with her.

Chapter 17

Penelope stood in the rose garden. The distant sound of voices reached her from across the space, and she bit her lip, trying not to let her tears fall. Lady Penrith's disdain clung to her, sharp and searing, like acid against her skin. She had been looked down upon before but that did not mean she had grown used to it. She hated the way it made her feel, as if she were something lesser, something unworthy.

She looked down at the baby, focusing on her duties. Thomas was still playing; some complex game he had invented that involved throwing pebbles and leaves into the water of the fountain. She had to smile. He was so intent on it.

"Should we go back to the house?" she asked him with a smile. He turned round sharply, as if he had been so absorbed in his play that he had forgotten she was there. His eyes widened. She laughed.

"You want to stay?" she asked him.

He did not reply, but he stared at her as though the merest thought of going to the house made no sense. Then he turned around and went to the fountain again.

Penelope giggled. The little boy was a source of delight.

"If only it was just you," she murmured, going to crouch beside him on the lawn. Even the earl confused her. She could not tell herself any longer that it was her imagination. He had leaned close, and she knew that it was because he wanted to kiss her. She had detected desire in his eyes—not too different from the longing that she felt whenever she was close to him.

"But what am I supposed to do?" she whispered under her breath. She was a maid, and he was an earl—the social differences between them were too huge to contemplate. And his world wanted nothing to do with her.

Lady Penrith had just made that clear.

Her heart ached, and she let herself cry, tears falling silently. The little boy played on, and she was glad that he was distracted. She did not want her tears to distress him. The judgment in that expression had scalded her. It reminded her too starkly of all the things that were impossible about herself and the earl. His world was so different.

"Miss? Whatever is the matter?" A woman's voice asked. It was a kind voice, and Penelope whirled round, surprise mixing with the initial shock of hearing a voice.

"My lady!" She shot to her feet, cheeks flooding with shame. The woman who addressed her was an older woman with white hair, wearing a blue dress.

She had blue eyes, and they sparkled in a friendly way, and a long, thin face that might have had some resemblance to the earl's slim countenance. Penelope stepped back, feeling wary. Lady Penrith's cruelty was too recent for her to trust anyone of her social standing.

"I did not mean to startle you," the older woman said softly. "You do look very much like Emily."

"I do?" Penelope blinked. "You know my sister?" That was the first surprise. The second surprise was that nobody had ever said that before. Emily was shorter, with a softer face than Penelope's own, blonde hair, and hazel eyes. In Penelope's opinion, Emily was by far more beautiful than she herself was. She herself could not see a resemblance. Most people did not, which meant that this lady, whoever she was, must be very observant.

"Yes," the lady replied gently. "You have the same long oval faces, and your eyes are the same shape. And you have a similar manner about you. A gentle manner. I like to see gentleness in people. It is a quality I admire." She smiled.

"Thank you, my lady," Penelope stammered. The kindness felt almost as bewildering as the cruelty that she had just received. It was hard to know the appropriate thing to say. She dropped a curtsey and then blushed, feeling foolish. It was so terribly difficult to know what the nobility expected. Her mind moved in another direction, drawing a conclusion. "Are you..." she began. The lady must be Emily's employer, Lady Sterling.

"I am Lady Sterling," the woman replied before she had time to complete the sentence. "Emily is the lady's maid to my daughter, Sophia. Who is somewhere over there, studying the roses." She gestured towards the other corner of the garden with real fondness in her eyes.

"I am honoured to meet you, my lady," Penelope replied, curtseying again.

"You are doing a grand job with the baby," Lady Sterling told her, gesturing towards Thomas where he sat playing with the leaves and the water.

"You truly think that, my lady?" Penelope gaped. She had thought that everyone would see her as Lady Penrith appeared to—as someone not quite human and failing even in that humble role.

"It is clear to me," Lady Sterling replied, nodding at the child. "He is happy. I need to see no more."

"Thank you, my lady," Penelope replied, inclining her head in acknowledgement. The words helped to heal the deep wound of Lady Penrith's disdain just a little. She smiled shyly at Lady Sterling, who smiled back.

"I wish you a good day, Miss Matthews," she said warmly. "I shall leave you take care of your young charge. He needs you more than I." She chuckled.

"Thank you, my lady," Penelope replied. She wished that she could ask the older woman to take her regards to Emily, but she could not find the courage, and Lady Sterling had already walked on down the path, almost out of sight. She turned to Thomas, who had stopped playing and was watching her, a frown creasing his brow.

"Little fellow!" she addressed him, grinning warmly. "Would you like to go indoors?"

This time, he grinned at her, and her heart melted. She knelt down on the grass beside him and opened her arms. He crawled onto her lap, and she hugged him tight. His little body nestled against her chest, warm and fragrant, and she kissed his hair, blinking back tears that were, this time, partly tears of joy.

"You're so dear to me," she whispered into his hair. "So dear."

He made a small cooing sound of apparent happiness, and she hugged him tightly, all of her own sorrow melting, diffusing in the love and calm in her heart.

"Come on, then," she murmured, grunting with effort as she stood up with him still in her arms. "Let's go indoors."

The nursery was warm, the midmorning sunshine slanting in through the big windows. Penelope put Thomas gently on the rug by the fireplace and tidied up while he sat and played with the few wooden blocks that she had found in the former nursery in the west wing. She glanced at her sewing-things. She had found some disused linen in the laundry and she had decided to make a doll for little Thomas. He had nothing to play with—or, nothing besides the blocks and a wooden cotton-reel that she had managed to find. He seemed to be reasonably content with his blocks—especially if she sat and played with him— but the lack seemed wrong to her. Poor as she and her family had been, she had never wanted for playthings as a child. They had been simple things, but there had always been something. And she had a sister, while he was by himself.

"Someone must know your story," she murmured to the child as she went to sit on the upholstered chair with her sewing.

She had just begun stitching the doll when someone knocked at the door. She stood and went to answer it, her heart thudding. If it was the earl, she had no idea what she would do. And what if it was his sister? That was something she would not be able to face.

"Who is it?" she called fearfully.

"It's me!" Anna called back. "Can I come in?"

"Anna!" Penelope felt her legs almost give way with relief, and she opened the door, grinning at her friend. "Do come in! How grand that you're here." Her heart soared to see her familiar, friendly face with its thin features and its big grin.

"Penelope! Grand to see you," Anna said warmly. "And how fares young Thomas?" she asked. She glanced at the hearthrug. She was dressed in her black uniform, as usual, but her cheeks glowed and there was a brightness in her eyes. Penelope smiled to herself. Perhaps there was a handsome man in Anna's thoughts.

"Thomas fares well," she replied, glancing at the small child where he sat playing on the hearthrug. His ear seems to pain him much less. He slept well last night," she added with a smile. She had slept well, too. It was such a relief to see him healthy and without pain.

"I am glad to hear it," Anna replied. "May I intrude? I have an hour or two before my mistress will require my help." She made a wry face. "It has not been long since I helped her dress for luncheon, and she seems occupied for the moment."

Penelope let out a sigh. She did not want to think about Lady Penrith. It must be horrid to work for her. "Is she very cruel?" she asked, frowning.

Anna chuckled. "Difficult, mayhap. Demanding, certainly. Terribly self-critical and aware of social etiquette—to the point that I think it hurts her more than it hurts anyone else around her. But cruel? No."

Penelope breathed out. Anna's view was reassuring. Seeing another side of Lady Penrith—not the cold, disdainful side, but a self-critical, hesitant person who clung to social rules because she had no other security—that helped.

"Good," she murmured.

Anna smiled. "No, I do not think I would work for someone cruel. Perhaps I would try to be a lady's companion instead, like Papa always thought I should. But imagine having to play the pianoforte to amuse someone? I think I would hate that." She chuckled.

"I think nobody would ask me to do that," Penelope said with a giggle. "Not if they had any liking of music. I can't play the pianoforte."

Anna grinned. "I can do so only barely."

They both laughed. Thomas, hearing the sound, crawled over with two blocks in his hands. He could toddle around, but he preferred to crawl, something Penelope thought was not worth changing—not given how anxious and insecure the child already seemed to be.

"Good morning!" Anna greeted him, making him sit up and look at her in puzzlement. "What do you have?" she asked, gesturing to the blocks.

"Box," Thomas informed her, grinning at her with a winsome grin.

Penelope giggled. "Blocks. Yes! You have blocks," she told him, her heart filled with warmth.

"Box," he repeated, dropping them both on the floor and then chuckling. They both laughed.

"Have you been playing all morning?" Anna asked the child. He was too busy with his blocks to look up, and Penelope replied.

"We went walking outside in the garden. Some guests came out to walk in the rose garden, and so we came inside again." She did not want to mention that one of them was Lady Penrith. She longed to talk about the earl, about the strange way he looked at her, but she felt too shy. Anna laughed.

"I can imagine," she replied, making a wry face. "It is very pleasant outside," she added.

"Were you in the garden too?" Penelope asked a little distractedly, bending down to sit with Thomas, who was banging one block on the other block and chuckling.

"Yes," Anna replied. Her voice sounded strange, a little tense, and Penelope glanced at her. She had gone a little pink, and Penelope grinned to herself.

"Was there someone there?" she asked. "Guests enjoying the sunshine, perhaps?" She teased.

Anna blushed redder. "Well, the viscount was there," she said in a small voice that made Penelope want to chuckle.

"Oh?" she asked, raising a brow.

"It was very decorous," Anna replied with a grin. "We talked about the weather. The viscount told me that he had gone riding and that the woods are very beautiful. He said that I would doubtless enjoy a walk." She was grinning broadly, unable to resist as she related the story. "He said that he would like to show me the woods."

Penelope laughed. "*Show* you the woods?" she teased. "Or have a chance to walk with you in the woods?"

"Penelope!" Anna smacked Penelope's hand, and Penelope giggled, smacking her in return on the upper arm. Anna laughed. "I am sure it would be entirely above board."

"Oh, what a pity," Penelope teased. They both giggled. Penelope's cheeks were warm.

"And you?" Anna asked when they were quiet. "Do you dream of a secret admirer too?"

"No!" Penelope insisted playfully, giving her friend a shove. Her face was hot, her entire body blushing.

"I do not think I believe that," Anna teased.

Penelope just laughed.

The church clock struck, and Anna gestured to the door. "I should go. I told the cook I'd help her collect some herbs. In return, I get jam tart." She grinned smugly.

Penelope chuckled. "Enjoy the jam tart. I'm afraid I have to keep an eye on our little rascal." She grinned lovingly at Thomas. "Or I would certainly help."

"Have a good afternoon," Anna said, rising to stand. "I will come up and tell you about the jam tart."

"Do that," Penelope giggled. "Enjoy the afternoon, Anna."

Anna bid her a good day and ducked out into the corridor. Penelope leaned back in her chair, her heart warm and full of happy thoughts. Her cheeks flushed as she thought about the earl. Was he an admirer? It seemed so. His gaze on her had felt like that.

"Don't be silly," she told herself aloud. She grinned. She lifted her sewing, musing that Anna saw no such barriers to her own interactions with a viscount. And, she reminded herself as she stitched, but for the fact that Anna's father was born fourth, she might have been the daughter of a viscount herself. Perhaps she was not silly.

She smiled at the thought. And, after all, a little daydreaming never hurt anyone.

Chapter 18

"And have you a fondness for visiting the museum when you are in London?"

Peter blinked. Lady Adeline was talking to him, but his mind was elsewhere and he had barely noticed what she was saying. Something about a museum. He frowned.

"I like museums," he replied cautiously, still not sure that he had followed what she had said.

"Splendid! I do love the museum! I insist on visiting it whenever we are in London. I am sure I drive dear Papa to distraction." She giggled.

Peter laughed uncertainly. His attention was unfocused. His mind kept on drifting to Miss Matthews in the garden. She had gazed into his stare with that compelling mix of trust and interest; an authentic, honest look that had no guile. He had longed to kiss her. He had fought the urge valiantly, but the depth of his desire shook him, and he had gone riding to attempt to put it out of his mind.

The time in the forest with just Wildfire, his horse, had not succeeded in distracting him—rather, it had done the opposite. Everywhere he went, he recalled that moment in the forest when Miss Matthews rode with him. He had returned home tormented and shut himself in his chamber to rest. Millicent had insisted on him attending dinner with the rest of the guests, and he had promised her that he would attend the card games and entertainments in the drawing-room afterwards, which he dutifully did. However, it was impossible to focus, and his mind kept wandering.

"...and did you see the exhibition at the British Institution?" she asked. "Fascinating!"

"Very fascinating," Peter murmured. He realised, belatedly, that he had no idea what she had said. He blinked again and tried to focus. He looked down at Lady Adeline.

She smiled up at him. Her dark eyes were bright and sparkling, her cheeks delicately flushed, a similar red to her lips, which were a beautiful bow.

Why is it that I feel nothing? he thought wildly. Barely five inches away from him was the debutante who had been acknowledged by several newspapers as the most beautiful woman in London. And yet, his attention remained barely focused, his mind elsewhere.

"Did you enjoy your ride this morning, my lord?" Lady Winthrop asked him. "Such a fine day! Adeline and I swore that we would spend every second of it in the garden. With parasols, of course." She beamed at Adeline.

"One must take care of one's complexion," Adeline agreed, smiling teasingly up at Peter.

Peter winced. Again, he felt as though the two women were looking at him expectantly and yet he had no idea what he was supposed to say.

"Would you care for some refreshment?" he asked. Lady Winthrop looked a little confused, and Peter winced inwardly, guessing that whatever response she had expected, it was not that. But Lady Adeline recovered faster.

"Oh, that would be most welcome, my lord!" she replied, fanning herself. "It is so hot in here." She swept her delicate hand across her brow.

Peter tensed. She was so beautiful, every gesture seemingly designed to show off her fine slim hands, her lovely pale skin and black hair. Yet he remained indifferent. He gestured to the table.

"What may I fetch for you?" he asked her.

"Lemonade would be lovely," she replied. "Thank you."

"It is my pleasure," Peter replied. "And you, my lady?" he asked Lady Winthrop.

"Oh! That is kind! Lemonade, too," Lady Winthrop replied, beaming at Lady Adeline.

Peter bowed to them both and hurried towards the refreshments table. He was glad to get there. He waited in line, relieved by the brief moments away from the demanding company. Millicent caught his eye and smiled. She was standing near the pianoforte, chatting to a group that included Aunt Marcia. Millicent, at least, seemed to approve of his spending time with Lady Adeline.

"Lemonade, please," he asked the liveried footman who was pouring drinks. "Two glasses."

"Very good, my lord," the man replied and poured two glasses of cool, pale liquid, passing them to Peter. He took them carefully and carried them back across the room to the two ladies, who beamed at him.

"Thank you, my lord," Lady Adeline murmured.

"Such a gentleman!" Lady Winthrop noted.

Peter reddened.

"Are you fond of walking?" Lady Adeline asked Peter as he stood with them uncomfortably, wishing that he could think of something to say.

"Um, a little," Peter replied. "I prefer a ride to a walk."

"Walking is so refreshing," she answered, smiling her bright smile. "I make a point of walking around the estate grounds at Winthrop Manor at least twice a day."

"Adeline is a very keen walker," Lady Winthrop put in.

Peter tensed. He could not think of anything to say. He was sure they expected some comment or other, but nothing came to his mind. He glanced across the room. Edmund and Millicent were still standing by the pianoforte. Millicent was nodding politely at something Aunt Marcia was saying, but Edmund looked quite disinterested. As Peter watched, the fellow's eyes moved to him, and Peter tensed, seeing that sharp, dark gaze narrow. He had never noticed before how watchful Edmund was, but the fellow was always staring at someone or other. He never said much, but his keen eyes seemed to miss little. He saw Peter watching him and looked away.

I do not like that man, Peter thought with a shiver. Something about Edmund's silent watchfulness always bothered him. The fellow appeared to be shallow and uncomplicated; the sort of man who read the *Gazette* and followed the races and made modest investments but had no real aspirations. But Peter was not so sure.

"Are you fond of whist?" Lady Winthrop asked him. Peter frowned.

"I do not play often," he replied. He tensed, seeing the card-tables set out. Some people were already sitting down to a game. He disliked cards, and the thought of being trapped at a table with Lady Adeline for half an hour for a game filled him with a need to escape.

"I regret, my ladies, that I must excuse myself," Peter murmured. "It is terribly warm, and I need to take the air." He gestured to the doors to the terrace, which had just been opened. He bowed and was grateful that neither of them suggested that they would accompany him.

"I trust you will feel better when you return indoors." Lady Adeline sounded sincere. Peter smiled at her. She was not a bad sort, he reflected guiltily. He just could not warm to her.

"Thank you, my lady," he said sincerely. He smiled at her awkwardly. Then, he hurried out of the room.

The balcony was cool, the night air almost cold after the stifling heat of the drawing room. It had been only half an excuse—he really did need to get outside and into the fresh air. There was a wooden seat under a creeper that grew up the wall, and he went to sit there, shutting his eyes tiredly.

Just another hour, he promised himself inwardly. *Then I will excuse myself and sleep.*

The confusion and the tumult of emotions that had tormented him for the last few days left him with little strength for anything else. Had he not promised to spend time with the guests to make up for his increasing absences, he would have already been resting.

He tipped his head back, opening his eyes. The stars showed in the dark sky, twinkling silver overhead. He gazed up. He had lost his mother when he was too young to remember her, and he had never felt such a need for her. He always imagined that she was there, somewhere, beyond the stars, watching over him. He longed for someone he could trust who could give him guidance. Millicent had her own plans and ambitions, and she was not someone whose advice he believed was neutral.

Miss Matthews's face filled his mind, and he groaned. He longed for her, yet every thought of her filled him with confusion. She was so far below his station that he could not entertain the idea of any sort of connection with her. And yet, every time he saw her, his heart soared. He longed to spend time with her, to talk to her. He longed to kiss her, yet it was not just her beauty that drew him. It was who she was—her tenderness, her insight, her complete lack of falsehood.

"Peter? Might I join you?"

Peter turned to see George coming out onto the balcony. He smiled. If he was in need of friendly company, George was as uncomplicated and friendly as he could wish. He nodded.

"Of course, cousin," he replied.

"Thank you." George sat down heavily on a chair behind him, sighing as he stretched his long legs in front of him. "Hot evening, eh?" he asked.

"It is," Peter agreed.

"Stifling in there," George noted, sipping a drink. It smelled like lemonade. "Had to escape the heat." He smiled at his cousin. "Yourself?"

"The same as you," Peter replied. He stared out into the night. He had not seen much of George in the last few days. The fellow had taken to spending time in the gardens, taking long, rambling walks. He always looked happy when he came back, and Peter did wonder what he found out there that made him seem so pleased.

"Fine stars," George commented, tipping his head back to gaze up at the blackness. Peter nodded.

"Very fine."

"Just the thing for when one sits out here alone. Something cheerful and bright," George noted. Peter inclined his head.

"Quite so," he agreed.

"I trust you're not still wondering about—about London and what happened there that night."

Peter sighed. He had been wondering about it; his thoughts just turning to it as George had arrived.

"I can't stop thinking that it was my fault," he murmured. He did not look at George but out at the vibrant stars in the darkness. "I wish I knew what had happened, and why." He looked down. If it had been murder, and not a robbery gone horribly wrong, then who had planned it? He wished he knew.

George turned to him. "Perhaps we won't ever know the truth," he said gently. "But whatever happened, Charles would not want you to blame yourself. Of that I am certain."

"I know you are right," Peter replied, letting out a sigh. "But I still need to know."

George inclined his head. "It is the nature of man to wish to know," he replied.

"Aristotle," Peter commented, recognising the quote. George chuckled.

"See? Cambridge did something to us, after all. Rammed some knowledge into our heads somehow."

"Somehow, yes." Peter laughed. "Not by our own desire to know, I think."

"Quite so."

They both smiled.

Peter gazed up at the stars again. George sighed.

"How many do you think there are?" George asked. "Stars, I mean."

Peter shrugged. "More than I can count, that's for certain."

George chuckled. "The world is so full of mysteries. What are the stars, and how did they get there? I don't think anyone really knows. Not really." He paused. "Some fellows think that they are distant Suns. Or so I heard, anyway. But I don't know." He shrugged. "I prefer to think there's something more romantic about them than that."

"Distant Suns," Peter murmured. "Is that romantic? I don't know. I'm not a romantic person."

George laughed. "That's what you say," he teased. "We all have a bit of romance in our souls, I think. We all love. We all dream. We all wish that our longings would come true." He sounded almost sad.

"That's so," Peter agreed. He shut his grey eyes briefly. George's words echoed what he felt in his own soul.

George sighed. He stretched his long legs out again and stared up. "So many questions," he murmured again.

"Quite so," Peter agreed. His heart ached. He had so many dreams and longings—Miss Matthews being the main one. But how could that ever come true? He did not know.

George sighed again and shifted on the chair.

"Don't sit out here too long, old chap. It's beautiful, but the quiet can drive one mad."

"Mayhap, yes." Peter nodded. He stretched his legs, considering going inside. George stood.

"I have to go in. I promised Sophia I would play cards with her." He grinned. "She's not half bad at whist, I must admit."

Peter laughed. "Not surprised, old fellow. Not surprised. Enjoy the game."

"I shall. Come in and join us when you feel ready to."

"I will," Peter told him.

George smiled and turned in the doorway, then went inside, his form yellowed by the candlelight as he went indoors.

Peter turned back to looking up at the sky. The distant stars glittered, and Peter wished he could float up there, far away from all that troubled him. Miss Matthews's face mingled with the distant memories of London, and he shut his eyes, trying to ignore all his worries. He longed again for guidance, for some word from a trusted person that could help him with his troubles.

He opened his eyes again just as a white moth flitted past, drawn by the candles. He watched it flap outside the window, circling and seeming to dance, as moths do; flirting with the light. The moth drifted upwards and eastwards, towards the nursery. Then it spiraled away, flitting over the wall and out towards the river that bordered the estate. He sighed.

"Mother? If that was a sign from you, I wish I understood what it was."

He stretched his legs again and stood. Perhaps he should go in again. Sitting out in the dark was not making things any easier. George was right.

He walked towards the door. George and Sophia were at a card-table opposite the doorway. George was smiling, and Sophia was laughing, clearly amused. Peter smiled to himself. If only his life was as simple and carefree.

Miss Matthews's face drifted into his thoughts again, and his heart ached. What if it truly was possible to do as he wished? What if George was right, and dreams could come true? The thought was wild, one that troubled him even more than his own attraction. He pushed it aside and went to join George and Sophia at the card table. Perhaps distraction was all that he needed. Even just watching their game would lighten his mood and lift his spirits somewhat.

"Peter! Come on! Join us!" Sophia greeted him. "You will have to sit out this round, I'm afraid. We've already begun. But next round, I am certain George will play with you. I am already undone." She giggled, pointing at the cards.

"I am certain you can make a victory out of the worst hand," George demurred.

Sophia just laughed.

Peter smiled, watching them and enjoying their honest, direct company. They were so different from the other guests, whose distant, cool, good manners always left him feeling as though he did not know what to say. He felt far more at ease in Miss Matthews's company—she made no demands, sought no particular response, but simply allowed him to speak as he wished, just as she, in turn, spoke her mind.

His thoughts drifted to the nursery and—despite himself—he could not help but wonder what Miss Matthews was doing and how she fared.

Chapter 19

Thomas wailed fretfully from his cradle, a sound of frustration rather than pain. His little legs kicked at the linen sheet that covered him as he thrashed about in annoyance and discomfort. Penelope hurried over from where she brushed and braided her hair for the night, lifting him. He turned away, limbs flailing.

"What is it, little fellow? It's the heat, isn't it?" Penelope asked gently. "You can't sleep either." It was a swelteringly-hot midsummer night. Penelope, in her long linen nightgown, could not sleep either. The window was open, a gauzy curtain shutting out the starlight. Not so much as a cool breeze stirred it to alleviate the heat.

Penelope wrapped her arms around the little boy, who pushed at her with the same frustrated gesture with which he had pushed at the sheets. His face was red, his little body clammy with sweat. His forehead was no warmer than usual, Penelope noted as she pressed her lips to his brow. He was not fevered, simply restless and hot.

"Hush, now," she murmured. "You can't find any rest in here, can you?" she said softly. She gazed out of the window. The sky was black, as dark as rich velvet, half-visible through the gauzy curtain. Penelope's heart thudded with a mix of excitement and fear. She barely felt bold enough to sneak into the gardens at night. She went closer to the open window, listening carefully. No music drifted up from downstairs, so it seemed that, whatever the guests were doing, they were not having a ball and there were no people on the terrace.

There's no reason not to go outside, she rationalised. *We'll only be a few minutes; just until he cools down and can sleep.*

"Wait a moment," she told the fussing baby, who was kicking and flailing in her arms as if even her body heat irritated him. She settled him on her bed, hurriedly unbuttoning her nightgown and donning a shift and her white uniform. Then she slipped her feet into her outdoor boots, lifted little Thomas in his flannel nightshirt, covered him with a thin linen sheet and carried him into the hallway.

They walked down the dark, silent corridor. She tensed halfway. Lamps still burned in the main hallway, and, as she neared the entrance, she could hear the laughter and chatter of guests—probably in the drawing room. She hesitated. It would have been more proper to use the servants' hallway, but it might already be dark in there and she could not risk a fall. She drew in a breath, steeling herself, and carried Thomas down the corridor and towards the stairs.

Nobody appeared in the bright-lit corridor and in the entranceway, the front door was open. She slipped out and walked down the stone steps towards the lawn. The cool air was like walking into water, refreshing as a gulp from a stream on a hot day. She felt instantly relaxed. Thomas, in her arms, stopped fretting and looked around, wide-eyed. The garden was entirely silent except for the chorus of cricket-song that hummed and burred in the background. No breeze so much as rustled the bushes or the trees, which stood utterly still and black against the blueish dark of the night sky. The air smelled fresh and cool with dew, and the lawn was soaking with it, the drops spangling the black expanse where the light from the windows caught them.

Penelope walked quietly down the stone path. The windows in the main part of the house cast bars of golden light onto the grass and she could see the way for a few paces ahead. She breathed out, and in her arms, Thomas seemed to rest more easily. He was making small nonsense sounds, something that he did when he was falling asleep.

"Just a few minutes," she told the child. Somewhere nearby was a stone bench. They would sit there until Thomas slept, she decided, and then go in. Delicious as the cool air was, she did not want either of them to remain outside too long and risk catching a chill.

Her gaze scanned the dark space. She spotted the bench, a glimmer of white in the dark. It was just a few paces away and she wandered there, sighing as she sat down. The stone was cold on her legs and she leaned back, shutting her eyes. Thomas was still babbling.

She rocked him in her arms, feeling drowsy. In the peace of the garden, with only the chirping of crickets to disturb the quietude, it would be so easy to fall asleep.

A twig cracked nearby. Penelope tensed. There were no fences around the estate, and it was quite possible for creatures from the woodland to enter the grounds at night. She had never heard of wolves being anywhere near human settlements in the middle of summer—if they ever ventured close, it was in the deepest cold of a very bad winter. Even so, a shiver ran down her spine. Every nerve in her body tensed. She stood utterly still, scarcely daring to breathe.

A twig cracked again. Whatever it was, it was bigger than a wolf. It was something large and heavy, and it was walking towards them from behind the trees. Penelope shut her eyes briefly, steadying herself. Then she tightened her arms around Thomas, who had gone silent as if he sensed her anxiety. She stood up.

The sound of steps was distinct now, and closer. It was a person. She had no doubt about that. She thought about running, but she could not risk a fall when she cradled Thomas in her arms and besides, her legs had locked with fear and even if she had wanted to, she could not persuade them to move. She looked around in terror.

The form of a man rounded the tree.

"No!" Penelope cried out.

The man stopped. His form was hard to see against the black shadow of the tree, but she could see the white collar and sleeves of his shirt and it was clear that he was quite tall. He called out.

"Miss Matthews?" His voice was incredulous with surprise.

"My lord?" she called back, surprise making her voice a few tones higher than its normal middle tone.

"Miss Matthews!" The male voice repeated. The shadow of the man stepped forward and, when he stopped just two steps away, it was clear that it was indeed the earl. He was in his shirtsleeves, his dark brown hair sweat-damp on his brow. He was smiling, his eyes wide. She could just see his expression in the mix of starlight and the light from the windows. Her heart thudded.

"My lord," she repeated, dropping a curtsey. "Forgive me. Thomas could not sleep. We sought the cool air of the garden. I will go indoors," she added, turning towards the path. Perhaps he would be angry. The staff did not generally wander around in the gardens at night, and perhaps it was forbidden. Perhaps he would disapprove of her exposing the baby to the colder air.

"You need not go," the earl said softly. "Stay awhile."

Penelope stared up at him. His voice was soft. His expression, or what she could see of it in the dark, was open and friendly. Her heart started to race wildly in her chest. When they saw each other in daylight, or in the nursery, there was always some tension, some briskness and reserve despite the gentleness of the interaction.

"I would like to stay until Thomas sleeps," she agreed. The baby had stopped his sleepy cooing, but she could feel that he was still awake, his small body tense. When she looked down, he was watching her warily. She stroked his head reassuringly. "You can rest, little one," she told him gently. "It is safe."

"Was he restless?" the earl asked. They were standing near the bench and Penelope settled down on it again. The earl remained standing opposite her. She swallowed hard. He was her employer and it felt odd that she should sit while he stood, but he had not objected and her arms were tired, so she remained seated.

"Yes," she replied. "The heat tormented him."

"He's not alone," the earl chuckled.

Penelope laughed. His smile was a flash of brightness in the dark. She drew a deep breath. Being alone with him outdoors felt forbidden somehow, and also wonderful. She wanted to stay and talk with him even after the baby fell asleep. The barriers between them seemed to soften in the darkness, blending away the rigid divide and making them two equals, restless on a hot night.

"It is a very hot night," she sympathised. "Is it always so warm here?"

"In Devon?" The earl lifted his shoulder. "We usually have a few hot days. I don't recall one as bad as this in a few years. My plants will love it."

"It is like the colonies?" she guessed.

The earl chuckled. "Only the explorers could say for certain how oppressive the heat is there," he replied. "But this does seem to be the sort of climate my plants favour. I only wish I could show you."

"You would show me?" Penelope asked. Her heart raced. The thought of visiting the greenhouse with him filled her with delight. She would love to see the plants that interested him so.

"If you care to look, yes," the earl said with surprising humility. "There are some oil-lamps in there, as I recall. Our gardener thought they might help to heat the place in winter, but really all they did was fill the place with a foul smell of burning oil." He chuckled. "As it is, they will give us some light. If they are still there," he added.

"If you wish to show me, I would very much like to see," Penelope replied.

The earl grinned. "Come on, then," he replied, standing back so that she could get up from the bench. "It is a rare thing for anyone to willingly subject themselves to my endless talk of plants." He laughed.

Penelope giggled. "I want to hear everything about your fascination with them," she assured him.

He smiled. "You're a bold lady," he told her.

Her heart raced. His gaze held hers, steady and intent, and the way he looked at her sent a rush of warmth through her. She lowered her eyes to the ground, her cheeks flushing.

"Thank you," she murmured, her throat tight with emotion.

"My pleasure," he said softly.

Penelope's heart thudded. She held Thomas close. He seemed to be aware of the strange excitement between them because he was wide awake, looking around with big, round eyes. Penelope held him close, supporting him on her hip.

She followed the earl as he led the way towards the side of the manor.

A stone path led towards the greenhouse. Penelope followed the earl, and when he reached the door, he lifted a hand.

"I will go in and light the lamps," he told her. "I do not want you to risk walking along the paths in the darkness with the baby. There are many benches and you might trip and fall."

"Thank you," Penelope breathed.

In the darkness, she saw a brief flare as he used a flint and striker to create a brief spark. He must carry a tinderbox with him—perhaps he smoked a pipe sometimes. She smiled. There was so much to find out about him.

A light flared and steadied, and the earl appeared in the darkness, his appearance a little distorted by the glass panes of the greenhouse. She slipped in through the door.

"Careful. Let me light another one," the earl cautioned, holding up his hand. She waited at the door while he lit two more lamps, and then he beckoned to her.

"Now you can see a little better. On your left are some bromeliads—they are a strange sort of plant. Pineapples are a sort of bromeliad. Have you seen a pineapple?" he wanted to know.

Penelope shook her head, feeling a little ashamed of her ignorance. "No, my lord," she murmured.

He grinned. His smile seemed as bright as the oil-lamp he carried. "Nor have I. I know of them from books, but I have never actually seen one. Millicent, my sister, claims to have seen two. She attends far more parties than I do, and they are prized centerpieces, so I can well believe it. Ladies tend to borrow pineapples from one another for decorating the tables, and a few are used until they are quite rotten. Can you imagine?" He laughed.

"No, my lord," Penelope replied honestly. He chuckled.

"It seems a little silly to me, too."

They looked at one another. The silence stretched. His smile was bright, and something about it made her heart thud.

She looked down, feeling shy. Thomas was awake, murmuring and wriggling. She soothed him and then looked up at the earl. He gestured to the table on their left, where clusters of plants stood. They had dark green, rigid leaves, some with pink tips and some with serrated edges. The leaves seemed to come from a central point, leaving a curious hole down the center of the plant. Penelope gazed at them in amazement. They were like nothing she had ever seen.

"These are remarkable," she breathed.

The earl chuckled. "They are some of my favourites, too. Look at this one," he added, indicating one that had white patches on its leaves. "Bromeliads are beautiful. They have several varieties in Kew Gardens that I do not yet have. I must collect some more, but I never seem to have time in London." he looked sad.

Penelope wondered why mention of London saddened the earl, but she did not ask. She gazed around the greenhouse. The two oil-lamps flickered at the far end, casting dancing shadows, and she looked over at them, the shapes of plants outlined in dark green by their light. She stared in fascination, her steps leading her in that direction. The earl noticed where she was looking and gestured towards the table.

"There are some rather interesting creepers there. I am eagerly awaiting their bloom." His grin was bright.

Penelope wandered closer to have a look. The plants had dark green leaves, and one or two had buds on them. She felt a frisson of excitement, wanting to see what they would look like when they opened.

"How beautiful," she breathed.

The earl grinned. "You know, you make me remember how much I love these plants." His tone was soft. "Very few people really feel the same excitement, or understand it, even, when I do."

Penelope gazed up at him. He had rested the oil-lamp on the table, and she could see him clearly. His gaze was soft. His smile was gentle and his eyes danced with the same longing that thrummed through her body. He stood so close to her. She realised that a strand of her hair had come loose from its confining bun, and she reached up to tuck it back, but before she could do so, he tenderly tucked it behind her ear. His fingers traced her cheek. She gasped. His touch was so tender, making every nerve in her body tingle and dance. She could feel the traces of his fingers even as he lifted his hand.

"I did not mean to alarm you," he murmured.

"You did not." Penelope gazed into his eyes.

The earl gazed back. He held her gaze. Penelope's heart thudded. It seemed as though he was about to say something, as though he had something to tell her. Thomas wriggled in her arms.

The earl chuckled, and the tension dispersed.

"We haven't forgotten you," he told the child gently as Penelope comforted Thomas softly. Thomas gazed up at him, bewildered. Then he began with his small cooing noises again. Penelope smiled.

"He is tired," she said softly. "I should take him to the nursery to sleep."

"Yes. You must be cold," the earl answered. He frowned. "That uniform cannot be very warm."

Penelope giggled. "It is not very cold out here," she replied. As it happened, the greenhouse was not particularly warm, and the thought of going inside, into the stiflingly warm house, was actually appealing.

"Perhaps not," the earl commented. "But you should go inside," he added, sounding worried.

Penelope nodded. "Thomas needs his sleep," she agreed.

The earl gazed at her tenderly. "Do not work too hard," he said softly. "You, too, need your rest."

"I will sleep as soon as Thomas does," Penelope assured him.

"I imagine so," the earl said with a wry smile.

Penelope smiled back and for a second, the tension of earlier returned. Her body thrummed with excitement as his grey eyes stared into hers. He was very close—so close that she could feel the heat of his body through the shirt he wore. She could see the firm, broad outline of his shoulders and his narrow waist, and she felt a sudden, strong and inexplicable urge to feel his warm arms around her, to lean against his firm chest and see how it felt.

"Allow me to walk with you to the house," the earl said softly. "It is very dark, and you might slip."

"Thank you," Penelope murmured.

The earl waited until she had reached the door of the greenhouse, then extinguished the lamps. They walked slowly back to the house in silence. Penelope was aware of his presence beside her, her every nerve tingling as they walked back towards the door.

"I should go around to the servants' entrance," she murmured. He shook his head.

"It is dark there. Go in through the front door. Nobody will see. And if they ask, tell them I told you to." He smiled.

"Thank you," Penelope murmured. She smiled up at him. Their eyes met. Light poured from the windows high above, and she could see his face clearly for the first time. She drew in a breath. She had forgotten just how handsome he was. His thin, chiseled features cannoned into her heart, and her blood fizzed with delight.

His smile widened as he saw the admiration in her eyes. She beamed back.

"I should go," she managed to say. She stayed where she was. She did not want to.

He nodded. "I also should. The guests will soon retire to bed."

Neither of them moved. Penelope took a deep breath and took a step up towards the door. She walked slowly, conscious of his gaze on her as she went. Her cheeks burned.

As she slipped into the house, she turned and saw that he was indeed watching her. She grinned and blushed and shut the door behind her, heart pounding, mind filled with a mix of delight and confusion.

"I do not understand him," she murmured to Thomas as they walked briskly up the stairs towards the sanctuary of the nursery. "I do not understand any of it."

Thomas was almost asleep. He had stopped making the small cooing noises and lay quietly in her arms, his eyes closed. Penelope gazed down at him; her heart filled with love. Slowly she settled him in his cradle so that he would not wake. Then she walked silently across the room to her own bed.

As she took her boots off, setting them before the fireplace in the hopes that the dew-soaked leather would dry more swiftly there, her thoughts strayed to the conversation with the earl. She recalled his gaze on hers, his touch tender on her cheek.

"I don't understand any of this," she said again into the silence of the room. As she lay down to rest, she was smiling. She knew thoughts of the earl would follow her into her dreams and fill them with warmth and happiness.

Chapter 20

Penelope gazed out at the clouds that hung, low and oppressive, over the estate. It was four o'clock in the afternoon, but it seemed much darker. The shadows under the trees were deep and an eerie light shone diffusely onto the lawn through the clouds, making the air prickle with the promise of a storm.

Thomas murmured to himself in his cradle, dropping off for his afternoon nap. Penelope glanced back at the big chair, where she had piled the garments that she intended to mend or sew while he slept. She stifled a yawn. She had slept well but woken early and been unable to sleep anymore, her mind tumultuous with thoughts. The strange evening with the earl in the greenhouse plagued her thoughts, making her alternatively elated and confused. It was impossible to guess what was in his mind, what he really felt or thought.

"He cannot love me," she said aloud. "Not truly."

The part of her that had seen the tenderness in his eyes, the quiet devotion in his gaze, fought against the part that clung to reason—to social order, to the weight of impossibility. What she had witnessed with her own eyes waged battle against the beliefs she had long accepted simply because they were the way of the world.

He cannot really love you. He can only be thinking of exploiting you. You are beneath his station.

The words hit her with the force of a fist. That, she was sure, was what any sane person would tell her. Nobody of the earl's standing could truly be falling for her. And yet, when he looked at her, she did not see only desire, but care. She did not see a lustful, selfish longing to exploit her—none of his behavior suggested that. She saw true interest.

"Let me make sense of this," she whispered. "I need guidance. I am so confused."

There was nobody at the manor she could truly ask for advice besides Anna, and Anna seemed very distracted of late, spending all her free time in the garden. She longed to speak to Emily. Her steps led her to the desk in the corner of the nursery, where a writing-desk stood. Perhaps writing a letter to Emily would help. She settled down at the desk, but stood restlessly as the wind stirred the curtains and a distant rumble of thunder sounded across the eerily-lit hills.

"Hush, little fellow," she murmured as Thomas stirred and moaned in apparent fright. "It's all well."

She shut the window, hoping that it might shut out the worst of the noise. It was stickily hot in the nursery without the slight breeze that had entered earlier and with the strange, oppressive heat of the previous night still hanging in the manor.

She went back to the desk, lifting the pen. Words came swiftly, flowing with ease, but none of them felt like something she could share. What had been intended as a letter was becoming a journal entry, filled with her deepest feelings and her wild confusion.

...And yet, I do not know what to feel, she wrote. *My heart is on fire, filled with wild joy every time I see him. Yet I am also afraid. Confused. What I believe to be happening cannot truly be happening. I must be mad to think it. But how else am I to interpret his looks, his words? His touch on my cheek? It is too hard to understand. I beg for guidance.*

She paused as a knock sounded at the door. She tensed. Was it a knock or a growl of distant thunder? She was not sure and she did not answer until the door opened a crack.

"Miss Matthews?" the earl called. "May I come in?"

"My lord!" Penelope shot to her feet, covering the letter with a sheet of blotting paper hurriedly. Her cheeks flared. She had been imagining his touch on her face; imagining that they had lingered longer in the greenhouse. His grey eyes held hers. There was no mistaking the longing in their depths, or the intensity of concern.

"Are you well?" he asked gently. "You seem flustered. Did I disturb you?"

Penelope shook her head. A tendril of her dark brown hair had come loose from her bun, and she tucked it hastily behind her ear.

"No, my lord. I am at ease. Thomas is sleeping," she answered, gesturing to the cradle where the baby slept peacefully, seeming unperturbed by the distant rumble of thunder.

"Oh." The earl looked over at the cradle tenderly. "How fares young Thomas? Is he more tolerant of the heat?"

"He seems so," Penelope replied. "He fares well." It was hard to find words—his warm gaze was making her body flood with heat, and it was difficult to think.

"I have you to thank for that," the earl murmured feelingly. His gaze was intense. "It is thanks to you that he thrives as he does. That he is as well as he is."

Penelope bit her lip, her cheeks flaring. "I cannot accept that praise," she said gently. "He is a hardy baby, I think quite naturally resilient."

The earl shook his head. "He was fretful and miserable before. His former nanny said so often enough, and I saw with my own eyes that he was not happy. You have done wonders."

Penelope shook her head but allowed herself to grin in happiness. "I am glad for his joy."

"As am I," the earl said gently. "Thomas is precious to me. When he was ailing as he was, I felt as though I had failed him." It was hard not to notice an audible shake in his voice, as if he fought against tears.

"You would never fail anyone," Penelope said gently. One thing she had noticed was that he was devoted to whatever he cared about. Whether it was Thomas, the estate, or even his precious plants, the earl took care of those things that mattered to him. She looked up. He was standing stiffly, as though she had slapped him. She tensed, afraid that she had upset him. His grey eyes were wide, his expression difficult to read.

"You cannot know that." His voice was almost inaudible. "You do not know what failings lie at my door."

Penelope glanced at little Thomas, lying so peacefully in his cradle. The emotion in the earl's voice shook her composure. It took her a moment to decide what to say.

"You are right," she agreed slowly. "I cannot know what lies in your past. But I do know this—whatever it was, you would have done your utmost. If things did not turn out as you wished, it was not your fault. I have seen how deeply you care, and I know you would always give your best for those you love."

She did not look at him, but focused on the window as she spoke. When she looked back at him, she was shocked to see tears course silently down his face. She tensed in horror. She had upset him beyond her power to correct it.

"My lord?" she whispered, horrified.

"Forgive me," he managed to say, his throat tight. "I cannot tell you how those words free me from a terrible burden. My cousin..." he paused, then began. "My cousin, who is Thomas' father, was killed. I do not know by whom. But I do know that..." he paused again. "Whoever it was, they targeted my coach. My cousin was using it. He and his wife were returning from the opera. I will never know what would have happened if they had not borrowed the carriage with my insignia emblazoned on it. Perhaps he would not have been touched. I will never know." The tears flowed again.

Penelope drew in a breath. That explained too many things. Thomas's presence and the earl's deep fondness for the child. The fretful, fearful wails that Thomas had made whenever she left him unattended for a minute or two. The earl's silence and apparent sadness. It all became clear. The earl took out his handkerchief and dabbed at his face, drying the tears that soaked it. He sighed.

"Sorry," he murmured. "You must think me weak."

Penelope shook her head. "It is not weakness to grieve in the face of such a loss. It is human. I am so very sorry." She paused, not sure what to say.

He smiled, his face still damp. "It is certainly not your fault," he said gently. "It is mine, if it is anyone's. But never yours."

Penelope shook her head. "It is the fault only of whoever organised it. I pray that you will find out who did that so that your mind may be set to rest. But it is not your fault. How could you possibly have known?"

The earl sighed. "You are right," he murmured, his shoulders slumping. "Thank you."

She looked up at him. "You are a good man," she said firmly.

The earl gazed into her eyes. His expression seemed almost shocked for a moment, his gaze widening, his grey eyes round with something like disbelief. Then he looked down, shaking his head.

"Your words move me beyond what I can say."

He stared into her eyes. The room was utterly silent. Penelope could hear only the beating of her heart. The strand of hair that had sneaked out of its bun earlier brushed against her cheek, and the earl reached up and stroked it behind her ear again. His palm lingered at her cheek, warm and soft. Then, slowly, so slowly, he leaned forward, and she leaned forward, and his lips pressed against hers. Her heart stopped beating for a moment, surprise rooting her to the spot; and then longing thrummed through her, and she leaned forward some more, moving into the kiss.

The earl's arms wrapped around her, and she leaned against his chest, the firm hardness of him warm against her body. His arms were strong and tight around her. She wrapped her own arms around him, feeling his narrow waist, his wide shoulders. He drew her close, his lips clinging to hers. His mouth was soft and warm, the feeling of his lips on hers making her senses swim.

A noise in the hallway made him tense. He stepped swiftly back. Penelope gazed up at him, her heart thudding. He blinked, staring down at her.

"Forgive me," he murmured softly.

Penelope tried to find words, but her mind had stopped working, her thoughts moving slowly through the haze of wonder and amazement that filled her.

"There is nothing to forgive," she managed, but her voice was almost inaudible.

"I must go," the earl said quietly. He turned to the door. Penelope stood still, part of her aching for him to stay, for him to wrap his arms around her and kiss her again, even longer and more deeply, but part of her was too confused and needed a moment to think before doing anything.

The earl opened the door and turned to her, his eyes a mix of the same confusion and longing she felt. Then he stepped out into the hallway, shutting the door behind him.

Penelope stood by the wall where she had been standing when he kissed her. She could not move, rooted to the spot by a torrent of feeling. Wonder was chief among the feelings that filled her, and amazement and joy. Confusion was there, too, and disbelief. Had that really just happened?

She touched her lips, the feeling of his own lips lingering there. She shut her eyes, reliving the beauty of the kiss. Her heart filled with blissful warmth, and she opened her eyes again, her smile stretching across her face.

"But what will happen?" she asked the silent air of the room. What he had done was wonderful; beautiful, and everything a part of her had secretly longed for. But what would it mean for the future? There was no route whereby they could express that love; no way for them to realise the beauty that was between them. Becoming his mistress was unthinkable—the shock would kill Papa entirely, and it was a dangerous life. And besides, if he had wanted that, surely the earl would already have suggested it? No, that was not the solution.

Penelope walked silently over to the window, gazing out on the storm-clouds there. The tumultuous scene reflected the mix of wild emotions that flooded her heart, and she leaned on the sill, gazing out at the lighting as it flashed across the hills.

The kiss was the most beautiful thing she had ever received, but also the most confusing. Like the storm, it unleashed a wildness and wonder inside her. But she could not help but wonder what it would bring.

Chapter 21

"What have I done?"

Peter spoke the words into the silence of his study, a question more than a plea, though no answer would come. He had retreated here immediately after breakfast, weary from a night spent mostly awake.

The thoughts of the kiss consumed him. Memories of Miss Matthews' soft lips parting under his played through his mind repeatedly. Longing surged up in him, almost irresistible, with the merest thought. And yet he could not allow himself to have such dangerous longings.

"It would ruin her."

That was his deepest fear and the thing that made the kiss so dangerous and wrong. Making her his mistress was the only route that would be even vaguely possible for them, since their social standings were so widely different. And yet, doing so was the last thing that he would wish to do. Ruining her reputation, robbing her of the one thing that could ensure her safety—her respectability—was the one thing that he would never do.

"But how else could it be possible?" he asked aloud.

If he had no earldom, and if Thomas was not reliant on him, he would run away. He would take Miss Matthews in his coach and travel far away, somewhere where neither of them would be recognised. He would wed her and use whatever small amount of money he could claim as his personal wealth from the estate coffers to support them. As for the earldom, its succession would follow the course dictated by law and tradition.

He and Miss Matthews would not have a plentiful existence, but they would have the bright and shining love that seemed to fill him whenever she was close.

The estate and its needs could not be forsaken, though; the burden of continuing what his ancestors had made was too strong. And Thomas. He could not take the poor child into a poverty-stricken existence with them, not after he had been born into a world of privilege; the life that Charles had wanted for him. He had promised Charles that he would raise his son in a way that he would approve of, and he had to fulfil that promise.

"But how can I make another choice?" he asked himself aloud.

Millicent expected him to find a respectable countess and continue the family line, and that was—if he thought about it—no less than duty demanded of him. He could not allow himself to indulge in wild fantasies. But those wild fantasies brought him the greatest spark of joy that he had ever felt. He would hand over the earldom in a flash if he could have Miss Matthews by his side.

He stood and went to the window, then paced back to his desk again.

As he sat down, someone knocked at the door. He jumped and almost swore but managed to contain himself.

"Who is there?" he called out in his most authoritative tone.

"My lord, I have a message for you. It is urgent," the butler's familiar voice called through the door. "Or, so the messenger informed me. It requires a reply."

Peter swore and stood up, opening the door.

"Thank you," he managed to say as the butler handed him a note. He frowned at the seal, which bore no insignia. He slid his finger under the seal to open it, and his eyes widened as he read the note that was scrawled there.

My lord, he read. *I will be in Brentdale village until early this afternoon. Please come and see me at your earliest convenience as I have news of an urgent nature to impart. I am staying at the Wheat Ear Inn. I await your reply, or your arrival at the inn. Yours faithfully, A. B. Irving.*

Peter let out a long, slow breath. His heart was racing. He had to know whatever news the man had to share. He gestured to the butler, who was waiting, tense and alert, in the doorway.

"Please have my horse saddled," he began, thinking as he gave instructions. "And fetch my cousin George," he decided. "I will go to my chamber to dress. I need to depart the manor for a while. If anybody requires my presence while I am out, please inform them that I had business of an urgent nature to attend to. I will return by lunchtime," he added. The butler bowed.

"At once, my lord."

Peter thanked the man and hurried to his chamber. There, he changed into his buckskin breeches and a velvet jacket—clothes for horseback riding. A knock sounded at the door as he sat to put on his knee-length riding boots.

"Peter?" George called through the door. "It's me. May I come in?"

"Please do," Peter replied, tugging his boots on and standing up.

George entered, and his eyes widened as he saw Peter in his riding things. "What is it, cousin? Do you need to go somewhere? The butler summoned me, saying you needed to talk to me."

Peter nodded. "Irving wrote to me," he began. George knew the name, and he inclined his head to show he understood. "He is at the Wheat Ear Inn in Brentdale village. He wishes to meet with me. I would value it immeasurably if you were to accompany me," he asked.

George smiled. "Of course, Peter. It is an honour to be asked. I am grateful for your trust." He looked around. "You're already dressed. I'll need a moment to prepare."

Peter inclined his head, grateful that his cousin had agreed so readily. "Thank you. I will have a horse saddled for you. Meet me at the stable," he offered.

George nodded. "I will be there in a moment or two."

Peter thanked him again and then hurried downstairs. When he reached the stable, Wildfire was already saddled and waiting. He mounted up at once.

"Please saddle Blaze for my guest," he instructed the stable hand.

The stable hand hurried to do as he was asked, and Peter rode Wildfire at a walk around the paddock, trying to calm down. He could not imagine what Irving might have to say to him. He hoped it was good news; that they had discovered whoever had ordered the attack. Perhaps, he reflected, they had evidence that it was not an attack but a simple robbery. Either thing would be a relief.

As he rode down the length of the paddock, he could not help but think of what Miss Matthews had said—about it not being his fault. About him doing his best. He sighed. It was easily the most reassuring thing that he had heard.

"Peter! I'm on my way," George called, hurrying towards the stable.

Peter walked Wildfire across the paddock and waited while George mounted up, and then they rode out together.

The road to the village led uphill, but the ride was not long—particularly when undertaken on two well-rested hunting stallions. They reached the inn within an hour. Peter reined in his horse in the inn yard, and George reined in behind him. They dismounted. Peter led his horse to the inn water trough for a much-needed drink.

"Stable and feed our horses, please," he instructed a stable-hand who ran up. Peter flipped the boy a coin, and his eyes widened.

"Cor! Thank you, my lord."

Peter waited a moment for George to join him, and then they both strode into the inn.

The taproom was crowded, and Peter stood in the doorway, narrowing his eyes to see if he could spot Irving. Farmers taking a mid-morning break from their labours sat at tables with carters, farriers and other artisans, drinking, eating or simply talking or playing cards. The air smelled of the wood panelling, smoke from the fireplace, and hay. Peter spotted Mr Irving sitting by himself at a table and gestured to him. His eyes widened, and he hurried to the door.

"My lord!" he greeted him, bowing low. "I did not expect you so early." His expression was troubled.

"No matter. I rode here straightaway. This is my cousin and trusted friend, Lord Chelmsford. He is welcome to join us. I will request use of the inn's private parlour," he added, looking around the crowded room. Not only would it be unseemly for an earl and his companion to linger in the common room, but it was also far too public. He had no desire for their conversation to be overheard.

"Thank you, my lord," Irving replied.

Peter located the innkeeper behind the front desk and soon they were led to the upstairs parlour, which was much quieter. The room had the same wood panelling, but the furniture was upholstered and green brocade curtains hung at the windows. Peter settled on a comfortable chair by the table and gestured to the innkeeper to shut the door as he went out.

"Please, tell us whatever you have to say," Peter asked Mr Irving. The fellow looked down nervously, hands clasped.

"My lord, a witness has been located. A labourer was on the road at the time of your cousin's death. Because of the heavy storm, this labourer was standing in the shelter of the trees not too far from the place where the carriage was halted by the brigands. He saw part of what happened. More importantly, he believes that he heard the brigands talking a little before the confrontation occurred. He claims that they were discussing the way that they would divide the pay they received from the job."

"How reliable is this man's word?" Peter demanded at once. He had to know if any of this story was believable. It changed everything. He could no longer choose to believe that his cousin's death had been a tragic accident.

"Very reliable, my lord," Mr Irving said at once. "He is an upstanding member of his community and well-liked and trusted. I do not see any reason to believe that he is lying. It was dangerous for him to come forward, and I cannot imagine any benefit that he might gain by giving false witness."

"True," Peter agreed.

"Did he see the men? Would he be able to identify them?" George wanted to know. Peter nodded in thanks to his cousin.

"He was unable to see them, my lord. It was night, and he was a few paces away from where they had concealed themselves in the trees with their horses. He claimed to be able to hear their words, but he could not see them."

Peter sighed. "What else did he hear?" he asked.

Mr Irving looked down. "He heard little else, my lord, besides the three men hidden there discussing how they planned to divide up their pay. They did not mention who had paid them, save that he was a "fancy toff", and that they were surprised he had not paid them more." He looked away uncomfortably.

"A toff?" Peter asked. It was a disparaging term for a wealthy or noble person. Whoever had paid the killers, they were of a similar social standing to Peter himself. He swallowed hard.

"Yes, my lord. Sorry about the word, my lord." Mr Irving added frowningly.

"No matter," Peter said quickly. "This man had nothing else to report?"

"No, my lord," Mr Irving confirmed.

Peter let out a long breath. He glanced at George. George looked back.

"What do you conclude from this, Mr Irving?" Peter asked respectfully.

The older man ran a hand down his face tiredly. Peter could imagine him riding directly from London with the news. He must be exhausted.

"It confirms what was already claimed, my lord," Mr Irving said wearily. "That this was not a robbery, but a planned killing. And it does suggest to us that whoever paid the killers was a nobleman, or at least a gentleman."

"It does," Peter agreed.

None of them said anything. George looked at Peter sympathetically. Peter cleared his throat.

"You have done well, Mr Irving," he said slowly. "I thank you for your news and for the time that you took in riding here to deliver it personally. Please charge whatever expenses you incur here at the inn to my name. My solicitor will see that it is paid."

"Thank you, my lord," Mr Irving replied. He looked pleased.

Peter pushed back his chair, glancing at George, who did likewise.

"Thank you," Peter said again, going to the door. "If you hear any other news, do not hesitate to write. I would like you to continue investigating. It would be excellent if we could uncover some information that might help us to identify the person who ordered this killing."

"Indeed, my lord," Mr Irving replied.

Peter and George departed from the inn and mounted up in the inn yard. They rode back to the house silently. Though conversation eluded him, Peter was grateful for George's presence. His mind was too burdened for words.

"Thank you for coming with me," he thanked George as they neared the manor. George grimaced.

"I am so sorry, Peter," he said caringly. "This news is hard to bear."

"It is," Peter agreed.

George said nothing more. Peter rode ahead wordlessly. The path was too narrow to ride alongside one another.

After ten minutes of riding, Peter stopped and turned. He could hear fast hoofbeats and he scanned the woods for George. As he watched, horrified, Blaze, George's horse, reared. George shouted in alarm.

"Whoa! Easy! What in Perdition's name is bothering you?"

Peter rode alongside, heart almost stopping as his friend was almost thrown.

"Easy, boy," he murmured to Blaze, who had stopped rearing and stood shivering as if flies bothered him. "What's the matter?"

As Peter reached out to touch the distressed horse's mane, he tensed. He could hear something. Hoofbeats. Loud and urgent; riding up behind them.

"Who goes there?" Peter shouted. His heart thudded in his chest. They were near the estate. Nobody ever rode in that part of the woods. His own horse stamped, and Blaze neighed; an angry challenging sound that made Peter blink in surprise.

Nobody replied. The sound of hoofbeats sped up, then slowed and then disappeared, as if the rider had taken a turning somewhere and was no longer behind them. Peter shivered.

"I think we should go back to the house," he murmured.

"I agree," George replied.

They rode back to the house in silence. Neither of them spoke, even as they dismounted at the stables, letting the groom take care of their horses. In the hallway, Peter drew in a deep breath. He had too much to worry about. The strange rider in the woods was just one more unexplained mystery. He had so much to think about and worry about, and yet, in all of it, the one thing that still plagued him as the familiar smell of the hallway enveloped him was the kiss and his aching heart. He had to think of something to do about that as well, and soon.

Chapter 22

"Sister, I am indisposed," Peter murmured. He was in the upstairs hallway, near the drawing room. His dark blue velvet tailcoat felt stifling, despite the fact that the evening was much cooler than the previous one, and his knee-breeches seemed to constrict his legs. He was dressed for a ball and he absolutely did not want to attend. He had far too much to think about. Mr Irving's news, the puzzling ride back to the estate, and the kiss from the previous night. He could not possibly stand around and exchange pleasantries with strangers all evening, and he could not even think of dancing with someone. He was too distressed.

"You don't have to stay all night," Millicent replied in a loud whisper. "But for pity's sake, brother, you have to come for the first hour at least! Lady Adeline expects it, and I would be upset, too, if you did not."

Peter sighed. "The first hour," he promised. He did not know what else to say. Millicent had put a great deal of time and effort into organising the event, and it would feel churlish not to attend.

"Thank you! Now, I must hurry down. Edmund! Have you seen my shawl?" she called out to her husband.

"Where did you put it?" he asked a little condescendingly.

Peter pushed the thoughts of his sister away, and tried, with them, to push away all the thoughts that preyed on his mind. His mind had been in turmoil all morning, since he and George rode to the village. He wanted to focus on the ball and the guests; on enjoying himself and doing some justice to Millicent's intense preparations. But Charles and Eliza hung like spectres on the edge of his thoughts, and with them mingled thoughts of Penelope Matthews.

"What am I supposed to do?" he murmured to himself as he went slowly downstairs.

He could not do anything about Charles and Eliza's murder—not until Mr Irving returned from London with the news that he had some information that could lead to the conviction of a suspect. And he had absolutely no idea what he was supposed to do about Miss Matthews. He knew what he wanted to do, which was to run to Ireland with her; but that was impossible in reality.

"Peter! Still warm, eh?" George asked as Peter spotted him in the hallway. Peter shrugged.

"I suppose," he replied. With all the other discomforts of the evening, the stifling heat in his evening clothes had slipped his mind.

Peter went to the door, waiting for Millicent and Edmund, who would join him in welcoming the guests. George, who was a guest, waited with him.

"Oh! Peter! Just on time. George! You're early," Millicent greeted George. "Welcome! I hope you enjoy the evening." She gave him a sparkling smile. George bowed.

"Thank you, my lady," he said a little teasingly. He nodded to Edmund and then inclined his head to Peter, grinning at him supportively. "Have a good evening, old chap," he murmured on the way into the ballroom.

Peter inclined his head. "I will try," he promised his cousin, though he felt sure that he would have a horrid evening. He shifted uncomfortably from foot to foot, wishing that he could be elsewhere.

"Lady Winthrop! Lord Winthrop. And dear Lady Adeline," Millicent greeted the next guests to arrive. "How grand. I trust you had a pleasant afternoon?"

"It was too hot," Adeline said poutingly.

Peter winced. Even Millicent looked a little surprised by the frank and somewhat churlish answer. Lady Winthrop giggled.

"Oh, Adeline, dear! How droll. I am sure she's teasing you," she said to Millicent, who smiled.

"Good evening," Peter greeted the guests, bowing to each of them in turn.

"Good evening, my lord," Lady Adeline breathed. She was restored to her former self. Her smile glowed, her beautiful ballgown of blue muslin seeming to glow as well. He drew in a breath. When she chose to, she radiated charm that made her almost irresistible. If he had not been aware of her self-absorbed and calculating side, he would have believed her as lovely as society claimed and simply felt guilty and stupid for failing to fall for her as so many others had. He watched as she drifted downstairs, a vision in blue, her thick black hair piled in an elegant chignon decorated with silver pins.

More guests arrived and he bowed and greeted them politely, the mannerly exchanges seeming false and meaningless to him. He could think of nothing besides Charles and Eliza, his mind going over the facts that Mr Irving had told them.

"That's almost everyone," Millicent whispered as Peter straightened from a bow, the guests drifting past and to the stairs.

Peter slumped for a moment, relief washing through him. He felt tense and the strain of having to pretend that nothing troubled him was almost unbearable.

The last guests drifted in. He stumbled back wearily as the butler came to close the doors.

"Peter! You really are unwell," Millicent whispered to him, her brow lowering with concern.

"Perhaps you should retire to your chamber," Edmund murmured. His gaze was hard. Peter frowned. Edmund had been decidedly strange all day; moody and withdrawn, barely speaking to anyone. Peter had caught him looking oddly in his own direction once or twice; an unreadable but certainly not pleasant look in his eyes.

Perdition may take the fellow! he thought crossly, pushing the worry away. Edmund was the last thing he needed intruding into his thoughts. He had far too much to worry about as it was.

"I agreed to stay for an hour," Peter replied firmly. He glanced at Millicent, who smiled.

"I say! It's hot in here," George murmured, wandering over as Peter tried to think of something to say. "Fancy a drink, old chap? I do."

"Yes, that would be very pleasant," Peter replied, giving George a grateful smile.

They wandered over to the refreshments table together.

Peter helped himself to a glass of lemonade. He wanted to keep a level head. He sipped it and, as he stared out over the ballroom, Lord and Lady Winthrop drifted over to join him. He tensed.

"Such a lovely ball!" Lady Winthrop gushed. "Your sister is excellent at organising entertainments."

"She is," Peter agreed, his voice level.

"The music was so fashionable at the previous ball," Lady Adeline replied, drifting up to join them. Peter bowed in polite acknowledgement. Etiquette had been schooled into him as a child, so that, when his entire mind was elsewhere and his soul was focused on anything and everything else, he could still manage to function politely, if in a detached, empty sort of way.

"It was. I will pass the compliment on to my sister," he said seriously.

"Please do!" Lady Adeline replied with a big smile.

"I wonder if the music today will be as controversial, in terms of dances?" Lady Winthrop mused. "Are there any waltzes planned?" she asked Peter. Peter smiled, but inside he groaned. He knew that they expected him to dance with Lady Adeline. His mind was racing.

"May I reserve the Polonaise?" he asked Lady Adeline. It was a lively dance, but nowhere near as intimate as a waltz. He could just manage a Polonaise.

"Oh! Yes, of course," Lady Adeline replied. She held out a hand to her mother, who passed her a pencil from the drawstring purse that she carried. Lady Adeline scrawled something on the dance-card that hung from her wrist. It was, Peter noticed, feeling less guilty, already quite full.

He chatted with them distantly, making polite replies without really listening to anything that they said. His gaze scanned the ballroom. Millicent and Edmund were at the far end. Millicent looked happy; Edmund seemed his usual self, except that he was even more withdrawn and quiet than usual.

"It is frightfully hot in here," Lady Winthrop murmured.

"Yes, it is. Might I fetch you ladies some lemonade?" Peter asked, using the statement as a way to escape.

"Oh! How gallant! What an exemplary fellow!" Lady Winthrop exclaimed.

Peter blushed and bowed, hurrying away.

When he had returned with the lemonade and with George in tow, he managed to extricate himself more easily.

"I am going to stay until the Polonaise," he whispered to George. "And then I shall go upstairs to rest. I feel quite indisposed."

"Of course, old fellow," George replied easily. "I'll stay a little longer. The music is good," he added, inclining his head towards the musicians, who had begun playing a quadrille. Peter sighed, glad that he had managed to escape some of the dancing.

The Polonaise, bright and lively, was played after the long, solemn quadrille, bringing some light relief to the ball guests. Peter danced it, amazed as he had been before by Lady Adeline's skill. She was a beautiful woman and a skilled dancer and he noticed more than one man watching him with undisguised dislike as he whirled with her around the ballroom. It might have amused him, or even made him feel proud to be dancing with a desirable woman; but rather, all he felt was sorrowful. He did not want to be dancing with her. He wished he could be dancing with Miss Matthews.

As he bowed low, an overwhelming weariness slammed into him. He smiled at her, but she frowned.

"Are you quite well?" she asked him.

"I am a little indisposed," he commented. "If you will excuse me, my lady. I think I must lie down."

"Oh! Someone should send for the physician!" she exclaimed, her gaze moving over the ballroom. Peter shook his head.

"No. Please. No physician is needed," he said swiftly, heart thudding. "I am just extremely tired. Matters of business tired me out, I am afraid," he added, making a vague gesture towards his study at the top of the house. "Please forgive me, my lady; and enjoy your evening." He bowed again.

"Oh. I suppose I must excuse you, then," she commented a little ungraciously. "Stay well."

"I will, my lady," Peter promised. "And thank you for the dance."

"Thank you, my lord."

Peter walked as fast as he could through the ballroom. His head pounded and he felt weary and lightheaded. He reached the entranceway and sat down heavily on one of the padded seats by the entrance. He felt sick.

As he sat in the cooler air, the music distant and the chatter and laughter almost too far away to hear behind the thick ballroom doors, the oppressive headache cleared. He blinked, feeling a little better.

He shifted on the chair, about to stand.

"Nephew!" a voice said from his right, making him spin sharply round, getting to his feet. The hasty movement made him lightheaded, the room spinning. "Oh, my dear nephew. Are you well?"

"I am well, dear Aunt," Peter managed to say to Aunt Marcia, who stood before him. He had to try to focus on her face, which was turned up towards him with a frown of worry on her furrowed brow.

"Are you certain?" she asked softly. "Sophia saw you earlier. She said you looked sick. You're very pale, nephew," she added concernedly.

"Just tiredness," Peter demurred. "I already feel better," he added, which was true.

Aunt Marcia looked at him; a long look with those wise blue eyes.

"You know, nephew," she said after a quiet pause. "One secret I can tell you, now that I am the age that I am, is that life is not infinite. It's far too short, in fact." She sighed. She looked sad, her eyes unfocused. "It is certainly too short to make decisions that we think will make everyone else happy. All we can truly know is what would make us happy, after all."

"Perhaps," Peter said lightly. He could not let himself think too carefully about her words—they stirred a wild joy within him, opening a world that had been shut away by his own sense of rightness.

"We should not choose what we think others want us to. We don't really know what they want," Aunt Marcia continued. "You deserve happiness, nephew. Wild happiness. All the happiness you never allowed yourself."

Peter looked at her in surprise. His heart jolted, feeling again the joy that he knew he could not permit himself.

"I have duties, Aunt," he said quietly. He was not sure who he was trying to convince—her or himself.

"Duties to do what you think others want of you?" Aunt Marcia demanded. "No, nephew. Duty should not dictate what we do, or one day we will turn around and blame all of those who put that duty on our shoulders for ruining our lives. Duty creates only bitterness and resentment, and for what? For nothing. Allow yourself happiness. Do what is written in the longings of your heart. That is where our true story is inscribed; the story meant for us."

Peter gaped at her. She seemed to be urging him towards Miss Matthews, but she could not possibly be. She could not know of the kiss. She could not have guessed the secrets of his heart. Yet her advice filled him with joy as precious as the most beautiful flowers in his greenhouse. He bowed low.

"I thank you for your advice, Aunt Marcia," he murmured, meaning every word. "If you will excuse me, now, however, I must go and rest. Please give my regards to Sophia and I hope that both of you enjoy the evening."

"I shall, nephew. And take care." Her voice was tender.

"Yes, Aunt," Peter replied. "Thank you," he murmured again.

He walked up the stairs to his chamber, his head reeling. The terrible feeling of sickness had worn off, replaced with a confusion that was almost as debilitating. He could almost believe that Aunt Marcia was speaking of Miss Matthews, about his feelings for her and how he should follow them, and yet how could she be? It was altogether too impossible.

He exhaled sharply, running a hand over his face. "What am I to do?" he murmured as he pulled off his shoes and lay down fully dressed upon the bed.

He shut his eyes, the headache that had plagued him for most of the ball returning to oppress him. His last thought as he drifted off to sleep was of Miss Matthews and that sweet kiss. And, for one aching moment, he wished that he could do as his aunt had suggested.

Chapter 23

"Flower! Flower." Thomas repeated, reaching with a small, plump hand for the flowers that stood in the middle of the table in a porcelain vase. Penelope chuckled.

"Yes! Yes. It's a flower, Thomas. Quite so," she affirmed. The little child gurgled in delight. In the past few days, he had been using words more and more; asking for what he wanted by name. He seemed more relaxed and happier and Penelope rejoiced to see it.

"Want," he told her. He pointed at the rose in the vase.

Penelope laughed. "You can't have it, little fellow," she said with a smile. "It's thorny." She pointed to the stem of the red rose, where spikes were evident above the edge of the porcelain container. "You can have a jam tart, if you want? Would you like one?" She gestured to the small plate of jam tarts that she and Anna had shared for afternoon tea. She had welcomed Anna's bright presence in the nursery—it was a welcome distraction from her own confused, tumultuous thoughts.

"Yes!" the little boy yelled. Penelope laughed.

"I shouldn't give you too many," she told him with a smile. "Or you shan't be able to sleep and you'll have a poorly stomach."

"Want," Thomas repeated.

Penelope laughed and passed him a tartlet—just the size of a gold sovereign—filled with jam. He grabbed it and stuffed it into his mouth, grinning blissfully. Penelope smiled.

When Thomas was awake, it was impossible for any dark thoughts to surface in her mind. He was a source of endless joy. But when he slept and the nursery was silent, it was hard not to be sunk in worries.

If the earl blames me for what happened, then he might send me away. I cannot risk getting sent away, she thought with a frown.

She wished that she had seen him again after that moment in the nursery, but he had not come to check on Thomas once, and she had not seen him in the hallway or even in the garden.

As Thomas leaned back contentedly, his mouth covered with pastry crumbs, Penelope reached to wipe at his face with a clean handkerchief. He chuckled and she laughed, making it a game. He ducked and she moved left, then jinked right, wiping the side of his face with the cloth. He shrieked and giggled.

A knock sounded at the door as she went to lift him to put him on the hearthrug. She frowned.

"Who is it?" she called. It was probably Anna, she guessed, coming to fetch the plate; but it sounded different to her usual swift, bright knock and she hesitated to open the door, unsure of who was there.

"It's Mrs Hallden," the older lady who was the manor's housekeeper called through the door. "May I come in? I have an urgent message."

"Of course," Penelope said at once, putting Thomas on the mat and hurrying to the door. Thomas sat where she had put him, seeming bewildered. He could clearly sense the agitation in the room.

"I am sorry to disturb," Mrs Hallden said carefully. "But a messenger brought this post-haste. I had to bring it to you immediately."

"Thank you," Penelope replied, her frown deepening. She could not imagine why anyone would have sent her a letter, much less post-haste. Her first thought was for Emily. She took the letter, thanked Mrs Hallden again, and hurriedly opened it. It did not bear a seal, and the writing was not a hand she recognised.

Her gaze moved down the letter swiftly.

My dear daughter, she read. *I asked Mrs White to help me with writing this letter because I am almost too ill to sit up. I trust you are well and I hesitate to disturb either you or Emily in your current places of employment. However, the physician assures me that this illness is of a serious nature. Much as I do not wish to disturb, it would mean an immeasurable amount to me were you and Emily to join me at the house at this time. I would welcome an opportunity to see you both again. Yours sincerely, your father.*

Penelope held the letter tight. Her heart jumped, pain lancing into her chest. It could not be! Her father could not be so ill. And yet, she could not disbelieve it. She recognised the script of Mrs White, their neighbour, who was the teacher in the village school. If Father had asked for her assistance in writing the letter, he must indeed be very, very sick.

"He wants to see us before he..." her throat stopped, unable to say it. He had written to call them back home, lest he pass away. She knew it. Mrs Hallden had departed and Penelope sank into the chair by the fire, heart twisting with grief and pain. She had to go.

"But what about Thomas?"

The little child was playing with blocks by the fire. He had blossomed in the last few weeks; going from the frightened, tense child who cried frequently and could not bear to be left unattended, to a confident, playful boy who ventured off by himself and talked to her as he explored the world.

"If I go, you will be frightened again," she murmured. It was too clear that the child's anxiety had been because of his parents' sudden death. Another loss would break him, undoing all the progress he had made. Her heart was sore.

She gazed out of the window. It was almost dinnertime, the sun low on the horizon, close to setting. The garden was awash with rich orange-gold light, the sky cooling to a whitish blue, darkening at the edges.

She glanced back to Thomas. He was playing happily with his blocks, and her heart twisted painfully. She needed to think, but here in the nursery, with the little child right beside her, she could not think clearly. Her father needed her, but one glance at the cherubic little baby and she could not even think of going home.

"I need to go outside," she said softly. She looked around. Someone could summon Mrs Aldham or another maid to sit with Thomas for a few minutes. She just needed a moment or two for thought.

Simply opening the door revealed a maid tidying in the hallway. Penelope called to her.

"Could you please fetch Mrs Aldham?" she asked the maid, who was little more than a girl; perhaps fifteen.

"Oh! Oh, of course, miss," she replied. "I must just brush this dirt aside before someone steps in it," she added.

"Of course. Thank you for helping me," Penelope replied, feeling a little guilty. The young woman rushed off and Penelope went back to the chair to wait. Thomas turned around and grinned at her, gurgling happily as he dropped a block on the mat, knocking two others that he had piled. He chuckled with delight and piled them again, then repeated the action.

Penelope laughed.

"Miss Matthews?" a voice called through the door. Penelope stood and hurried to it.

"Yes, Mrs Aldham," Penelope replied. "I am so sorry to disturb you," she added, stepping aside so that the older woman might enter. "But if you have some time, might I ask you to sit with Thomas? Just for a few minutes, I promise. I have to fetch something in the garden."

"Oh. Of course, miss. Just a few minutes, mind. I have to go to the kitchen later to help with the banquet."

"Of course. Thank you," Penelope replied, heart full of gratitude. "I'll not be more than ten minutes," she assured the older woman. Ten minutes, she reckoned, would be more than enough. All she wanted was time to gather her thoughts and frame a reply to her father.

Mrs Aldham sat down by the fire and Penelope explained swiftly to Thomas that Mrs Aldham would watch him while she went downstairs. Then she hurried away.

The garden was cool and she drew her shawl about her shoulders, grateful that she had thought to bring it with her. The air smelled of dew and the sun had set, a blue dusk hanging over the lawns. Penelope's stomach rumbled. It was almost time for dinner. She walked lightly down the path, hurrying towards the rose garden.

Her feet led her to the secluded area near the fountain where she had been sitting that afternoon when she and the earl had spoken in the gardens. Her heart ached.

"I cannot go home," she murmured. The thought of leaving—of not seeing the earl—pained her more than she cared to admit. She longed for clarity, to understand his feelings, to find some resolution. Even a single day away felt unbearable.

And yet, how could she hesitate? Her father's face drifted into her mind—pinched and drawn, just as it had been the last time she saw him. He had been unwell then, his illness the very reason she and Emily had sought employment. Their wages had been necessary to pay for his care, as his stipend alone had never been enough.

If he was now calling for her, if he truly believed the end was near, how much worse must his condition have grown? A pang of guilt tightened in her chest. However much she wished to stay, her place was by her father's side—not only because he needed her, but because she could not bear the thought of failing him now.

She wandered to a bench and sat down, tears running down her cheeks. She had found a home at Brentdale—a child, a dear friend, and a man who fascinated and drew her towards him. She had never imagined finding so much. And yet, she could hardly—and would not want to—turn her back on the home she already had. Emily was there, and Father. She needed to go there.

She exhaled shakily, pressing her hands together as though grounding herself. "There must be a way," she whispered into the silence. "Some way to make this right."

The sky was darker than it had been, a rich sapphire blue in which the first stars showed. She tipped her head back, gazing up. The scent of the dew was cool and damp in her nostrils. A cricket sang once, a brief trill, and then was silent. The stillness was absolute.

Penelope frowned. The stillness had been absolute, but, when she listened closely, she could hear a human voice. It was not far from her, and it seemed to be coming nearer. It was a male voice and she instinctively shrank back into the arbour, hiding herself from direct view of the path. The voice—whoever it was—sounded angry and embittered and she felt afraid of it.

"...he knows. I know he knows!" the voice raged. Footsteps drew closer and Penelope gasped, realising that the man was walking along the path that headed to the fountain. She looked around for an escape, but the roses grew on all sides and it would be impossible to slip quietly away. She would need to blunder through the flowerbeds and her skirts would get snagged by the rose branches. She stayed where she was. The voice drew closer.

"That wretched investigator," the man hissed.

Penelope frowned. That made no sense. What investigator? She froze where she was, hidden behind a trellis of climbing roses.

"He knows. I heard it all!" the man said quite loudly. Penelope tensed, sure that there must be another person strolling with whoever spoke, but when the speaker continued, it was the same voice. "He did not see me, but I followed him. And now I know the truth. It's only a matter of time. They are hunting me."

Penelope tensed. There was a strange note in the person's voice. That they were not sober, she did not doubt. She could smell brandy and she realised that whoever it was must be standing very close.

"Damn that Peter Blakefield," the voice hissed. "It should all be mine."

Penelope frowned again. Blakefield was a surname she recognised. It was the surname of the family she worked for, the personal surname of the Earls of Brentdale. Was Peter the current Earl? She strained to hear. What the person was saying might affect the earl.

"It should be mine," the voice slurred. "And it will be. When I find a way to get him. It should have been him. Damn that coach," he swore again.

Penelope's brow creased. What coach? What the man was saying made no sense and she longed to see who it was. She risked taking a step forward when there was a snatch of silence.

"If that damned Charles had not been in the coach that night, it would be done. I would be in charge here. I would be in charge and all my debts would be paid."

Penelope's blood went cold. She understood all too well what he was saying. The coach was the one that the earl's cousin had borrowed. He had been attacked in the coach, but he had not been the intended target. The earl had been. This man, the one in the clearing just a few feet away, had been the plotter who had sent the killers. He had wanted to kill the earl.

Penelope took a deep breath. She had to see who it was. Whoever it was, they intended to kill the earl. She had to tell him. Had to warn him. She took another step forward and stuck her head around the trellis. She could see a silhouetted figure just five paces away. It was too dark to see his face clearly and she stepped forward again. A twig cracked. The man's head jerked up sharply.

Penelope froze. He was looking straight at her.

"You!" the man hissed. Penelope tried to scream, but her throat was tight, her mouth dry. Her legs buckled and she almost lost control of her bladder.

She could not take a step. She could not run. "You were spying on me. You heard me."

"No," Penelope whispered. His voice chilled her blood, the threat of violence strong in every syllable he said. She could not think. She could not move. The only word that came to her mind was "no". She repeated it, tears of pure terror running down her face as the man approached. "No. No, no."

His expression was a mask of hate, his eyes slitted with rage. "You'll run off and tell him." His voice allowed no argument.

"No," Penelope said in a hushed tone. "No. Please." Tears continued falling.

"You'll run off and tell him and ruin everything," the man raged. He towered over her. He was quite tall; around as tall as the earl. In the part of her mind that was not frozen in terror and able to think, Penelope was sure that she had seen him walking with the other guests. He was part of the earl's house party.

The man was towering over her and he had a wooden staff in his hand that she had not noticed before. She squinted at it in terror. It was a walking cane, or perhaps the handle of a rake or a spade.

"No," she whispered, sure that he was about to hit her.

"You'll tell him and ruin me!" the man shouted.

"No!" Penelope screamed. The ability to move returned and she tried to run, but the man was much faster—too fast. The blow came hard and swift. The wooden staff struck her skull with brutal force, pain exploding through her head. A sharp cry tore from her lips as her hands flew up, instinctively grasping at the wound.

Then, the world blurred. Blackness swarmed at the edges of her vision, swallowing her whole.

And everything went dark.

Chapter 24

"Peter, dear... do come away from the window and join us?" Millicent murmured. "Dinner is about to be served."

Peter turned from the window, where blue dusk was just settling on the estate garden, to where his sister stood a few inches away. The drawing room was packed with chattering, laughing guests. His head hurt and he stayed by the window, staring out into the garden, which was just cloaked in blueish dusk.

"I feel ill," he insisted.

Millicent sighed. "I know. I do wish you would see the physician. You've felt ill since yesterday evening. Adeline was most upset that you left the ball early, though she did her best not to show it." Millicent looked at him a little crossly.

Peter sighed. "I am sorry, sister. But I cannot help it," he replied, feeling a trifle impatient. His head truly did ache and he was starting to suspect that he might have caught a fever; though he had no other ills to speak of besides the pain in his head and he was sure that was mostly from worrying.

He could not stop thinking about Miss Matthews. Beyond even the news from the investigator, it was his concern about what had happened that plagued his thoughts. He could not regret it—the kiss was beautiful, magical. And yet, it tormented his dreams. What if she had taken offence? Aunt Marcia had hinted at an unfair dismissal in Miss Matthews' past. What if part of the unfair treatment had been the unwanted attentions of her employer? He had done something that could have hurt and offended her greatly. And yet he still could not feel remorse or regret. It was still too wonderful. He shook his head to clear it, realising that Millicent was talking and he had not heard anything she said. He tried to focus.

"Do come and join us for dinner? The staff have been working all day on the banquet and it took me an age to plan it all," she said a little crossly. "It is in honour of a special occasion, after all," she added, raising a brow.

Peter inclined his head. "I know," he said wearily. "I will come down, but please do not be offended if I depart early," he added. Millicent looked up at him, eyes wide and mouth set in a tight, irritated line.

"You've been departing early all week, brother. I do wish you'd see a physician. If you are ill, he can cure you."

Peter sighed. What he had could not be cured, and he knew that. The worry and guilt that the investigator's report had called up in him, combined with his pain and concern about kissing Miss Matthews, were not curable.

"All I need is bed-rest and some peace and quiet," Peter insisted.

His sister made a small, exasperated sound, turning away. "I need to organize the guests. We will proceed downstairs. Do try and stay for the banquet, at least until the fish course has been served."

Peter nodded. He was genuinely not sure if he would be able to eat anything—he felt too sick and he had no desire for food. But he did owe his sister something for all her intense effort and he would sit there if she wished it, even if he could not so much as taste a spoon of soup.

"I will try," he promised.

Millicent smiled gratefully at him and he watched as she moved to the door, subtly gathering the higher-ranking guests in her wake. While he insisted that dinners were informal, Millicent and Edmund could not loosen their rigid London manners and she insisted that the guests depart the drawing room in order of rank—the highest-ranking first, and the hosts last, as was proper. Peter stood back to wait. The guests began to move to the door, drifting out into the hallway.

As Peter walked downstairs with Millicent beside him, he frowned. Edmund should have been with them. When he thought about it, he realised that he had barely seen the fellow all day. He had only seen him once or twice for the last two days—Millicent said that he was off riding by himself quite often.

"Odd," he murmured.

The door to the dining room was open and he went inside. The candlelight was blinding, shining, as it did, off clean white tablecloths and glittering on polished silverware and candleholders. Peter winced. It made his head hurt.

He took his seat at the head of the table, Millicent on his left. Lord and Lady Winthrop had managed to take the place closest to him on the other side, with Lady Adeline on his right. He winced. His head started to pound.

He took his seat at the head of the table, Millicent on his left. Lord and Lady Winthrop had managed to take the place closest to him on the other side, with Lady Adeline on his right. He winced. His head started to pound.

"My lord! Are you feeling quite well?"

Peter shook his head, but the motion only worsened the throbbing in his skull. The headache that had hovered at the edge of his awareness all evening was now pressing in with full force, growing almost unbearable. He turned to Millicent, who he could see was looking distressed. He could barely make out the details around him, everything blurring with the pain in his head.

"Please excuse me," he murmured. "I am sorry, Millicent. But my headache is worse than I thought. I must rest."

"Brother, of course," Millicent replied. "Please let me send for a physician?" she asked. Peter bit his lip. He had never heard the genuine care in his sister's voice before and his heart twisted. He had assumed her motive for having a party was mostly self-serving—preserving the family's status in society, and thereby assuring her own status as well—but it seemed as though perhaps she really cared.

"I am sorry, Millicent," he repeated caringly. "But I must go somewhere cooler and quieter for a moment. I will try to come back as soon as I feel well. Please start the meal in my absence," he added. He pushed back his chair and stood, hurrying out of the room.

The entranceway was too bright, the noise from the dining room still audible, even if as a low burr of sound from inside. He walked half-blind to the windows near the library, his head pounding. The library shared part of the terrace with the ballroom and he walked in, then out through the big doors and into the coolness of the garden.

"Just some rest," he promised himself. Then he would return to the dining room and try to appreciate all Millicent's effort.

He leaned on the railing of the terrace. The garden was cool and still, the blue dusk just settling. He could see across to the trees that grew densely around the big lawn, screening the rose garden from the house. He frowned. There was movement there. The guests were all inside, yet he could have sworn that he saw a person moving slowly and laboriously down the path that led from the rose garden. He narrowed his eyes, heart pounding. His first thought was that it was a burglar or a brigand.

He strained his eyes to see the considerable distance across the lawn towards the thicket of trees where the figure was headed. There it was again—a jerking, uneven motion, as though the man was pushing a heavy barrow, or dragging something across the lawn right at the back, where the garden met the trees. His first thought was that it must be a gardener, but he dismissed it instantly. No gardener would be working—why would they, when it was increasingly impossible to see what one did? The darkness would fall in a matter of minutes, the blue night slowly swallowing the colours. Peter narrowed his eyes again, watching. He could see the man fairly well—he had brown—mayhap chestnut—hair and he was wearing a white shirt that stood out sharply against the blue-black scenery around him, and dark trousers.

Peter looked down towards the object that the man was dragging. It was white, and lay low on the ground—certainly not a wheelbarrow, nor a pile of twigs or leaves. He gazed in horror as, suddenly, it became clear what it was.

It was a human body.

A woman's body.

"No!" He tried to shout, but his throat tightened, and only a hoarse whisper escaped.

Long, dark hair spilled across the shadowed ground, unbound and tangled. She was not tall, but nor was she short, her slender form dressed in a white uniform. Recognition struck him with a force greater than any blow.

Miss Matthews.

His stomach turned violently, horror clawing at his chest. Was she breathing? Was she alive?

His pulse roared in his ears as he sprang forward, panic and fury propelling him across the lawn. He had to reach her before it was too late.

Chapter 25

Penelope blinked.

The first thing she noticed was that the world was no longer black but a deep, endless blue—the sky stretching above her. The second was the unsettling sensation of movement, the cold earth scraping against her back as she was dragged along, faster than was comfortable.

Then came the third realisation—someone was pulling her. By the ankles.

Panic surged through her, tightening her throat. She fought the urge to scream, forcing herself to stay silent, to think.

"It's not right. It's not fair," a man was muttering. Penelope lay very still. Memory flooded back. The man was the one who had hit her into unconsciousness; the one who had tried to silence her because she had overheard his confession to a murder.

A cold dread settled over her, far sharper than the ache in her skull. She was in mortal danger.

The man was dragging her under the trees. She had no doubt that he intended to murder her. He could not risk that she would tell someone what she had heard him saying. *Perhaps,* she thought wildly, *he believes me dead, and he is planning to bury me.* She sobbed aloud in fear and the man stopped pulling for a moment. His voice changed.

"You're awake?" he demanded.

Penelope did not respond. She lay perfectly still, her mind warring between two fears—the fear of alerting him to her consciousness and the equally chilling terror that he might not yet realise she was alive.

Neither fear made it any easier to move or speak. Her body felt frozen, her breath shallow. She remained motionless, too frightened to utter a single word.

"No, not awake," the man muttered and began dragging her again. Her head jolted, and she winced with pain, but some instinct told her to keep still, not to move or utter a sound. She obeyed it in spite of the knowledge that it might be safer or better if he knew she was alive. "Damn you," the man swore, making her blood freeze with the hate in his tone. "You're just another one of those trying to make life hard for me."

Penelope said nothing, but he had stopped dragging her for a moment, and she tried to think. She could smell the damp, rich earth, the smell of water even stronger than the earlier, cold scent of dew in her nostrils. She shut her eyes and listened. She could hear water, too; the slow, rushing voice of a river. Horror chilled her. Was he planning to throw her in? She could not swim. His hands were still at her ankles but her terror of drowning was greater than her terror of anything else he might do and she jerked back, struggling to free her legs from his grasp. He swore and grabbed at her uniform, keeping hold of one leg.

"You are alive, after all," he said in a cold, heartless tone. "But not for long. You heard me. How soon before that rat Peter knows, eh? I know... you'll go running off to tell him. Edmund is a murderer, you'll say. He ordered your cousins killed. All I need to do is break your silly neck, and then no one will stand in my way."

His voice was trembling, something almost like madness in his tone. "Bet you didn't know that if an earl dies without a son, his wealth—at least, what isn't entailed—passes to his next of kin, eh? With Peter gone, Millicent inherits everything that can be transferred, and as her husband, that fortune will be mine. No more debts, no more creditors hounding me. A comfortable life, all within my grasp. But you had to interfere."

He let go of her ankle and bent down, kneeling on the grass. Penelope gasped in terror and shot backwards, trying to find her feet, to stand up. Her legs were weak, her ankles sore from being pulled and her right leg buckled, bringing her collapsing to the ground.

She screamed as his hands closed around her throat, fingers tightening like a vice. The sound was cut off instantly, strangled into silence as she fought desperately for breath.

"Just a few seconds, and then I'll have it all," the man was shouting. "First you, then Peter—once he's gone, it will all be mine. I'll finally have what I deserve. The wealth, the freedom, everything that was denied to me."

Penelope struggled to breathe. Her vision was becoming grey, her head pounding, coughs and gasps struggling to rise in her throat. She could not breathe. Terror swamped her senses.

"He had everything," the man snarled, his face contorted with rage. "The fortune, the name, the power. It should have been mine. Penelope stopped being able to hear. Her body was writhing, her head throbbing and she could not see; her vision blacking out. She could not release herself from his hold, and she began to weaken. She was sure she was going to die. She hated the idea. She did not want to go. She wanted to stay; to see Thomas grow bigger. To see Emily again. To see her father.

Suddenly, without warning, she tumbled over backwards, the hands released from her throat. Air rushed into her lungs in a great, rasping breath, but it brought little relief—her body convulsed as she coughed violently, gasping and choking, her throat raw and burning. Mucus and tears streamed down her face as she lay curled on her side in the damp grass, her body wracked with shuddering breaths.

Slowly—painfully—her senses began to return. Her thoughts cleared, piece by piece, and with them came the awareness of her surroundings, of the cold earth beneath her, of the desperate, aching relief of simply being able to breathe again.

"You scoundrel!" someone was shouting. It was a voice she knew, although it was so full of anger that she barely recognised it. It was the earl, she realised slowly. He was there. He must have been the one who knocked her away, or who knocked the man over. She had no idea what had happened.

"Get your hands off me," the other man was snarling as her attention returned to the moment.

"You were trying to kill her. You were trying to kill Miss Matthews," the earl yelled. "I'll not take my hands off you until the village Watch can be summoned to arrest you."

"You wretch," the other man yelled.

Penelope rolled onto her side, blinking against the darkness. The night was so black that she could make out only the shadowy forms of the two men locked in a desperate struggle.

The man who had attacked her—the one who had nearly taken her life—was in his shirtsleeves. The earl, distinguishable by his dark jacket, fought fiercely against him.

As she watched, horror tightening in her chest, her attacker twisted sharply, using his weight to roll sideways and throw the earl onto his back.

A strangled cry rose in her throat, but no sound came. Her limbs felt heavy, her body too weak to respond. Her head throbbed viciously, and when she tried to push herself up, her strength failed her. Instead, she rolled aside, desperate to avoid being caught in the fray.

As she watched, the two men fought. They were a few feet away, wrestling in the grass. The earl reached up, clawing at the man's face, and, when he yelled out in pain, he turned sharply sideways, tumbling the man in the white shirt onto his back. The earl righted himself immediately and she heard a loud crack as he punched the fellow.

"You could have killed her!" the earl was shouting. "Perhaps you have." He was sobbing, Penelope realised, and as he drew back his fist to slam into the other man again, she coughed and spat.

"Here..." she tried to say. Her voice was weak and rasping, but he must have heard her because he stopped with his fist about to strike and turned to gape at her.

"Is that you?" His voice was shrill with amazement.

"Yes..." Penelope whispered. She could barely speak.

The earl let out a sound like a sob, and Penelope almost cried out as the man he had cornered tried to get up. The earl hit him again, and he fell back, apparently unconscious. After a second or two, the earl risked moving. He crawled over to where Penelope lay.

"Miss Matthews?" he whispered. His breath was rasping, and Penelope reached out to him. His hair was wet with sweat, plastered to his forehead. She could not see him clearly, just make out his face in pale blue-greys in the dusky light. His dark brown hair framed his face, clinging to his brow. His eyes were damp. His face was just two inches away from her own. She managed to smile at him. He gazed at her in wonder. He reached over and rested his hand on her cheek. She gazed into his eyes, her own filling with tears.

"You saved me."

He shook his head. "You almost died," he whispered. "I almost lost you."

Penelope gazed at him in amazement. She had never imagined that he could care about her—that he did care about her. She had seen longing in his eyes, but—even though it had never seemed lecherous or felt wrong, it had been too easy to dismiss it as such. She had never allowed herself to truly believe that he actually cared.

"Thank you," she whispered.

The earl coughed, then chuckled. "That is a very proper thing to say at such a time," he said, grinning. "May I say that it is my pleasure?"

Penelope breathed out slowly. The way he said the word lit fires that she did not fully understand somewhere deep inside, but she was far too tired to do anything about those feelings, and she chuckled, then coughed.

"My throat hurts," she whispered.

"I am sure." The earl's smile tensed. "You should see a physician. I have no idea how much damage that scoundrel succeeded in doing, but you should be properly tended."

"I'm... quite well," Penelope rasped. She rolled over, trying to sit up. She did not want to go anywhere. She did not want to see anyone. All she wanted was to stay there, lying on the dew-wet grass with his face inches from her own.

"Whoa," the earl said gently, rolling so that he was sitting hunched on the grass beside her. "Careful. You've taken quite a blow—you shouldn't be trying to move around."

Penelope grinned. He was sitting beside her, his shoulder next to hers, so close that the warmth of his arm seemed to seep through to her own skin through his coat.

"I can move," she managed to say. He shook his head.

"You shouldn't. You're shivering. Have my coat." He shrugged it off and draped it around her shoulders. Penelope drew it close, holding it shut around herself. It warmed her instantly.

"Thank you," she whispered.

"You need to get indoors," the earl said gently. "But we also need to take care of him. I will tie his hands and feet and then escort you in. Then we need to fetch the village Watch."

"You are also not well," Penelope managed as the earl crawled towards the unmoving man who lay on the grass.

"I am quite well," the earl answered. He had removed his cravat, and he was using it to tie the man's hands. As she watched, he removed one of his own silk stockings and tied the man's feet together with it. Then he rolled over and crawled back to where she lay.

"Can you stand?" he asked.

"I will try to." Penelope pressed down on the earth, managing to push herself up into a crouch and then slowly to standing. Her head spun, and little flares of light danced in front of her as she stood up. She gasped and almost fell.

"Whoa," the earl said gently, steadying himself as he stood. He reached for her, and she, too weak to hold herself upright, let go of the effort and leaned into him.

He did not pull away. Instead, he held her, his arms wrapping around her as if anchoring them both. For a long moment, neither of them moved—his body pressed against hers, solid and steady.

She clung to him, her arms tightening around his back, drawing him closer. A deep breath shuddered through her as she fought the overwhelming urge to weep—not from pain, but from sheer, unrelenting relief. It had been terrifying.

"Shh," the earl murmured gently as her tears ran. He was crying too, she realised; a stifled sob sounding where his head leaned against her own.

"I thought I was going to die," she whispered. "And that dreadful man was going to kill you." That had been another one of her fears—if she was killed, she could not warn the earl.

"He tried," the earl said with a small smile. "What I cannot forgive him is that he sought to harm you. The scoundrel! The wretched, vile scoundrel." His voice was full of rage.

"He tried," she whispered.

The earl laughed. He gazed into her eyes. "You are right. He tried. But he did not succeed. You're rather resilient, Miss Matthews."

"As are you, Lord Brentdale."

"Peter. Call me Peter," he said firmly.

Penelope gaped at him. Her heart stopped. He could not mean that. He could not mean that she could use his name. She was a servant in his household; not truly a member of the gentry, let alone the nobility. She could not address him by his name. And yet...

"Please," he said firmly, when she said nothing. "Call me Peter."

"Peter," she whispered.

He smiled. "Good," he said. "And might I have the honour of knowing your name?" he asked her softly.

Penelope swallowed. "Penelope," she managed to say.

He grinned. "Thank you." He paused. "Thank you, Penelope."

Penelope did not say anything. She gazed into his eyes. The river was rushing past, the sound loud and roaring in her ears. Neither of them moved. It seemed as though everything stood still. He gazed into her eyes. His own were wide and darker than usual in the evening's darkness.

He leaned forward and she gasped as his lips pressed, briefly and swiftly, to her own. Her heart soared, love flooding her body and stealing her senses. She opened her eyes and stared at him.

"But—but..." she stammered.

"That is how I feel," he said firmly. His voice was tight with unspoken emotion. "Now, let us go into the house. It is cold out here and you are unwell."

Penelope followed him slowly across the lawn, too dazed to do anything else. She leaned against him; too unsteady to walk unsupported. He was limping, too, she realised. Neither of them was unhurt.

They walked slowly to the door. Penelope hesitated. She should not go through the front door—especially not without Thomas—but through the servants' entrance around the back of the house. He opened the door.

"Come on," he said gently.

"But..." Penelope stammered.

He looked at her wordlessly and she walked in.

The hallway was warm, almost hot, after the cold outside. She blinked; the light so bright it hurt. The butler appeared beside them, and a man Penelope distantly recognised. She blinked again to clear her vision, and she realised where she had seen him before. He had been the man she had seen when she and Anna were searching for the cart. The man Anna often talked to.

"Peter! There you are," the man began before the butler could say a word. "I heard shouts. We were worried about you. Whatever happened? Were you attacked by bandits?" He frowned. His gaze was worried.

"Almost," Peter said in a small voice. He glanced at Penelope. "Someone tried to strangle Penelope. I will tell you the particulars later. She needs help. We also need to summon the village Watch."

"Perdition! Someone tried to strangle her?" The man gaped at Peter. Then he nodded. "The Watch. Of course. I will see to it. Are these brigands still in the gardens?" he asked, frowning.

"One brigand. He is unconscious. I hope he remains so until the Watch arrives," Peter added. He turned to Penelope. "You need to go upstairs where it is warm."

Penelope hesitated. She did not want to disturb Thomas, though guilt suddenly flooded her. Mrs Aldham was watching him—she must have been watching him for almost half an hour. She had promised ten minutes only. She turned to go up the stairs.

"Wait," Peter motioned. He whispered something to the tall man, then turned to her. "I will come with you."

"Thank you," Penelope breathed. Guilt had driven her to hurry away, but in truth, she felt frightened. After being attacked and almost killed, she did not want to be alone.

Peter walked over and took her hand, leading her up the stairs. Penelope gaped at him, but she said nothing. Her heart was soaring, full of love, amazement and appreciation.

They walked slowly up the stairs.

The drawing room was empty. Peter gestured to her to go in. She walked in, feeling dazed. Cutlery and crockery were set out on a long table, along with a host of delicacies and drinks. The guests would retire into the drawing room after the meal. Penelope tensed, gazing at the fine furniture and silken wallpaper. She had never been in such a room. She turned to Peter, heart thudding.

"I shouldn't be here," she said awkwardly. "I need to go to Thomas." Her hands were mud-stained and she gazed at them worriedly.

"We will both go to Thomas in a moment," Peter said gently. "But for the moment, please, sit down and get warm. You have had a shock. You need to take some care of yourself."

Penelope nodded numbly. She gazed at him. In the bright light, she could see him clearly. His hair was wet with sweat. A bruise showed on his jaw. His shirt was loose at the neck where he had removed the cravat and his jacket and trousers were covered in mud and grass-stains. His grey eyes held hers; weary but with a level, intense gaze.

"Penelope," he murmured softly. "Are you hurt?"

She shook her head. "Just tired," she replied. She reached up to touch her brown hair, which had come loose from its chignon and cascaded around her shoulders, the strands wet and clinging to her sleeves. "I must look awful." Her face, she was sure, was swollen from crying and from the terrible coughing. He grinned.

"You are wet from the dew, and tired. But you look beautiful. You always look beautiful."

Penelope swallowed hard. Her heart hurt. She did not know what to say. She loved him with all her heart, and yet their love was impossible. Why acknowledge it when to do so would only cause pain? She looked down.

When she looked up again, he was still staring at her. She swallowed hard, taking a deep breath.

"Miss Penelope Matthews," Peter said, his voice low and gentle. "I love you. I wish you to know that. I know we are not meant to speak such things aloud. It is not done. But I cannot keep silent. I love you, and I do not care for the rules that would keep us apart. I want to share my life with you. If you wish it, I will walk away from the earldom. We can go to Ireland, where no one will know us, where no one will care about titles or propriety. I have savings enough for us to live comfortably—more than comfortably. If you would go with me, I would take you there in an instant.

His gaze was intent, his voice unwavering. "I love you, Penelope Matthews. I love you, and nothing else will do but for us to be together."

Penelope gaped at him. Her eyes filled with tears. He loved her? Truly loved her? He would turn his back on his world, on his status, on everything. He would walk away from the manor, from his family, from all the things he had been born to, for her? It was too much. It made no sense. She could not let him do it.

"Peter," she whispered. "I love you. I love you with all my heart. I love you more than I can ever say; more than I could ever imagine loving anybody. I want to be with you. I want it more than anything. But—but how can I? How can I make you walk away from all this? I cannot do it." She started to cry.

"Penelope. Penelope." He was inches away, his hand resting on her cheek. He reached up and wiped a tear away, gazing into her eyes. "I want to. I love you."

"But..." Penelope began. At that moment, the door burst open.

"Oh!" Peter's friend—the tall man who spoke with Anna and who had gone to summon the village Watch—gaped at them, cheeks reddening. "So sorry, Peter. I was just... I did not mean to interrupt. I wished to tell you that the stable hand is on his way to summon the village Watch. They should be here any moment. Whatever is the matter, Miss Matthews?" he asked gently, staring at her.

"Peter said he would give up the earldom for me, and I cannot let him!" Penelope blurted. She had not meant to say anything, but his kind gaze and caring words made it hard not to.

The tall man looked at Peter. Then he looked at Penelope. Then, suddenly, he started laughing.

"What?" Peter demanded. He sounded angry.

"Sorry, old chap!" His friend said, chuckling. "But you don't have to give up the earldom. You don't have to go anywhere. Penelope has noble blood. I can't believe nobody told you. Her grandfather was a baron. You don't need to give up anything. You can wed her and society will have nothing to say. I should have told you ages ago, but I didn't know about...this." He looked at them awkwardly.

Penelope gaped. Peter looked at her, eyes round.

"Is that so?" he demanded. His voice was low and level, as if he could barely believe it. "Is that true?"

"Yes! Yes, it is true," Penelope whispered. "But—but how do you know?" she demanded of the tall man. She guessed the answer almost before he said it.

"Anna told me. Anna Peterham. She is the great-granddaughter of a viscount, too; would you believe it?" he beamed at Peter, and Penelope wanted to smile at the joy in his eyes. "There is no reason at all why you two should not wed. So, now, will you stop crying, both of you?" He grinned at them. Penelope sniffed. Peter gaped at him and then turned to Penelope. His eyes were wide.

"Penelope..." he breathed. He turned to the other man. "George?" he asked. "I'm sorry. But might I have a moment with Penelope by ourselves?"

George nodded. "Of course, old chap. Excuse me." He went to the door.

"Thank you for summoning the Watch," Peter added. George smiled.

"Of course, old fellow. Now, if you'll excuse me, I'll return to the banquet."

Peter smiled and nodded at him. The door closed softly. Peter turned to Penelope.

"I can barely believe it," he said in a whisper.

Penelope smiled at him. She was crying—she could not help it. "It's true," she said softly. "It's true." She would have thanked her grandfather if she could, but she had never known him.

"This is wonderful," Peter said. He was crying too, not even trying to hide it. "It is so wonderful. I would have wed you anyway," he said softly. He was smiling.

Penelope grinned. "I know," she said. She swallowed hard, tears of joy making it impossible to say anything else.

"I loved you from the moment I saw you, I think," Peter said with a grin. "I will never forget that night when I spotted you around the doorway of the nursery. You captivated me then, and you still do. You are a beautiful, remarkable woman."

Penelope swallowed hard. His words touched her soul. Her heart was singing like a lark. She smiled. "I think I fell in love with you then, too. Or perhaps when you knocked me over in the hallway." She chuckled at the memory.

"I was so embarrassed," Peter said with a laugh.

"So was I. But you were so kind, and considerate, and I could not help but be amazed by you," Penelope murmured.

Peter grinned. "Well, I am rather glad it happened, then. Though I hope I did not hurt you." His brow lowered in concern.

She chuckled. "Not at all," she said softly. She took a step back. She really was tired; her legs almost giving way under her. He must have noticed, because he walked over and took her hand.

"Come. We will go to the nursery together. And then you are going to join me in the small parlour, where you can have some tea and become warm again and recover properly from what happened."

Penelope blinked at him. "Are you sure...?" she began. He nodded.

"Yes," he said firmly. "Yes, I am sure."

They went to the nursery. Mrs Aldham was still sitting there. She beamed at them when they came in, then her eyes widened in shock. "Miss Matthews! My lord! Whatever happened?"

"We were attacked," Peter said grimly. "But all is well," he added, holding up a hand as Mrs Aldham lifted her hand to her mouth in horror. "The man who attacked us is under arrest. We are all safe."

"Oh. Oh, thank goodness," Mrs Aldham murmured.

"Thank you for sitting with Thomas," Peter continued. Penelope was at the cradle, staring down at the baby, who was asleep and looked peaceful, his golden curls against the pillow, his eyes with their long lashes closed. "Might I ask you to sit with him for a while longer? Miss Matthews is hurt and needs tending."

"Oh! Oh, of course, my lord," Mrs Aldham said at once. "He's fast asleep. It's no trouble at all. I will sit and mend while he sleeps," she added, smiling at Penelope.

"Thank you, Mrs Aldham," Penelope said softly. "Thank you so much."

"No trouble at all, my dear. Go and get well," she murmured.

Penelope thanked her again and ducked wearily out of the room. She was barely aware of where Peter was leading her, but soon he opened a white-painted door and she found herself looking into a small private parlour. The chairs were upholstered and a fire burned in the grate. She watched him walk to the mantel and light the lamps, then ring the bell at the bell-rope in the corner.

"Please, sit," he said firmly. "I have summoned the butler to fetch some tea for us."

"Thank you," Penelope breathed. She sank, exhausted, into a chair.

She closed her eyes and she was almost asleep when the butler arrived with the tea. She was aware of Peter coming to sit beside her and taking her hand in his own.

"I love you, Penelope," he murmured as she gazed up at him.

"I love you, too, Peter."

He smiled. "Tomorrow we will talk some more," he told her gently.

Penelope nodded. She closed her eyes and she just managed to open her eyes again and drink some tea and eat the corner of a sandwich before she fell deeply asleep.

Chapter 26

The room was dark, except for the flickering of two oil lamps. Peter bent down over Penelope, hearing the slow, steady rhythm of her breathing. She was fast asleep. He put one arm under her knees and the other behind her shoulders and lifted her up in his arms. Her dark hair hung in wet curls around her face, which was pale. Her chest rose with her breath. He gazed at her for a long moment. His heart ached with the love that filled it. She was so beautiful; so vulnerable yet so resilient. He bent down and kissed her brow. She sighed but did not wake. He carried her carefully to the door, pushed it open and crossed the hallway to the nursery.

"My lord! What is..." Mrs Aldham, the maid who sat with Thomas, began, rising to her feet, a frown of consternation wrinkling her forehead.

"She's asleep," Peter told her firmly. "I will put her in her chamber to rest. Please, help her with her wet clothes if she awakes?" he asked.

"Of course, my lord!" Mrs Aldham replied. She looked a little flustered, and Peter could well imagine why. It was unheard of for an earl to take such interest in the care of a maid in the household. He was sure that all the servants would be scandalised.

Just as well we have already discussed what to do, he thought. He smiled to himself. He carried her through into the next room, placing her gently on the bed. It was a small, stark chamber with no personal touch except for the black uniform hanging on the door. His heart twisted. Soon, she would be able to express herself a little better, both in furnishings and apparel.

His heart ached as he recalled how she had looked in the green gown. She would look magnificent in a ballgown made especially for her. In whatever colour she chose.

He smiled to himself and walked softly out.

In the hallway, he was met almost immediately by the butler. The man had a worried frown on his face. Peter tensed.

"My lord, it..." the butler began, but Millicent was there before he could say more.

"Where is Edmund?" Millicent demanded. She gaped at Peter. "Whatever happened? Why are you here? What should I tell the guests who are waiting in the drawing room for you? Why are you covered in dirt?" she added, frowning.

Peter took a deep breath. "Sister." He did not know what to say. How was he supposed to explain to her that Edmund was the man who had organised it all? Who had ordered the death of Charles and Eliza? That he had tried to kill Penelope, and himself? He had heard all of what Edmund was saying, the confessions he made to Penelope before he hurt her.

Before he could speak, George stepped out of the drawing room up the hallway. Peter let out a sigh of relief as, clearly understanding the sensitivity of the situation, George hurried up.

"Millicent," he began gently. "Peter and I have something to tell you. You might not believe us, but it is true. I saw it myself."

Millicent gaped at him. Peter coughed.

"Millicent, sister, it was Edmund. He did this. He attacked me. He attacked Penelope—Miss Matthews. He was behind it all. The murder of Charles and Eliza. He planned it and paid for it. I can prove it," he added. She shook her head.

"No," she said firmly. She looked at him. "No."

Peter swallowed hard. George began.

"Millicent, dear cousin...it's true. I swear it." George tensed. "He really did."

"No," Millicent began, but Peter could see in her eyes that she believed them. His heart ached. She looked horrified. The shock had been bad enough for him, and he had been too focused on getting Penelope to safety to think about it.

"You need to rest," George said gently, resting a hand on Millicent's shoulder. "Let me lead you to your room," he added.

"No," Millicent began. Peter looked down, his heart aching. George was managing better than he would have. He watched as George led his sister down the hallway. She walked as if she was sleepwalking. Peter's heart filled with guilt and sorrow. As he watched, the door opened.

"Please, take care of her," George said to a young lady with long auburn hair and a slim face who stood there.

"Of course. Come, my lady. Come and sit down. Do you need some tea?" the young woman asked gently.

Millicent said nothing.

"She has had a shock," George explained, and he whispered to the woman. She nodded and led Millicent inside.

Peter ached to sit down. He was exhausted. Relief from having that part of his duty complete almost knocked him off his feet. George came over to join him.

"Anna will take care of her," he said gently.

"Anna?" Peter asked, then grinned. "Ah, yes! How could I forget? Penelope's colleague and companion." His grin widened.

"Yes. That Anna," George said a little awkwardly. He smiled.

The hallway was silent. Peter blinked, shaking himself. He was almost asleep.

"I should dismiss the guests," he said after a moment.

"Already done, cousin," George said gently. "I told them myself. You need rest. Your face is a terrible mess."

"Is it?" Peter asked grimly. He ran a hand down his face, feeling for bruises. His right cheekbone was swollen, and his brow. He grimaced.

"Not really." George smiled fondly at him. "Nothing that won't make you more interesting to a lady."

Peter hit him playfully on the shoulder. George grunted and shoved him back. They had not sparred since Cambridge and they both laughed.

Peter stifled a yawn. "I should go to bed," he said softly.

"Yes. You should," George said firmly. "You need sleep after all that hard work."

Peter shook his head. "Thank you, George," he said gently. "Your help was invaluable. All of it," he added softly. Without George, he might never have discovered that Penelope was a baron's granddaughter. He would have married her regardless, would have cast aside the earldom without hesitation if it meant being with her. But now, the most extraordinary thing was that he had no need to do so. She could take her place within the peerage—an active part of it. By birth, she was not so far removed from his world after all.

He smiled. His mind filled with thoughts of her. He imagined how wonderful it would be to share their life together, how much fun it would be to do the things that were tedious to him, like balls and evening parties. She would enjoy them, and that would make it worthwhile for them both. His grin widened.

"Goodnight, old chap," he murmured to George, who was still standing with him in the hallway. "Thank you."

"It was not exactly taxing, old chap," George said warmly.

Peter just smiled. His friend had come along at just the right moment, possibly saving both of their lives or at least helping a great deal. He shoved him playfully again.

"You probably saved my life, old chap," he murmured.

"You would have been fine without me," George said gently.

Peter smiled and George smiled back and then Peter, stifling a yawn, turned up the hallway.

"Goodnight," he called again. "I will see you in the morning."

"See you at breakfast," George called back.

Peter walked slowly to his chamber. He undressed slowly, rinsed his face and hands in the bowl of water on the nightstand, and then buttoned on his nightshirt and got into bed. He lay back on the pillows, exhausted. As he fell asleep, his mind was full of memories of Penelope and plans for tomorrow.

***

The next morning, he awoke to find the cloudy daylight filling the room. He blinked and limped to the curtains, drawing them so that he could get dressed in privacy. His legs ached. His head hurt. His hands ached, too, and he gazed down to find that his knuckles were a mass of bruises. At least one bone had cracked, he guessed, the joints swollen and one crusted with a little blood where the impact cut the skin. He winced, rubbing his fingers over the swollen skin.

His thoughts turned to Penelope as he went to dress. How much pain was she in? He recalled how her face had been swollen, her throat rasping as she coughed and struggled to take in even the smallest breaths. Any compassion or sorrow he might have felt for Edmund disappeared. Whatever happened, that fellow had to be dealt with. He was dangerous and he had committed unthinkable wrongdoing already.

His thoughts lightened as he went to find something to wear. He blushed as he chose a blue jacket, wondering what Penelope would think. He had never paid particular attention to what he wore—his manservant often picked outfits for him, so that they were modish and acceptable to society—but Peter had never really bothered about how he looked before. He gazed in the looking-glass, wondering how he would look to her.

A livid bruise showed on his cheek and his temple and he winced. His eye on that side was a bit swollen, and something had grazed the skin on the other side. He sighed.

"I was in a fight," he reminded himself. He was hardly going to be unscathed after something like that.

He shrugged on his shirt, put on riding-breeches and the blue jacket, and limped down the hallway to breakfast. He could hear voices in the breakfast room and he tensed. The guests were still there and he did not want to face them. George had declared the party concluded, but they needed time to get home and some of them might linger all morning. He nodded and walked on.

At the door to the nursery, he paused. His heart soared and his hands were damp. He was unsure what she would think or say. Perhaps she had simply been too tired to refuse. And yet, she had seemed sincere. He drew a deep breath and knocked on the door, shyness making his cheeks flood with colour as she opened it.

"Penelope!" He breathed. She was dressed in her black uniform, her dark brown hair pinned back from her brow. Her face was pale and grey rings of exhaustion framed her beautiful eyes. Otherwise, she looked exactly like she usually did, but for the livid bruise on her temple. "Good morning," he murmured. He bowed.

When he straightened up, looking into her eyes, she gazed into his stare tenderly. She dropped a swift curtsey.

"Good morning, my... Good morning, Peter," she corrected, grinning.

"Quite so." He grinned. When she smiled, she was breathtaking. His heart flipped and for a moment he could not think of anything to say. He stood in the doorway, hesitant and shy.

"Did you wish to say something?" she asked gently. Peter inclined his head.

"Have you broken your fast yet?" he asked carefully. When she moved her head to indicate "no", he smiled. "Might you have your breakfast with me?" he asked swiftly. The words came out in a rush.

Penelope gaped. "But, Peter... your guests. And Thomas, and..." she glanced into the room.

"Is he sleeping?" Peter asked. She nodded. "Bring him with you," he replied. "We will take breakfast in the small parlour upstairs," he added. "The guests are departing today. George organised it."

"He was very kind," Penelope murmured.

"He's a kind person," Peter replied warmly. He smiled at her. Her smile widened, eyes sparkling in a way that made his heart race. He stood back and she went to fetch Thomas, wrapped in a shawl and sleeping soundly, then hesitantly stepped out to join him in the hallway.

Peter walked with her to the small parlour, standing back for her to enter. He rang the bell, summoning the butler.

"Please fetch breakfast for two," he instructed the man. He had to admire the way the butler simply bowed and withdrew, though Peter could see disbelief on his face. He smiled grimly to himself. The staff would have to be informed. And he wished to make things official quickly.

Breakfast arrived swiftly, and Peter poured tea. Penelope accepted the cup.

"Thank you," she murmured, sipping it delicately. He gazed at her. She was so beautiful. He could have sat and watched her, but for the fact that he had so much to say, and that she seemed to be shy, looking down awkwardly.

"We have to plan a great deal," he murmured.

She smiled at him, eyes sparkling. He held her gaze. She frowned.

"The man..." she began. He cleared his throat.

"Lord Penrith has been taken to the village. He will be tried in Lynton." That was the nearest large town. He hesitated to say that the sentence would be harsh—most likely exile in a colony.

"He cannot hurt us anymore," Penelope murmured. Peter's heart twisted.

"He cannot," he agreed. His heart filled with relief as he thought about it. They were safe. He no longer had to worry. Charles and Eliza's deaths were at least explained and the murderer had been found and brought to justice. He could begin to heal from the horror of that.

He noticed Penelope gazing at him with a worried expression. He frowned.

"My father..." she began awkwardly. "He is very ill. I must travel to see him." She swallowed hard.

"We will travel together," Peter said quickly. "In the main coach, it will not take long. How far away is your home?" he asked.

"Fifty miles," Penelope said softly. "Twenty miles from Sterling Manor," she added. "My sister works there."

"Then we will fetch your sister on the way," Peter said firmly.

"You would...?"

He inclined his head. "Of course," he said quickly.

"Thank you." She breathed the words.

"Of course," he said again. His heart ached. He remembered all too well the gnawing worry he had felt when his own father had been ill, despite the distance that had always stood between them. Penelope, he suspected, was far closer to hers. The sorrow in her eyes, the quiet fear she tried to mask, struck something deep within him.

She smiled at him lovingly and he smiled back. His mind wandered, filling with thoughts about her home and her life, eager to find out all he could about her. He knew so little and he wanted to change that. He wanted to find out more and keep on finding out, drawn to her by fascination and love as he had been for so long.

He looked up as Penelope bit into a crunchy slice of toast. She blushed and giggled. He smiled.

"Sorry. I'm very hungry," she murmured.

Peter chuckled. "Me, too," he agreed. He buttered a slice of toast, added some of his favourite marmalade, and bit into it. The room was mostly silent as they ate, the fire popping in the grate, sunshine falling through the half-open curtains to paint golden bars across the carpet by the hearth.

Peter sighed. He could not recall a time in his life when he felt more content, more at peace. His gaze lingered on Penelope, straying to the small baby who slumbered on the big chair by the fire, tucked in with shawls and pillows; and then back to her.

"This is... pleasant," he said shyly. He did not know what else to say; how to express the love that filled his heart. She smiled. Her smile made his heart soar, glowing with warmth.

"It is," she said softly. She seemed shy, too, and he smiled.

"I never felt so happy before," he managed to say.

"Me, neither," she whispered shyly. She had butter on her cheek and he leaned forward and cleaned it off with a napkin, grinning. She blushed. His hand remained where it was, his palm against her cheek. She was sitting rather close, and it was not difficult to lean across and press his lips to hers. His heart ached; his body flooded with heat as their lips met. She leaned against him, her kiss as eager as he felt.

He sat back, dazed and smiling. She grinned. She looked a little dazed too. He grinned back.

She reached across and took his hand. He held hers; the slim fingers cool against his skin. His heart swelled with a blend of love and steadfast devotion. He gazed at her, unable to look away. Her lovely dark hair framed her face, one curl coming loose, as it sometimes seemed to do, from the bun in which she had scraped the rest back from her forehead. Her big green eyes regarded him steadily. His heart filled with love.

"I love you, Penelope Matthews," he whispered, his heart almost too full to speak. She beamed back.

"I love you, too, Peter Blakefield," she replied softly.

He smiled and gazed into her eyes, and he knew that he had never felt so happy.

Epilogue

Penelope swallowed hard as she heard the music of the church bells ringing out across the village green. Brentdale village church stood a few feet away, and the peal of bells was loud, incessant and joyful. She turned to her father, who stood at her side, his white collar proud around his neck. His thin face was pale in the morning sunshine. He grinned, his brown eyes with their hazel flecks—so like Emily's own—lighting up with his grin.

"Well, daughter. Here we are." His voice—which had been truly beautiful, so much so that many of his parishioners loved simply to hear him read—was weakened by the long months of sickness, but he was smiling.

"Here we are, indeed." Penelope's own voice cracked. She was close to tears. She gazed into her father's eyes. He looked back, his gaze level. His eyes shone and she knew that he was also about to cry.

"Know that I love you, daughter," he murmured gently.

Penelope swallowed hard. "I know, Papa," she said quietly. "I love you, too."

"I am blessed, daughter," her father replied, squeezing her fingers tight. "Now, let us go in so that you may begin your life together."

"Yes, Papa," Penelope murmured, energy flooding into her at the thought of who was waiting for her within the church. "Yes."

Her father opened the door and they stepped in together. Someone played the organ, the notes joyful, uplifting. Penelope barely listened to the tune they played. Her white silk skirts rustled around her ankles, the pure white dress with its fashionable high waist and puffed sleeves fitting perfectly. She had wanted it plain, though Peter had insisted that she allow some embellishment, and so the low oval neckline was edged with white French lace and the waistband was a white silk ribbon. She looked down briefly, checking that her white silk shoes did not step on the long skirt, and then she walked—practically floated—up the aisle on the arm of her father.

She caught sight of Emily sitting in the front pew and she smiled as her sister grinned dazzlingly at her. Emily was wearing a pale green gown that drew out the green flecks in her hazel eyes and harmonised with her fine blonde hair. Her grin seemed to light the church, lighting up her small, fine-boned face. Penelope swallowed hard. She looked up, and her eyes moved to the front of the church. Her gaze caught Peter, where he stood by the aisle, and she stared, her heart filled with love for him as he stood there.

He wore a dark blue tailcoat—almost black in the darkness of the church—and long trousers in grey. His dark brown hair framed his pale, slim face and his mouth was a thin line above his well-formed chin. His eyes widened as he saw her and Penelope blushed in pleasure, glad of the gauzy veil that hid the flush from the rest of the church. She grinned at him through the thin fabric and he beamed back. She was still smiling as she walked up to the front of the church to join him.

The village vicar—a round-faced, merry man a few decades younger than Papa with thick dark hair and a friendly smile—stood waiting to begin the ceremony. He beamed at them and then opened his prayer book and began to read.

Penelope listened intently at first, then she could not help that her thoughts wandered to Peter, where he stood beside her, and she risked a glance upwards. He was listening intently to the ceremony, but he seemed to sense he was being watched because he turned and caught her eye. She tried not to smile, but she could not help it and her stomach tingled as he grinned back. She made herself look away, not wanting to disrespect the ceremony, but she was still smiling as she listened to the words. A bubble of happiness was rising inside her, growing steadily all morning until she thought the joy would simply make her drift away, lighter than air.

"...and do you, Penelope Marcia Matthews, take thee Peter Alfred Blakefield to be your husband?"

"I do," Penelope said solemnly. She meant it more than she had ever meant anything in her life.

The vicar turned to Peter. "And do you, Peter Alfred Blakefield take thee Penelope Marcia Matthews to be your lawful wedded wife?" he asked Peter.

"I do," Peter said in a low, deep tone. Penelope's heart soared. She gazed up at Peter and he gazed back and she thought her heart would melt, she was so happy.

The vicar continued the ceremony, his solemn voice carrying through the still air. Then, at last, he turned to them with a nod, and Penelope's heart nearly stopped.

Peter reached forward, his movements slow and deliberate, lifting the veil from her face with careful hands. As their eyes met, his gaze was steady—filled with warmth, tenderness, and something deeper that made her breath catch.

Then, in a gesture both reverent and intimate, he bent his head and brushed a gentle kiss against her forehead.

Penelope closed her eyes, the warmth of it settling deep within her, as though sealing a promise. His lips lingered there for the briefest moment, firm yet soft, before he straightened. When he smiled down at her, she could not hold back her own answering grin, her joy too great to contain.

They turned to face the congregation and Penelope's heart soared as she saw the smiling, loving faces looking back at them. In the back pew sat Mrs Hallden, her eyes damp and a big smile on her face as she looked at them with quiet pride. There were not many pews, since the village church was small, and in the next pew sat Peter's Aunt Marcia, and beside her was her daughter Sophia. Thomas sat on Sophia's knee and gurgled happily, grinning at them in apparent delight. Penelope's heart filled with love.

Her smile widened as she saw the familiar faces in the front pew. George sat there, and next to him was Anna. She wore a beautiful gown of ocher silk, her long reddish hair arranged in a chignon that left some locks loose to frame her face. She looked regal. She looked happy. She and George had wed in a small private ceremony on his estate just two weeks previous. Peter and Penelope had been their witnesses.

Penelope's gaze moved to Emily, who sat beside their father. She beamed at Penelope with love, and Penelope's heart ached with the love and joy she felt to have those two beloved people there.

Papa smiled at her, a quiet, gentle smile full of warmth. A lump rose in her throat as she met his gaze, overwhelmed by the depth of feeling in that simple expression. She had feared she might never see him strong again, and yet here he was, watching her on her wedding day.

She looked back at Peter, her heart full. Thanks to him, not only had Papa's bills been paid, but his home had been supplied with firewood, coal, and every necessity to ensure his comfort through the winter. She had no doubt that his care and generosity had played as much a part in Papa's recovery as the careful tending of Emily—and the strength of their own quiet hopes.

She looked up at Peter, her eyes full of love.

Together, they walked out of the church and into the sunshine.

The coach awaited them and Penelope flushed as Peter took her hand and helped her up into it. He smiled at her and then produced the purse of coins that was customary for the groom. He stood before the coach and hurled the coins up into the air, causing a yell of delight from the village children, who had gathered on the green to wait for just that moment. They ran towards him, grinning and shrieking in delight, hurrying to grab the coins that lay scattered on the grass, shining brightly in the sun.

Penelope's heart filled with love as she looked at the happy smile on his face. He clambered up into the coach and sat down across from her. The coach was not large, and their knees almost touched. Penelope grinned, and her blush grew more intense as he shut the door.

The coach set off.

Penelope smiled at him across the small space. Her heart was soaring, her entire body flushing warmly with delight. Peter leaned closer.

"I do not think I have ever been so happy," he said with a grin.

"Nor I!" Penelope declared.

He laughed and leaned forward, resting his hand on her cheek. He stared into her eyes and her heart thudded with the depth of love she saw there.

"I can hardly wait to celebrate with our friends," he began, "but I must admit, I shall also be glad when we have the manor to ourselves once more." He smiled shyly.

"So shall I," Penelope replied. Her gaze held his, and her heart throbbed with love and excitement.

He leaned close, and his lips trapped hers in a sweet kiss; one that made her heart race with wild joy, and her body tingle with a pleasure hitherto unimagined.

He was breathing heavily when he leaned back. She grinned at him.

He grinned back. The coach jolted, and they both laughed.

They arrived at the manor, and Peter helped her out. They walked up the stairs to the front door, and he lifted her over the threshold. Their guests were waiting for them inside, and they cheered. Penelope blushed.

"Congratulations, Penelope," Emily said, rushing forward and giving her a hug. Penelope shut her eyes, hugging her sister. The smell of lavender and flowers was strong in her nose, a particular scent that Emily always wore and which tore at Penelope's heart, filling it with memories of when they were both looking after Papa.

"Thank you, sister. I am so glad you are here."

"I will visit often," Emily promised. Peter had suggested that they could either travel regularly to call on Papa and Emily or send the coach to fetch them, as the journey was hardly an arduous one and could be managed within a day.

"Good," Penelope replied, swallowing. She would still miss Emily, even if they saw one another every fortnight, she was sure.

"Best wishes to you both," Lady Sterling murmured, coming forward next. Her fine-boned face seemed to glow with her soft smile. Her blue eyes were bright.

"Thank you," Penelope murmured. Lady Sterling had always been kind and supportive. She beamed at Sophia, who was resplendent in a pale blue gown and had Thomas—who wore a blue velvet coat and breeches and who looked quite bewildered—in her arms.

"Thomas!" Penelope said with a grin. His little face lit up, and he giggled. He reached out to her, and she lifted him out of Sophia's arms, holding him against her chest. He sighed and seemed to relax. Penelope looked up at Peter.

"He is happy," Peter murmured.

"He is," she replied. "I am so pleased to see him."

They proceeded into the dining room. Millicent had asked not to attend the wedding, since her health was still poor and she was recovering from the shock and trauma of what had happened. She was thin and pale as she came forward to greet them, but she smiled at Peter with genuine care. Penelope smiled at her.

"Thank you, Millicent," Peter said gently. "It is all beautiful. You have gone to such trouble."

Penelope had to agree. The dining room looked beautiful, with roses in elegant vases decorating the main table and the daylight glinting off the polished silverware that awaited their use.

"Thank you, Peter," Millicent said simply. "Congratulations," she added, turning to Penelope. Penelope had been a little apprehensive about Millicent's reaction, but oddly, she seemed to accept Penelope despite the circumstances under which they had met one another, when Penelope worked in the household. The sneer with which Millicent had regarded her then was replaced with a wary respect. Penelope felt much the same for Millicent, whom she had to admire for her courage. She looked beautiful in her blue gown and proud. Peter had suggested that, in some way, Edmund being ten thousand miles from her did her good.

They thanked her for the congratulations, and then they went to sit down at the table.

Mrs Aldham, grinning and wearing the same black uniform that Penelope had worn, came forward to take Thomas from her. He was almost asleep, and he did not protest as Mrs Aldham gathered her into her arms. They had decided to promote her to the position of nursemaid, though Peter and Penelope both agreed that her role in Thomas' life would be somewhat secondary, since they intended to do a great deal themselves.

Peter's relationship with the child had blossomed, and it moved Penelope close to tears to see him with the baby, holding him and playing with him with an expression of true care and love on his face.

Their guests gathered around, and soon the air was filled with the sound of happy laughter as people talked and chatted and chuckled together. The atmosphere was warm and loving, and Penelope gazed at Peter, her eyes full of love.

The luncheon was a simple one—or as simple as they could persuade Peter's sister to allow. They ate three courses, followed by a delicious dessert of syllabub. When the syllabub had been delivered and eaten, the delicious syrup sticky and flavoured with cherries, Penelope blinked, feeling sleepy and full. She turned to Peter with a smile. He smiled lovingly back.

"Perhaps the guests would like to go for a walk in the garden after luncheon?" he suggested.

"Yes. That is a pleasant idea," Penelope agreed. She glanced across at her father. Rooms upstairs in the manor had been set aside for him and for Emily, as neither would be travelling back immediately after the celebrations. Emily would remain for a few days, and Papa, still too weak for two thirty-mile journeys in as many days, would stay as well. It had been mutually decided that their presence at the manor would be a welcome one.

Penelope was certain her father would appreciate some rest after the long day, and she resolved to suggest that he retire to his room to recover from the meal in comfort.

Peter made the suggestion of going for a walk to George, who sat beside him.

"Capital idea," George agreed warmly. Penelope smiled to herself. She had liked George from the moment that she had met him, and his love for her best friend Anna only made her like him even more.

Slowly, the guests drifted out through the big doors and out into the sunshine.

Penelope and Peter walked slowly, going to the rose garden. Neither of them had spoken of what they wanted to do, but they both seemed to want to go there, and their steps led them towards the bench in the shade overlooking the lawn. The guests walked around peacefully or made their way to other, shadier parts of the garden. Mrs Aldham was there, walking slowly with little Thomas, who held her hand and made slow but steady progress across the grass on his small, chubby and sturdy legs. Penelope saw Emily talking happily with Anna and George and smiled.

It was good to have their friends and loved ones surrounding them.

Peter settled down beside her on the bench, and Penelope leaned against him, shutting her eyes for a moment in pure contentment. The sunshine beat down warmly onto her skin, and the closeness of Peter made her heart thud.

She opened her eyes to find him gazing lovingly at her. She blushed and looked away, feeling shy. Then she looked into his eyes, and she could not help but smile at him. He smiled back.

"This is a wonderful day," Peter murmured softly.

"It is. So wonderful," Penelope agreed. She took her hand in his, and he looped his fingers through hers, their entwined hands resting on her lap. Her heart thumped wildly in her chest as he gazed into her eyes.

"It is the best day of my life," he murmured.

"And of mine, too," Penelope replied warmly.

He smiled. His eyes widened as they stared into hers, and she smiled back. He leaned closer, and her heart soared. He held her gaze, his expression tender and loving.

"I love you, Penelope Matthews," he said softly.

"I love you, too, Peter Blakefield," she said with a grin, joy making her heart thud.

He leaned forward, brushing his lips against hers in a tender kiss. She closed her eyes, savouring the warmth of it, the quiet certainty of their love. When she opened them again, she rested her head on his shoulder, a sigh of contentment escaping her.

Side by side, they sat in peaceful silence, watching their loved ones stroll through the sunlit garden, laughter and conversation drifting through the air like a melody.

Extended Epilogue

The sunshine sparkled on the river, the sound of its rushing water pure and clear and refreshing in the summer heat. Penelope leaned back against the tree trunk behind her, dappled shadows dancing on her eyelids as she closed her eyes in blissful sleepiness. Her green-and-white muslin gown was spread out around her on the picnic rug, its skirts cool and light. Made of white muslin decorated with a pattern of green sprigs, it was a beautiful dress; one of her favourites. The novelty of having any fabric she chose for her gowns had not worn off in five years of being a countess.

The sound of laughter and giggles drifted across the lawn to her and she opened her eyes, her lips lifting in a smile.

Charlie and Amelia, her son and daughter, were playing on the lawn. At three, their son was a little faster and steadier on his feet than two-year-old Amelia, but that did not mean that Amelia was not capable of cornering him occasionally if they played catch. Both toddled with real determination and Penelope smiled as Amelia caught up with her brother, both of them tumbling into the fresh green lawn.

"I don't think either of them is hurt," Penelope said gently, as Peter, sitting beside her, tensed as if he would get up and go over to them. He was always attentive and protective and she smiled to herself, seeing the frown on his face as he glanced over at the tussling children.

Amelia stood up first, saw her father watching and toddled over towards him where he sat with Penelope on the picnic blanket. Her face shone with a big smile as she gazed over at him.

"Papa! Papa!" she said excitedly. At two, she had a good stock of words and she used them to good effect. Her little legs raced as fast as they could across the lawn, Charlie hurrying behind. Penelope's heart ached with love as she watched them toddling over.

Charlie's hair was the thick, dark brown of Peter's, and he had inherited Penelope's green eyes, which made a striking combination. His little face still had the softness of a child's face, but Penelope guessed that his father's fine bone structure underlay it and that he would have the same slim, gaunt beauty when he grew up. Her gaze flickered to Peter, her heart filling with the love she felt for him.

In the five years since she had met him, his dark brown hair showed strands of white here and there, and the wrinkles around his eyes had deepened slightly. He looked contented and happy, a father watching his children with a loving gaze as they ran over to him.

"Papa! Papa!" Amelia yelled. "Look!" She gestured to the grass-stains on her white skirt. "Fell."

"Are you hurt?" Peter asked gently as she promptly sat down next to him, her big hazel eyes gazing up at him. She had inherited the hazel eyes that Penelope's papa and Emily both had, and from somewhere—Penelope thought perhaps from her own mother—she had a head of blonde curls.

"No hurt," Amelia told him, grinning. "Dirty."

Penelope had to laugh. Peter chuckled, his eyes crinkling at the corners as he laughed. While some nobles would certainly have had a nursemaid to care for the children continuously, they loved the fact that they had chosen to spend almost every waking moment with their daughter and son.

"No harm done, young lady," he said warmly. "Are you thirsty?"

"Uh-uh," she said, shaking her head adamantly. Penelope grinned.

"I ran fast!" Charlie informed his father, his thick dark hair falling over one eye.

"That's grand. You did. I saw you," Peter said with a smile. "You're a very fast boy."

Charlie grinned proudly at the praise. Then he flopped down on the rug on Peter's other side. He gazed with mesmerised eyes at the picnic hamper.

"Cake?" he asked.

Penelope giggled. "There is a blackcurrant tart, young man," she agreed. "Do you need some lemonade? Are you thirsty?"

"Thirsty!" Charlie's eyes lit up, as if he had only just realised that he was thirsty. "Lemonade."

Penelope chuckled. Thomas was usually quite eloquent for his age, possessing a surprisingly large vocabulary that he often put to use. Yet when he set his mind on something, he became singularly focused, his responses reduced to short, determined replies.

Peter often jested that he sympathised with the boy, being a man of few words himself—an observation that never failed to amuse Penelope. Like Charlie, however, Peter was eloquent when he chose to be.

"Penelope? Do you have some mineral water?" Anna asked, appearing at the picnic rug. Penelope nodded.

"There is still some in this bottle," she replied, reaching over and lifting it. Papa was quite fond of mineral water, having read about its health properties, and they had included the bottle in the picnic-hamper mainly for him.

"Thank you!" Anna replied with appreciation. She lifted the bottle. "Little Henry is thirsty and I am disinclined to give him lemonade." She grinned.

"Of course," Penelope replied. Henry, Anna's youngest son, was just a little younger than two, and as a former nursemaid, Penelope had to agree that she would be disinclined to give so small a child much of Mrs Gracechurch's fine lemonade. It was full of sugar and the likelihood of it upsetting the delicate stomach of a small child was quite high.

"Thank you," Anna said again and, grinning, hurried across the small space of lawn to where she and George reclined on a picnic rug in the sunshine. Little Henry was resting on the rug beside her in the dappled shade. Penelope watched fondly as Anna poured the water into a little cup and held it for the child to drink.

She smiled to herself as their eldest child, a daughter named Portia, ran over to join them. A beautiful girl with thick pale brown curls and George's dark brown eyes, she was four years old and graceful like her mother. She would be tall and slender, Penelope guessed, like Anna was. Their middle son, a three-year-old named Mark, was playing on the lawn close to where Emily and her husband Luke sat.

Penelope's heart lifted as she gazed over at them. Emily had met Luke at a ball that she and Peter had attended with her at a nearby manor. Luke had been smitten with Emily almost immediately. His father was a viscount and he lived at an estate just six miles from Peter's own. They could visit Emily, Luke and their young son Gerald whenever they chose. Papa still chose to continue his ministry and live at their family's cottage, but he spent increasingly more time staying either with Emily or Penelope, a fact that they both appreciated.

Penelope's gaze moved sideways to her father, her heart flooding with love and tenderness. He was so much stronger than he had been, though the illness had left him with a prematurely-white head of hair and more wrinkles than he might otherwise have had. He looked older than his age, but with a grace and dignity that melted her heart. His gaunt face was peaceful as he gazed out across the lawn, watching Gerald crawling across the picnic rug.

"Mama! Mama!"

A voice behind her made Penelope turn sharply, and then she laughed aloud as Thomas, five years old and tall for his age, cannoned into her. His squarish face was lit with a smile, and his hazel eyes—usually solemn—were bright with joy as Patches—their dog—raced after him. A white wire-haired terrier with black spots, Patches was a bundle of enthusiasm, determination and thick wire-haired fur. Penelope laughed in delight as Thomas ran after the dog, then tumbled in the grass, the little creature leaping onto his chest and covering his face with enthusiastic licks.

"Easy, Patches," Peter called the dog, who turned and bounded towards Peter instead, then flopped onto the rug and lay in the shade, panting. Thomas ran over to join him, lying down on the picnic rug with much the same attitude. Penelope had to laugh. It was wonderful to see Thomas so confident, so happy.

Peter had agreed with her—in fact, she could not remember who had said it initially. They had formally adopted Thomas within a month and, though he had been told of his true parents, and the portrait of them hung in the gallery, he regarded Peter and Penelope as Mama and Papa. His own parents occupied the realm of heavenly guardians, watching over him, and Peter and Penelope agreed with his assertion that they were so. Peter sometimes talked of Charles and Eliza, but more often with fondness and love than with sorrow, and Penelope was glad to hear him doing so.

"Would you care for some jam tart?" Peter asked Penelope, reaching towards the picnic hamper. They had eaten a leisurely afternoon luncheon, beginning with cold meat pie and sandwiches and moving on to cheeses, pickled vegetables and fresh fruit. The jam tart reclined in the bottom of the hamper wrapped in a checkered cloth. Penelope grinned as Thomas and Charlie gazed at their father.

"Jam tart," Charlie echoed.

Penelope laughed. Charlie never stopped eating, though his physique was very much modelled on that of herself and his father—tall and slim. The pudginess of childhood blurred the long, slim bone structure in a way appropriate for a three-year-old.

"Amelia?" Penelope called to her daughter, who was sitting with Mark on the lawn, playing with pebbles. "Would you care for some jam tart?"

"Jam tart!"

Amelia, curls bouncing as she ran, raced over as fast as her little legs ran. Penelope chuckled as the little girl sat down with a thump on the picnic rug beside her, eyes focused on the food as Peter cut some slices for them all.

Mark was toddling over behind Amelia, and Anna called to him, chuckling.

"Mark, dear! We have some tart too. But you can sit with Auntie Penelope too if you want." She grinned at Penelope, who made room for the little dark-haired boy, who flopped onto the rug beside Amelia and gazed hungrily at the slice of tart that Peter was cutting for him.

"Papa?" Penelope called to her father, who was sitting peacefully on the low stool the butler had brought down for him, watching the river. "Would you care for some tart too?"

"A small slice, perhaps," her father agreed. "Thank you," he added, smiling at Penelope and Peter warmly.

Penelope grinned back. "Of course, Papa," she said fondly. She thanked Peter as he passed her a slice. Blackcurrant was her favourite and she smiled gratefully at Peter, whose eyes sparkled as he handed it to her. He turned to the children, laughing as they set about eating heartily. Both Charlie and Amelia were able to eat by themselves, though Amelia occasionally needed help, and

Penelope noticed gratefully that Peter had cut her piece of tart into little cubes that she could spear easily with a small, blunt cake-fork. She did so with dexterity, chewing contentedly, her mouth stained with blackcurrant jam.

Emily was resting with Gerald in her arms, leaning against a tree while Luke chatted happily with them both. Penelope smiled fondly at Emily, who looked deeply contented and restful where she lay back in the shade, a smile of bliss on her face. She wore a blue muslin gown, her blonde curls soft around her lovely face.

Thomas and Charlie had already eaten their pie, and Penelope watched lovingly as Peter carefully wiped around both of their mouths with a handkerchief, cleaning away the purplish stains from the blackcurrant jam.

"Should we make a boat?" he asked the boys. Charlie's eyes lit up.

"Yes! Yes, Papa! Make a big one!" Charlie asked enthusiastically. Patches, seeing the delight on Thomas and Charlie's faces, leapt up and started barking excitedly. Peter chuckled.

"We need some wood for that," he reminded the boys fondly. "Will one of you fetch a branch? Let's see if we can find a good one. Amelia, dear? Do you want to come too?" he asked Amelia, who had almost eaten her fill and had joined Mark in pulling out handfuls of grass, scattering them on the edge of the rug. It must have been part of some sort of game that they both understood.

"Going where?" Amelia inquired.

"We're going to make a boat," Peter explained. "Do you and Mark want to play too?"

"Boat!" Amelia said joyfully. "Yes. Come on!" she added, authoritatively, to Mark. He got to his feet and toddled playfully after her as she ran over to where Charles and Thomas were already searching, with Patches, for sticks to carve into a boat.

Penelope leaned back against the tree trunk, enjoying the afternoon warmth. The sunshine already seemed more golden, the day lengthening towards late afternoon. She guessed it to be around three o'clock, though she had not heard—or not noticed—the church bells chiming the hour. Butterflies flitted lazily over the flowers, and somewhere, a grasshopper chirped in the long grass. The garden was peaceful, filled with the sound of children's laughter and the low murmur of chatting adults.

"Should you not go in soon?" Papa asked, bringing Penelope's attention to the moment. "Are you not expecting other guests?"

"Yes." Penelope nodded. "I think it must be three o'clock, Papa... or thereabouts. We have another hour," she added, looking up at where the sunshine shone goldenly on the trees.

"It is exactly three o'clock," her father commented, taking out his pocket watch and opening it. Penelope chuckled. A few seconds later, the church bells rang.

"You are quite right, as usual," she said with a grin.

Her father smiled warmly. "And, I must say, the church bells are also very prompt," he added, grinning. "I should commend the vicar."

Penelope laughed. "I will tell him when I next see him," she promised.

Her father just smiled. They sat quietly and listened to the happy sound of the children, whooping and shouting happily as Peter carved a little boat to send down the fast-flowing waters of the river.

Emily, Luke and Gerald came and joined them on the mat. Penelope smiled, watching Gerald crawl about and listening to Emily relate a funny story about Gerald managing to escape their watchful eyes in the drawing room and hide under the chaise-longue.

"We could not fathom where he had gone! I was horrified," Emily said with a laugh, recalling her terror. "I was convinced he had crawled out of the door and fallen down the stairs. Luke spotted him. How we laughed!" She grinned.

"He crawls remarkably fast," Luke added, gazing in admiration at his small son. "I would never have expected him to reach the chaise-longue in the few seconds our attention was on the fireplace."

"He is very quick," Penelope agreed, watching the little boy crawling with appreciable speed towards the edge of the mat. He was eight months old, and a sturdy fellow, big for his age, with Emily's golden curls.

Anna and George stood and came over to join them. Anna had Henry in her arms, while Portia, who looked sleepy, clung to George. They all sat down on the rug and George wrapped his arm around Portia, who lay down beside him and fell almost instantly asleep.

"Poor dear. She's quite worn out," Emily commented to Anna. Anna smiled.

"I think it was the long coach ride, combined with all the excitement of the afternoon," she replied, gazing fondly at the little girl, whose pale brown curls tumbled around her face. At four, her long hair was down to her shoulders already, the strands fine and thin, like silk.

"What a lovely neckline that dress has," Emily commented to Anna, who wore a dark red dress, the sweetheart neckline embellished with ochre binding.

"Thank you. I did the decorating myself," Anna replied, flushing with obvious pleasure at Emily's comment.

"I love to sew! I made a white-on-white embroidery for a collar for my new gown," Emily told her proudly. Penelope smiled to herself.

Anna and Emily, having both been lady's maids at one time, shared a love of hairstyles and fashion that she herself had never really embraced, though she had to admit that she enjoyed being able to have more choices when it came to clothing. Even after five years, the sheer delight of choosing any fabric she desired for a gown had not entirely faded. The novelty of such freedom still lingered, and each visit from the seamstress to the manor brought with it a genuine thrill of anticipation.

"...and the new fashion for ribbons as hair adornments is quite pretty," Emily was commenting as Penelope's thoughts returned to the present.

"I rather fancy it, too," Anna agreed. "Though I prefer pearl pins."

"And flowers!" Emily chimed in. "I love the fashion for flowers in the hair."

Penelope smiled. Anna and Emily could discuss dresses and hairstyles for hours, but, then, they could discuss almost any topic for hours. They both liked the pianoforte, though neither of them claimed any form of expertise, and Anna admitted that there was a time she had not enjoyed it. Poetry, reading, painting, even riding—they had an interest in all sorts of fields and pastimes. Penelope loved poetry and reading, and the library at Brentdale had been a source of delight for her from the moment she went in through the doors. Peter had loved showing her the collection, and they still spent long evenings curled up in the library together, reading books.

The church clock chimed again, the chimes indicating half an hour past three. Penelope blinked in surprise.

"Should we not start gathering the little ones?" Papa asked carefully. Penelope smiled.

"It does usually take half an hour to round them up," she agreed. She glanced at Portia and Henry, both of whom were fast asleep. "Shall we try to find our errant sons and daughter?" she asked Anna, who chuckled.

"A capital idea," she agreed. "George, dear...?" she asked, lifting the sleeping Henry who was lying in her lap, his head cradled to her shoulder. She passed him to George. The baby stirred but soon fell asleep again in George's caring hug.

Penelope stood, and she and Anna went across the lawn towards the excited yells. Peter, surrounded by children, was standing around the corner, where the river curved around in a graceful arc. The children were shouting excitedly, pointing into the water. A little boat sailed there, about the length of an adult's forearm, carved out of an oak branch.

"Look! Look, Mama!" Thomas yelled. "It's still floating."

"It is, indeed." She smiled fondly at Peter, who grinned back. The children watched the boat, yelling excitedly about its progress. Even Mark and Amelia, who were the youngest children there, seemed highly excited about it.

"Look, Mama!" Amelia called, pointing.

"It's beautiful," Penelope agreed softly.

She glanced over at Peter, who must have understood why she and Anna had come to join them, because he clapped his hands.

"Ladies and gentlemen!" he addressed the children, making them all laugh. "I am afraid we must go indoors soon. We will watch the boat until it reaches the trees there," he added.

"Hurrah!" Thomas yelled, already sprinting towards the trees. Patches hurried after him, Charlie racing behind them. Mark and Amelia toddled along as speedily as they could, Peter walking next to them to stop them from accidentally falling into the river.

Penelope and Anna fell into step behind the small group. Penelope smoothed her hand down her patterned day-dress, the skirts a little creased from sitting on the rug for so long. She had decorated her dark brown hair with a green ribbon tied around the simple bun she always wore.

The children protested as Peter gestured towards the house.

"Come on! I'll catch you!" he yelled. The children whooped in delight, scattering in delight and excitement. Peter ran behind them as slowly as he could, giving some advantage to the little legs of Amelia and Mark, who shrieked in delight as he caught up with them.

Anna smiled. "I should help George," she replied. "He cannot carry both Henry and Portia."

"No. Of course," Penelope replied. "I will see you at the house."

"We will retire for a rest, I think," Anna replied, stifling a yawn.

"Of course," Penelope agreed. Anna and George did not live altogether too far away, but the ride was much further than that for Emily and Luke. Anna and George were staying at the manor for a few days, as was Papa. A suite was set aside for them in the west wing.

Penelope turned to check on them as she walked back towards the manor. Papa was walking with Emily and Luke. Emily had Gerald in her arms and Luke walked protectively beside them. Anna and George were with them. Anna carried Henry and George had Portia in his arms, her tousled head on his shoulder as she slept.

In the hallway, the children ran about in noisy delight. Peter was instructing them to go upstairs, and Mrs Aldham came down as Penelope walked in.

"Master Charlie! Miss Amelia!" she called. "You should have a rest now."

"No!" Charlie protested. He was hand-in-hand with Thomas, and Patches danced around them both.

"You can join us in the drawing room later," Peter promised the two little children. "And Thomas and Patches will come and play with you awhile," he added, glancing at Thomas, who, although he was five years old, still looked rather sleepy.

"Do you promise we can?" Charlie asked, stifling a yawn.

"Yes. I promise," Peter agreed. "And we'll read stories from the big green book," he added with a grin at Charlie and Amelia, who whooped with delight.

"Come now, boys and girls," Mrs Aldham said cheerfully, leading the three little children upstairs. "Will all the children be taking a rest, my lady?" she asked Penelope. She seemed to take delight in using the title, which made Penelope grin.

"No. Thank you, Mrs Aldham. Lord and Lady Chelmsford are going upstairs with their children for a rest. Emily?" she asked her sister. "Will Gerald join his cousins in the nursery?"

"Thank you, Mrs Aldham. I think he would like that," Emily replied, gently passing the sleeping Gerald to the nanny, who beamed.

"I'll take the best possible care of them," she promised Emily and Penelope, cradling Gerald tenderly.

"I know you will. Thank you, Mrs Aldham," Penelope told her fondly. She appreciated the older woman's care and devotion to the children a great deal.

She waited with the others while the children made slow but steady progress up the stairs. Mark remained behind with his parents, clinging sleepily to his father's leg. Peter lifted him.

"Thank you," George replied warmly.

"No trouble," Peter replied. "You will use the Peach Suite. There is a room for you and Anna, and a room for the three children, and a small parlour."

"Thank you. That sounds grand," Anna replied warmly. She smiled at Penelope, who smiled back. They walked upstairs together, Emily, Luke and Papa behind them. Penelope squeezed Anna's hand fondly as she went up the hallway towards her chamber. Anna smiled back.

Penelope joined the other guests in the drawing room to wait for their teatime visitors.

A light tea had been set out—a few sandwiches, slices of raisin loaf and buns waited on the table along with the teapot and cups. Penelope gestured to Emily, Luke and Papa to be seated and she poured the tea for them, knowing that Peter would prefer it if she did not wait. He came in to join them just as she stirred her tea. He smiled fondly at her.

"A fine day, eh?" he said with a smile. "The little ones are exhausted."

"Even Thomas," Penelope agreed with a chuckle.

"Even him," Peter agreed, smiling warmly.

They chatted with their guests and before they had even drunk their tea, the butler came in.

"Lady Sterling, Lord and Lady Aldham, and Lord and Lady Pinehurst."

"Please show them upstairs, Mr Harris," Peter replied instantly.

Penelope's heart thudded. She felt a little tense about meeting some of the guests, though she knew that she had no reason to. Peter had assured her that all would be well, and she believed him, but she still could not help a little apprehension at the thought.

Lady Sterling walked in first, resplendent in a blue gown, her lovely white hair styled elegantly. She curtseyed to everyone. The men had all stood up as she came in and Penelope stood to return her curtsey, smiling warmly at her.

"Welcome, Aunt Marcia," Peter said warmly. "Please, do be seated."

Penelope gestured Lady Sterling—or Aunt Marcia, as she insisted on being called—to a chair. Sophia was next, with her husband Johnathan, Lord Pinehurst. He was a wealthy baron who lived not far from Sterling House and Sophia had blossomed since she met him. Her big smile was as big as ever, her very presence seeming to radiate quiet contentment.

"Peter!" she greeted her cousin, smiling warmly at him. "Grand to see you. Penelope!" She hugged Penelope fondly. "Where are those wonderful second cousins of mine?" she demanded.

Penelope smiled. "Resting, I am sorry to say. You will see them shortly, however. Thomas, at least, will be bounding out of bed at any moment."

"Grand! Grand," Sophia replied, turning her bright grin on Penelope.

Penelope smiled and gestured for Sophia and Johnathan to join them at the table. Johnathan had middle-brown hair and a thin, serious face. He gazed at Sophia with adoration and Penelope had to smile whenever she saw them.

The next guests made her tense a little. Millicent, Peter's sister, came in, followed by Stewart, Lord Aldham. He was tall, with dark hair and a lined face; a few years older than Millicent and seemingly very serious. However, the tenderness in his gaze when he looked at Millicent was impossible to ignore, and her quiet joy radiated through the room. Edmund had passed away in the colonies of a fever, and Millicent and Stewart had married a year later. Their son was just six months old, just old enough to travel.

"Where is little Alfred?" Peter asked Millicent, who smiled.

"On his way. The nursemaid has him. He's fast asleep. May we take him to the nursery?" she added, glancing at Penelope.

"Of course," Penelope replied at once. "Welcome," she added. Millicent smiled, dropping a curtsey to Penelope and to the other guests.

"Thank you," she said sincerely.

Penelope smiled warmly at Millicent. Though she had been terribly unsure of having her in the house, she had hosted Millicent for the first time a year ago, after her wedding, and she had been amazed by how pleasant it had been. Millicent was no longer so tense and obsessed with etiquette. She seemed lighter and happier, and her care for Peter shone through whenever Penelope saw them together. She could not be angry with her, not even for her dismissive treatment all those years ago.

"I trust you had a pleasant journey?" she asked Millicent, who settled herself in a seat next to Papa.

"Very pleasant, thank you," Millicent replied. "Alfred slept most of the way."

"I imagine," Penelope said fondly.

She poured tea for the new guests and everyone sat and chatted happily. Thomas and Patches sneaked in and Sophia let out a small yell of delight. Thomas saw her and ran to her, climbing onto her knee.

"Auntie Sophia!" he greeted her with a big smile. "You're here."

"Yes, I am," Sophia replied warmly. "You must tell me all about what you have been doing."

She went to sit with Thomas by the fire, Patches falling asleep on her lap as they talked. Penelope gazed fondly at them both. Sophia and Johnathan often visited at Brentdale, and Sophia's interest in gardens was almost as intense as Peter's own. The greenhouse was a constant source of delight, and Peter always let Sophia take seeds or clippings for her own burgeoning greenhouse at Pinehurst Manor.

Penelope glanced across at her father, who was chatting happily with Lady Sterling. He looked tired, and she looked over at the clock. All of their guests would be staying for the night, with Lady Sterling, Sophia and Johnathan, Millicent and Stewart, departing the next day. Millicent and her family intended to stay with Lady Sterling for another week before returning to their home further north.

"Would anyone care to retire to dress for dinner?" Penelope murmured to Peter, who repeated her question so that everyone could hear.

"Yes. Yes, we would like to," Millicent said at once. Penelope smiled to herself. Millicent was still more aware of manners and etiquette than any of their other guests. Emily stifled a yawn.

"I think we will retire to rest," she told Penelope. Penelope smiled fondly.

"Of course, Emily. Dinner is at seven o'clock," she reminded the guests, all of whom were pushing back their chairs and standing, ready to retire for a rest before dinner.

When the rest of the guests had departed, Peter gently lifted a sleeping Thomas from the floor and rested him on the chaise-longue. Patches woke up and jumped on beside the child, then curled up and fell asleep. Penelope smiled to herself.

"Shall we sit outdoors?" Peter asked.

Penelope nodded. "That would be lovely," she agreed.

The drawing room balcony was wide and overlooked the lawn, the treetops seeming close from the height of the second floor. Penelope sat down on the bench and smiled as Peter settled down beside her. The day had lengthened towards early evening, the sky a cool turquoise-blue, the sunshine painting long golden rays on the lawn and the shadows long, dark bars like spilled ink on the grass.

"It's a beautiful day," Penelope murmured, leaning against Peter. She smiled sleepily, feeling contented.

"It is. A very beautiful day." He wrapped his arm around her fondly. "Thank you for having organised such a grand picnic."

Penelope smiled at him fondly. "Mrs Hallden did help," she reminded him gently.

"And my clever darling did most of it," he replied, leaning in and kissing her hair. Penelope smiled, resting her head on his shoulder, her heart filling with love as she sat beside him. She wrapped her arm around him, holding him close.

"It was a lovely afternoon," Penelope agreed, feeling tired. "You were so grand with the children." She smiled up at him.

"It was most enjoyable," Peter replied warmly.

Penelope hugged him tight. "You are a remarkable man," she told him gently. "So caring and loving and just wonderful." She giggled.

"Thank you. And you are a remarkable woman," he said, leaning close and kissing her cheek in a way that sent shivers through her body. "Loving and wise and just generally wondrous as well."

Penelope chuckled. "Thank you, dearest."

He laughed and hugged her tight, and they sat silently for a moment, watching the sunlight on the grass, the breeze ruffling the grass blades as the day lengthened towards night.

"I love you, Penelope," he murmured, holding her close. She turned and stared into his eyes. His grey gaze, so serious and so beautiful, was full of care and tenderness that made her heart ache.

"I love you, too, Peter," she murmured.

She hugged him tight and knew that she had never been so happy.

The End

Printed in Great Britain
by Amazon